The Planner

THE PLANNER

TOM CAMPBELL

BLOOMSBURY CIRCUS

LONDON · NEW DELHI · NEW YORK · SYDNEY

First published in Great Britain 2014

Copyright © 2014 by Tom Campbell

The moral right of the author has been asserted

Extracts appearing as chapter headings from *The London Plan: Spatial
Development Strategy for Greater London*. Greater London Authority, 2011.
Reproduced with kind permission of the Mayor of London

Bloomsbury Circus is an imprint of Bloomsbury Publishing Plc
50 Bedford Square
London
WC1B 3DP

www.bloomsbury.com

Bloomsbury is a trademark of Bloomsbury Publishing Plc

Bloomsbury Publishing, London, New Delhi, New York and Sydney

A CIP catalogue record for this book is available from the British Library

ISBN 978 1 4088 1826 8

10 9 8 7 6 5 4 3 2 1

Typeset by Hewer Text UK Ltd, Edinburgh
Printed and bound in Great Britain by CPI Group (UK) Ltd, Croydon CR0 4YY

To Mum and Dad

25 January

At its best, London can provide what is amongst the highest quality of life to be found anywhere. Unfortunately, this is not the universal experience of Londoners.

– The London Plan, Section 1.44

'Fuck you,' said Adam. 'Verb.'

'Fuck you, you fuck – noun,' said Carl.

'Fuck you, you fucking – adjective – fuck.'

'Well, fucking – adverb – fuck you, you fucking fuck.'

Adam laughed. 'You bastard,' he said.

'So what, swearing is funny now?' said Alice.

'No,' said Adam. 'Swearing isn't funny. *We're* funny.'

But James wasn't sure how funny they were. He may not have been much of a comic himself, but at least he usually knew *when* to laugh. Tonight, though, it seemed he couldn't even manage that: there was a dullness to him that made even smiling an effort. There was a woman there with them he'd never met before, Olivia, and she wasn't being particularly funny or laughing much either. But that was no consolation because she had other, unspecified talents. She wasn't what one would ordinarily call pretty – she had one of those flat, old-fashioned faces – but she was really posh, posher even than Adam, and James knew that meant she had to be assessed differently. In fact, for all he knew, it might mean that she was actually very beautiful.

It didn't help that the restaurant was just about the most expensive he had ever been to in his life. The address in Farringdon could have meant anything, but the inconspicuous entrance, tucked away on a terraced side street, its dark front door and small square windows should have raised alarm bells. The booby traps and unamusing quirks scattered across the English class system were not something James had ever navigated with ease, but he did know this much: anything this understated had to be classy, which meant that it had to be costly. He had no idea how much his meal was, but certainly enough to ruin every mouthful, and the drink was just as problematic for Carl, like James, was only capable of judging wine on the basis of price and so had ordered the most expensive bottles he could find.

But the real problem tonight was Alice. Even more than Adam and Carl, he was worried about Alice. She was on especially good form, which was likely to mean one of two things – either she was notching up another of her triumphs at the newspaper, or else she'd met someone. Another glamorous and improbably well-known boyfriend. It was getting out of hand: the last one, an incredible sod, had kept cropping up on the radio, and Alice herself was starting to become someone who wasn't famous, but who famous people knew and liked – something, James had learnt, which was actually much better, more desirable and harder to achieve.

In truth, ever since Alice had stopped being a teacher, James had found their friendship difficult to sustain. He was reasonably confident that he still earned more than her, but that was no comfort. She was in the kind of profession where success was measured in ways other than money and anyway, crucially, she owned her flat. Eight years ago, with help from her parents, Alice had shrewdly bought a two-bedroom flat in Highgate that had immediately and relentlessly risen in value every month since.

James stared down at his plate. It was a Silk Road fusion restaurant, with dishes originating from Turkey, Lebanon, Iran, Armenia and a number of other countries he was unlikely ever to visit. In the face of such a range, it was almost inevitable that he would choose poorly, and he was now facing a pretentious, unpalatable mess. James's semiotic analysis bordered on the dysfunctionally superstitious. Was his dinner a symbol of globalisation? Or did it represent more personal failings? He looked across the table – Adam had chosen some crisp and attractive spinach pancakes and Carl was oafishly enjoying his skewed kebab and chips. Christ, he thought, it never used to be like this. When did enjoying oneself become such terribly hard work?

'Mine isn't any good either,' said Felix, with a friendly smile. 'I think this place is overrated. Just like everything else.'

James smiled back. As seemed to happen more and more often, the person he was getting on with the best was the one he knew the least: Felix Selwood, whom he knew nothing about other than he was clever and worked in advertising. It was another of Adam's achievements that he had managed to acquire a varied and high-quality collection of close friends *since* leaving university.

'And, sorry – what is it you do? Adam did tell me, but I'm not sure if I quite understood him. Something to do with local government?'

'Sort of. I work in town planning,' said James with immense cautiousness.

'That sounds interesting.'

Yes, his job was interesting – at least James had thought so once, and there were, in theory, still interesting things to do: masterplans to produce, jobs to create, leisure centres to build, homes to knock down, communities to displace. These were all real and substantial things – more real, surely, than what the others did for a living.

'So what does a town planner actually do every day?'

By way of a response, James decided to go to the toilet, though it was hardly a sustainable solution. At least with the washrooms he was getting some value for money for, in contrast to the restaurant itself, they were idiotically overwhelming. Here, everything was superfluous, far too large and symptomatic of a civilisation on the brink of collapse. Limestone basins with gushing brass taps, dramatic mirrors with elaborate gold-gilded frames, a mosaic of cool cream and blue glass tiles, all pointlessly serviced by silent black men with soft hands. He removed his glasses, held his wrists and then temples under very cold water and breathed slowly. The basin was so wide and deep that he could comfortably fit his entire head in it while he wondered what on earth he was doing here.

In theory they were all there to congratulate Adam on a significant promotion. But that was hardly a cause for celebration. James tried to think back to the last time he had actually enjoyed his friends' success. He could recall being drunk and happy at Alice's twenty-eighth birthday party, and had been genuinely pleased when Carl had got engaged to Jane. But that was all a long time ago. Since then there had been many successful parties, many promotions and Carl was now going out with Zoe. How bad had things got? Had it got to the point where he actually disliked his closest friends? When had that started? Of course, that was one of the principal problems in doing your degree at the London School of Economics, the thing that they never mentioned in the prospectus: all the friends you made would go on to become insufferable wankers. Or was it just capitalism that had fucked everything up for them? Surely things wouldn't be so bad if Adam and Carl worked in the public sector? Wouldn't it be better if *everyone* worked in the public sector? All James knew for sure was that he couldn't stay with his head in the basin forever, and that he very much wanted to be home.

'Are you okay?'

James jerked his head up and put his glasses back on. It was Felix. Time passed differently under water and he couldn't be sure how long he'd been there.

'No,' said James. 'No, I don't think I am.'

Felix nodded. He didn't look like Adam, he didn't have vigorous dark hair and a big upper-middle class forehead, and he didn't look like Carl with pale proletariat skin and a brutish square face. For the moment, that would just have to do, and James had the sense that he was safe, that Felix wouldn't make things any worse.

'Have you had too much to drink?'

James probably had, but that was hardly the problem. It wasn't him that was ill, it was everything else. The whole migraine world.

'I hate my friends,' said James. 'They're all awful.'

'Yes,' said Felix. 'I think they probably are.'

A black man handed James a white towel and he held it to his face and hair. It smelt of apples and lemons.

'We don't have to go back,' said Felix. 'It's fine to stay here if you're not feeling up to it.'

James nodded. It would be nice to put his head back into the sink and stay there indefinitely, for his heart to slow down and his blood to cool, perhaps to let water erosion take its course and shape him into someone else.

'No, it's fine,' said James. 'Don't worry. I'll be along in a minute.'

James waited until Felix left, and then felt inside his trouser pocket for where he knew there was a ten-pound note. He didn't really know what he was doing, he didn't really like what he was doing, but he wanted to give some money to the only person in the building who had less than him. He put the note on a little silver dish. The attendant was at least fifty years old. He looked at it with eyes full of sorrow, but didn't say anything.

When he got back to the table, things were only marginally better. People weren't making jokes any more and so he didn't have to laugh or try to say something funny. Instead, they were having an argument. But the difficulty was that they weren't arguing about music or sport or even politics – they were arguing about the economy. And it wasn't something easy like what a bunch of fuckers the bankers were, but rather what seemed to be a reasonably technical discussion around the merits of fiscal investment versus monetary expansion, and their associated inflationary risks. Again, James could only look at his friends in dismay. Okay, Carl worked in finance and Alice wrote for newspapers, but how on earth did Adam get to know about this kind of shit? He was a lawyer, with a degree in English Literature, and yet here he was sounding perfectly knowledgeable about macroeconomics. God, he even seemed to know something about *micro*economics.

Increasingly, on nights like this, James felt as if Adam and Carl and Alice and everyone else were the adults, and that he was no more than their teenage nephew. They had grown up in ways he never had, and maybe, he was now beginning to fear, never would. It was more than simply wives and careers, money and mortgages – they had mastered the very principles of adulthood, while he was still watching, learning, aping them. Having an informed position on the economy was part of this, and James was frantically trying to think of something wise and insightful to say, but it was no good – anything he could come up with would either be truthful and naive, or else false and pompous. It was so much hard work, having to pretend he understood what was going on in the world, to have a view on what was going to happen next. And God, hadn't it been so much better when all that anyone ever did was get pissed and talk about girls?

The race of life, so people were often saying, is a marathon and not a sprint. But if that was really the case, why was everybody else sprinting? None of the others seemed to be pacing themselves, taking it easy and slowing down a bit. They had come flying out of the blocks immediately upon graduating and now, ten years later, seemed to be going faster than ever. Even the recession didn't seem to be holding them back. James had had high hopes for it, he had watched banks implode and stock markets fall with mounting excitement, but incredibly – and this was scarcely believable – it now seemed to be affecting *him* more than any of the others. It was Southwark Council that had frozen salaries, instigated redundancy programmes and now wanted to renegotiate his pension plan. And it was his landlord who had announced that his monthly rent would have to go up, while everyone else kept marvelling at how low their mortgage repayments had become.

It was a sorry state of affairs – James wasn't just lagging behind his peers, he was in danger of getting *lapped*. Other people were dismantling their marriages, resigning from executive management positions, going back to college to study non-vocational subjects and embracing ancient and exotic religions. A colleague of Adam's had given up being a director in a law firm and was currently doing the pilgrimage to Santiago on his knees, Alice's brother was training to become a violin maker. Their cleverest friend at university had sold his digital marketing business and then drowned himself in the river Nile. But James could take little solace from any of this. All he could do was wonder at the exciting and expensive ways in which people were now able to make themselves unhappy.

'I really have to be going,' said Alice. 'I'm horribly late, but it's been completely fabulous. Huge fun.'

Alice was leaving. It was almost midnight but, not actually all that amazingly, she had another party to go to. A party in Notting Hill that sounded dispiritingly good and which she hadn't invited them to. It seemed that for Alice, the days of turning up at parties with unannounced guests were over – particularly if none of them were well known or powerful. In the meantime, and this wasn't really any help at all, Carl had ordered the rest of them a round of brandies.

Alice kissed them all on the cheek with great enthusiasm, but as far as James could tell there was no more tenderness in his kiss than any of the others. In fact, she seemed to linger for at least three seconds longer with Felix.

'Have fun,' said Adam. 'We mustn't leave it so long next time. Apparently there's a fantastic new Vietnamese restaurant your way. Justine keeps badgering me to take her there.'

'Oh, the Lemon Grass. Do you know, it's just round the corner from me, and I still haven't been. The food editor at work won't stop talking about it. Let's fix something up. I'll email. I've got to go. Bye! Bye! Bye!'

Part of the problem was that James had left London. Or rather, that he had come back. For nearly three years he had worked as a junior planning officer in Nottingham. A perfectly cheerful and well-functioning town with planning issues that challenged rather than overwhelmed. Those had been what Adam had called his lost years, but which now seemed more like a golden age. He had walked to work in the mornings, he had spent a small proportion of his income on rent, he had prospered at work in undemanding circumstances and been promoted twice. He had captained his pub quiz team. For six months he had gone out with a maths teacher. And he had left all of this to move back to London, to work in the borough of Southwark, live in Crystal Palace and to spend evenings with friends from university who earned five times more than him.

'I've decided that your friend Alice is a good-looking girl,' said Felix.

'She's lost weight,' said Carl. 'And she dresses miles better these days. You should have seen the nonsense she used to wear. Plus,

she wears contact lenses and make-up now – makes a big difference. Christ, when she was at university she didn't even use
deodorant.'

'That's all true,' said Adam, sipping his brandy judiciously. 'But
there's something else about her now. She seems a different person.
Much more confident and self-assured. She knows exactly what
she wants from life, and that always makes a woman attractive. She
looks more Jewish as well. I know she always was, but these days
she actually looks it.'

'Really? I don't think she's very pretty at all,' said Olivia.

But Olivia, who clearly didn't have a fucking clue about anything,
was wrong. Alice did look good – really good. And Adam was
right. It was more than her clothes and figure. There was a prettiness that didn't just accompany her cleverness – it was part of it. Her
dark eyes glimmered with bright curiosity, her nose curved intelligently. Even her fringe that evening had been witty. She was
altogether a vastly better proposition than she had been all those
years ago when, once upon a time, James had gone out with her.

'I don't think she's all that different,' said James. 'She's still very
political.'

'Yes, but not in the same way,' said Adam. 'She isn't banging on
all the time about Palestine and women's rights in Timbuktu. She's
discovered irony. She's become a modern feminist, or maybe a
post-modern one. I don't know – a better one anyhow.'

'I'm sure her breasts have got bigger as well,' said Carl.

'So has she got a boyfriend?' asked Felix.

'Oh a few of them, I imagine,' said Adam. 'But I'm not sure if
there's anyone in particular.'

So now they *were* talking about girls. But not, thought James, in a good way. They were talking about Alice in much the same way that they had been talking about the global economy – with poise and expertise, and also with great detachment. The others could afford to be objective on such matters – they had never gone out with her, and besides Adam was engaged to Justine, a highly attractive all-rounder whose selection as a life partner resolved at a stroke many problems, and Carl was in a relationship that he described as messy, but actually sounded brilliant. And not having a girlfriend, which could be liberating and exciting, was actually becoming a major fucking problem.

But it was only now that the worst part of the evening, the bit James had really been dreading, was upon them. The bill. It was every bit as bad as he'd feared – a truly astounding amount of money. There had only been six of them, and Olivia had barely ordered a thing, and yet there it was: £713 plus service. It was just as well that Olivia had eaten so little, for it seemed she had no intention of paying anything, and nor did anyone else have any intention of asking her to. That was okay, James could understand that, but what was really unacceptable was that they had no intention of asking him to pay anything either. Instead, it was something to be settled by the grown-ups, and paid for by the private sector. He was being subsidised.

'Okay,' said Carl. 'Let's toss for it.'

'Good idea,' said Adam.

James should have expected that. Gambling, which for moral and psychological reasons was just about his least favourite thing, was also one of the things that nowadays Carl most liked doing. He had recently joined a private casino in Knightsbridge and started to lose glamorous amounts of money playing poker with comedians and actors, which he then won back from foolish young Arabs. Before too long, he would doubtless be joining a golf club and taking up pheasant shooting.

'Hold on,' said Felix. 'How's this going to work? There are three of us.'

Carl began to expertly arrange things. It was, after all, what he did for a living. He was a broker and it wasn't his job to make money – although he did, in fact, make a great deal of it – but to efficiently facilitate ways in which other people could win or lose even larger amounts.

'Okay, this is how it works. Adam – if you call it right, you get to buy dinner tonight. If not, then I do. But first, Felix gets the chance to call on your call. If he's right, then he's lucky enough to pay for the drinks. If not, then one of us gets that privilege as well.'

As he spoke, Carl tossed the coin, neatly caught it in one hand and slapped it flat against the back of the other. Adam and Felix nodded. James couldn't even begin to follow all this, but he had grasped the substantial point. Those atrocious fucks weren't playing a game of chance in order to avoid paying for dinner. They were playing for the *right to buy dinner*. They actually very badly wanted to spend more than £700. They wanted to demonstrate their kindness and senseless generosity, to do to him exactly what he'd done to the toilet attendant.

'Okay,' said Felix. 'I predict Adam is going to get this. He's the lawyer and the lawyer always wins.'

'Tails never fails,' said Adam.

'Tails it is,' said Carl, lifting his hand with an exaggerated grimace. 'Well, so be it. Dinner and drinks are on you two. But next time it's my treat, and we go somewhere *really* fucking expensive.'

More than an hour later, James still wasn't home. It had gone two in the morning and, to his disgust and shame, he was waiting for a night bus. In fact, it was worse than that – he was waiting for his second night bus. The first, populated by over-excited teenagers, foreign-language students and drunk poor people, had got him as far as London Bridge station. But now another one was required for the much longer journey to Crystal Palace. A bus that would hopefully be more sombre, but which also came much less frequently. Ominously, he'd been there for twenty minutes and still seemed to be the only person waiting.

It was January, there was no wind but the air was cold in a way that James had no way of protecting himself from. It was a mark of how serious things were that he had considered trying to look for a taxi. But no, he couldn't, and it wasn't just the expense – he had been driven stubborn by sadness, and he was now determined to get home by public transport, even if it took all night.

James was thirty-two years old. It was such a big, cocksure kind of an age. Not young any more, not callow and soft-hearted, but by no means old either. It was an age to be energised and just the right side of over-confident. It was the time when you should be making all of your really critical life decisions, armed with experience and optimism but without the debilitating weakness and caution. But instead, what was he doing? What decisions was he making? He wasn't contemplating marriage or divorce or procreation. He wasn't choosing a house to purchase or sizing up the job offer in North America.

No. For his was a life of small decisions. He was trying to decide whether to buy a bicycle or not. And how had he got here? Because, again, of all the small decisions he'd made, and all the ones that he hadn't. It was an existential failure that had got him here. Above all, it was his twenties that had got him here. His not-so-roaring twenties. Wasn't that the decade in which you were meant to get everything out of your system? The thirties were different. As far as he could tell, if you fucked up your thirties then you really were in trouble. But you were allowed to fuck up your twenties, that was the one good thing about them.

And what, exactly, had he done with his twenties? Well, he'd spent an awful lot of it in the office – waiting for his computer to boot up, eating sugared biscuits in meetings, reformatting Microsoft Word documents, filling in Excel spreadsheets, agreeing to things that he had no powers to disagree with. Where were the mistakes: the entertaining misadventures, the expensively learnt lessons, the-disastrous-at-the-time-but-now-fondly-remembered blunders? Maybe he hadn't made any. Maybe what he'd done instead was just make one very big one.

And why weren't any of his experiences *bittersweet* ones? Did such a feeling really exist? He would, he supposed, need to have had a major love affair in order to know for sure. A reciprocated but doomed romance, ideally with someone of a different social class or ethnic group. There had been little opportunity at work. As far as he could tell, the office had never been much of a place for that. Or was it going to be like university all over again – would he discover, in ten years' time, that everyone had been fucking everyone else? That all those evenings when he'd worked late or gone home early, everyone else was round the corner doing far-fetched things in a nightclub. Somehow, as unlikely as it seemed, it wouldn't entirely surprise him.

The bus rolled up. It always did in the end. But it was a ghostly vehicle with no passengers or lights, and heartbreakingly it simply stayed where it was, its engine rumbling good humouredly, its doors closed. As James well knew, this could easily go on for half an hour. The driver at least would be warm. He looked down at his phone. It was 2:25 a.m.

How had it got to this? Waiting for a night bus, hiding in toilets, getting drunk on wine he couldn't afford, having friends he was scared of seeing, living in Crystal Palace, working in local government, and wanting to cry a lot of the time. Those were hardly the ingredients for a happy and successful life. It was hardly what he had *planned*.

2

28 January

People should be able to live and work in a safe, healthy, supportive and inclusive neighbourhood with which they are proud to identify.

– *The London Plan*, Section 7.4

'Agenda item two: review of last meeting's minutes.'

There was a movement of papers, a little anxious pause as no one said anything. James sipped his tea, confident that he alone had actually read the minutes.

'So, are you happy for me to sign these off?' said Lionel.

There was some gentle nodding and benevolent murmuring. It seemed that everyone was happy for everyone else to sign them off.

'Okay, good. Item three: the main event, and I know there's been considerable interest in this one,' said Lionel, with a small chuckle. 'Neil here is going to give us a briefing from his transport study.'

It was Monday morning, just after nine o'clock, in Meeting Room Two on the fourth floor of Southwark Council. With a little preparatory cough, Neil Tuffnel, Senior Planning Research Officer, launched into his PowerPoint presentation on the interim findings of his study on long-term surface transport projections.

James sat back in his chair. The meeting, which was scheduled to last for two hours, stretched comfortably ahead of him.

James could identify each of the Planning Directorate's four data projectors by the pitch and rhythm of its hum, and this happened to be his favourite – not necessarily the quietest, but the least irregular. Rachel, sitting opposite, gave him a resigned smile. The room was over-warm. Already, Jane Nichols, Environmental Policy Manager and just two years away from retirement, was looking sleepy. The Assistant Director of Road Networks from Transport for London, a well-known prick, had sent his apologies, rendering the meeting worthless, but there could be no question of not going ahead with it. James started to think carefully about which biscuit to select from the plate in front of him.

Neil moved on to the second slide. James had already read the presentation, which had been emailed along with the agenda, and Neil was not the kind of man to deviate from it. For thirty minutes, he carefully took them through every bullet point and figure, every graph and calculation.

Lionel was chairing the meeting with great experience but not much skill. Poor old deciduous old Lionel, with his dry skin and wet eyes, his pink nose and unhappy pouch. The seasons hadn't been good to him. He had ineffectively chaired too many meetings, watched too many PowerPoints and dunked too many biscuits into mugs of sugared coffee. His career had peaked: he had reached the top band of his salary grade some years ago, and barely survived the last round of budget cuts. He breathed through his mouth too much and it was almost certain that at some point he would die of cancer.

Wanting to rest his eyes on something else, James looked out through the glass wall of the meeting room into the office beyond and, as he did so, he felt a surge of primitive and irrational tenderness for his colleagues. It wasn't like his friendships – there was affection here and there was intimacy. All these people, for all these years, who he had lowered his head to look at so that they didn't have to crane theirs to look up. He knew without asking how Lionel, Rachel and many others took their tea, whose mug was whose, and who minded and who didn't if they got someone else's. He knew that Neil liked coffee but no more than one cup a day or else he got anxious, and that since her heart scare Rupinder only drank green tea from her own packet. He knew the type of biscuits and confectionery they preferred, and which football teams they supported, and on Monday mornings he would ask them about the weekend and be rewarded with long friendly conversations that he had no interest in.

Of course, they couldn't all be friends. That wouldn't work. They needed other things, other people to bring them together. They didn't have business competitors, but they did have common threats and predators: senior managers, who were mostly terrible bastards, and the politicians, who they hardly ever got to meet but who were stupid and could make bad things happen to them. And there were lots of other, more minor, villains, bullies and dickheads for them to fill their days complaining about. There were those pernicious idiots in the Communications Team who made unfair demands and didn't understand anything that the organisation did, the entire Human Resources department, the drunkards in the postroom, and the IT officers with their foul manners and obscure powers.

There was an unexpected pause. Neil had finished, but it wasn't clear that the others had been following him closely enough to realise. Lionel hadn't been concentrating, and was looking elsewhere, and even Rachel didn't seem to have been listening. Neil was looking up, unsure what to do next. But this was the kind of situation in which James thrived, and he had already designed a suitable question to ask.

'Sorry, Neil, could you just talk us through the methodology you used for these estimates? Was it a telephone survey? It would be good to get a handle on the sample sizes as well.'

'Yes, of course. I'd be very happy to go into more detail if that would be useful,' said Neil. He looked round the room hopefully.

'Yes, please do,' said Lionel. 'I think that would be very helpful.'

Although not highly regarded as a public speaker, James was undoubtedly a talented listener. It wasn't just that he efficiently absorbed information – he actually looked like he was listening. As Neil started up again, he made a tight mouth, kept his eyes fixed, and from time to time would give earnest little nods of his head. Crucially, he never tired, but would maintain a purposeful demeanour broken only by quick, occasional smiles. It was at least partly because he was kind.

Neil kept talking. Lionel nodded happily – the meeting was going well. The data projector, no longer needed, continued to hum soothingly to itself, like an old uncle mumbling in his sleep. James ate a chocolate biscuit.

It was half past twelve. James was eating a sandwich, Rachel was smoking a cigarette and, across the road, they were coming out of the office. Blinking in the low winter sun, frightened by the traffic, the senior members of Southwark Council's management team were ineptly trying to navigate the city that they helped to run.

James looked at them grimly. Just as the military had its veterans, so too did the public sector. Of course, none of them were battle torn – they weren't maimed or limbless, they didn't limp or breathe noisily or make you feel disgusted and ashamed. But they were wounded nonetheless – misshapen, mangled, crushed. They leant, whispering to one another, with their inefficient hearts, their clapped-out livers and withered imaginations. James could recognise what had happened from all those geography undergraduate field trips. The steady application of erosive forces – day after day, meeting after meeting, year after year. Whether it was thermal erosion, sun blast, wind abrasion or just twenty-five years of public service, they had been worn away, their edges smudged and their centres softened. Of course, it didn't happen to them all in the same way. Like clay men, some had buckled and swollen under the stress, while others had stretched and disappeared under the tension. But they all looked terrible.

Which way would he go? He was tall now, but that counted for little. He could get still taller, he could become stretched and pinched and gaunt until he was no more than a shadow, a whispering, charcoal-grey presence with poor eyesight and thinning hair who quietly sipped sweet tea in meetings and nodded in agreement to things. Or he could go the other way. His round shoulders could get rounder, his stoop more pronounced. His spine would curl and his neck would contract, his chin would move upwards and his cheeks would sink. He would become compressed, spherical, red and always cross, his life based round energy-dense pub lunches and pints of dark bitter.

Meanwhile, Rachel Harris, stalwart of the planning team, was talking. 'One of the less obviously lethal punishments in North American prisons is to order inmates to dedicate an entire day from dawn to dusk, digging a big deep hole, and then spend the next one filling it back up again.'

'What are you talking about?' said James.

'That's what's happened,' said Rachel with a wave of her cigarette. 'Those poor wrecks have spent the last twenty years digging and refilling holes. Eighteen months to develop a new strategic framework, and then another eighteen months to revise and dismantle it. Again and again and again, year after year. That's why they look like that. That's why we'll end up looking like that.'

James looked across the road again. There was another explanation. *We make our buildings, and then our buildings make us* – wasn't that the first thing that every town planner gets taught? In which case, maybe it was the building that had done this to them? For the planning offices of Southwark Council were stupendously foul. So bad, in fact, that they had been nominated for a prestigious architectural award in 1967. A mysterious twenty-year property boom had transformed the city and wherever you went, every patch of land was being developed, built upon, improved, ruined. But not on this street, where it seemed an equally mysterious force was resisting. Offices were not, as a rule, haunted – but this was a special case, and anything may have happened. Had the architect done something dreadful in its foundations? Was it a site of one of those spectacular medieval atrocities? James was a geographer – nothing less, nothing more. He wasn't a human geographer, and he certainly wasn't a psycho-geographer. But in this instance, he was prepared to accept that other forces, forces beyond his understanding, were at work.

'Actually, I didn't think that meeting was so very bad,' said James.

'Oh, come on – don't be a sop. And you know we'll have to do it all over again with that knob from Transport for London.'

Rachel didn't just smoke cigarettes. She also drank half pints of Guinness, and ate packets of crisps in the pub. Her dark hair was formless and unprincipled without being especially innovative. She had a Midlands accent, which had probably held back her career, and a weakness for hyperbole and melodrama. She thrived on organisational discord and personal misfortunes, and adored restructures.

But Rachel's strengths were immense and well known. There were no stars or heroes in planning, but there were stoics and know-alls, and she was the finest of them: industrious, wildly competent and with an in-depth understanding of social-housing regulations. She could talk about many other things too, for she was also the most friendly and conversationally skilled town planner in the team, possibly in all of London. James suspected it might have had something to do with her education. Rachel had studied geography just like him, but at Newcastle or Hull or somewhere else where you actually had a good time and made friends that didn't go on to make you unhappy for the rest of your life.

'Well, time to go back inside,' said James. 'I've got loads to do.'

'We've always got loads to do. Generating work is what this organisation does. Even if there wasn't such a thing as Southwark, everyone at Southwark Council would still be busy.'

For the entire afternoon, James sat at his desk and worked. Although he could perform in meetings, this was what he did best, his default state. That had been apparent from an early age. Even by the standards of ten-year-old boys he had brought unusual levels of care to his pie charts and cross-section diagrams. He was diligent. He was very good at absorbing knowledge – at learning facts and remembering things in the correct order. In another age, before databases and search engines, when clerks and administrators ruled the world, he would have thrived, but you needed to be able to do other things now. You needed to do the kinds of things that Carl or Adam could do – to think on your feet, to say things that sounded perfectly credible even if you weren't sure if they were true, and to be able to make stuff up.

Part of the problem, although he hadn't quite appreciated this at the time, was that James had gone to what was probably the worst school in the country. A school that had given him no educational gifts or valuable professional contacts, like Adam's had, but no life skills either. If it had been one of those mad inner-city comprehensives attended exclusively by the children of the criminal classes and recently arrived immigrants, then he might have got something genuinely useful out of it: a bit of hard-won character, some street-wise toughness. But no – he had gone to school in the semi-urban dreary pleasantness of Leicester, and it had been, of all things, a grammar school. And the problem with grammar schools was that they were full of grammar schoolboys – nerdy little shits desperate to study Computer Science at university and with no greater ambition than to earn more money than their parents and to have children who would grow up to earn more than them.

'Do you want a drink?' said Rachel. 'I'm going for one with Lionel and Neil.'

James looked up. It was now five o'clock, and the office was emptying.

'I might join you in a bit,' said James.

But still he worked. He read the draft supplementary planning guidance on retail development, underlining in thick pink marker the sections that were significant, or else making undulating lines in the margins, where something was unclear. What were other people's jobs like? Adam would be at his desk, his head down, doing much the same as him, but more lucratively. Alice's job was indistinguishable from socialising and at the moment she was probably drinking Prosecco and having a well-informed discussion with an attractive male who was in a position to further her career. And what was Felix Selwood doing right now? Giving a presentation without the use of PowerPoint, confidently pitching something to clients, preparing some dastardly marketing campaign? For some reason, James would like to know about him more than anyone. He had been very good to him that night in the restaurant and, what's more, he hadn't actually needed to be. It wasn't what you'd expect from an advertising executive.

James's knowledge of such things was limited: he had only had two jobs and unlike many of his contemporaries, he hadn't thought long and hard over his choice of career. He hadn't deliberated over a dazzling set of adventures and rewards, in which one weighs up the respective merits of a high salary against stock options, wielding power and influence against international travel. But nor had he blundered into it. Local government was, he knew, a refuge for many, but he at least hadn't ended up there because the professions were too daunting and business too disgusting. No, this was it – and he wasn't under any illusion, as so many others were, that it was merely transitory. There was no Plan B. He didn't play in a rock band on Friday nights and he wasn't studying part-time for a qualification in art conservation. He wasn't even, for some reason, saving any money.

It was seven o'clock. It had been, he would have to say, a good day – and that, of course, was the problem. Before turning off his computer, he checked his personal email. There was a series of group emails from Adam and Carl celebrating the success of last Friday. There was an email from Alice, apologising for leaving while making it clear that the party she had left them for was well worth it. And there was an email from Graham Oakley, Director of Planning at Nottingham City Council.

James,

Haven't spoken for a bit. I know you're thriving in the Big Smoke, but . . .

Guy Wood is leaving us unexpectedly (long story). If you are interested, then there's a Deputy Director job going here. Let me know what you think and whether you're tempted at all – if so, will fill you in. Guy's working out his 3 month notice and you know we'd love to have you back. Lots going on here. That Science Park still hasn't happened yet!

All the best,

James read it through carefully. It was just about the most interesting email he had received in months. Out of the blue, someone was offering him a job. That was, by any standards, a big deal. Okay, it was actually his old boss asking if he'd like to go back and do something similar to his old job, but still – he was wanted. And it was a promotion: Deputy Director of Planning at Nottingham Council with all that it implied: an increased salary, better pension, professional progress, surrender.

He turned off his computer. The office was deserted, but he still risked going down in the battered little lift, in which Neil Tuffnel had once been trapped for six hours, and out through reception. He nodded goodnight to the nameless security guard and looked at his phone. There was a text message from Rachel: 'We're going for an Indian if you fancy it.' But James didn't fancy it. He walked to the train station under the communist weather, his shoulders hunched, his face bowed, looking for answers in scuffed shoes and the cracks in the pavement.

Why not just take the job? He'd be a bloody fool not to. Deputy Director – a big job in a small team, but all planning teams were small these days. Lionel didn't even have a deputy any more. Besides, he was through with London. He had done London twice, he had studied here and he'd worked here. He'd written masterplans, analysed traffic patterns and compiled spreadsheets. He'd given it a good go, and it just hadn't panned out – it was a perfectly honourable defeat.

No, he should leave, and leave soon, for he knew it was going to end badly. He could see it in the crowds outside the pubs, gently cupping their cigarettes and grievances, and the bottles of beer spitefully dropped next to the recycling bins. The imprecise and rudimentarily structured anger, the poorly evidenced suspicions, all slowly souring and thickening into something else, something more dangerous. The people of London, all seven million of them, had come to realise who was to blame for all this and it turned out that it wasn't the bankers after all. Nor was it the television presenters or East European labourers. It wasn't even the politicians – no, it was their servants. It was the public servants who had fucked things up for everyone. It was the *planners*.

There was no use looking anywhere else for support. For the ones that needed him the most were actually the ones that liked him the least. The economically functional treated him with suspicion, but it was the others who were most bitter: the bewildered old men on social security benefits and the crowds that build up on the steps of post offices on a Thursday morning. Little pools of zero-utility people, trapped and held together by nothing more adhesive than a disused bus shelter and their anger. They all hated him, they hated everyone who tried to help them. And James did try to help – it was what he had just spent the whole day doing. It was what he did every day.

Well, maybe it was time for that to change. Maybe he needed to start helping himself a bit more. He should go to Nottingham, and not because Graham Oakley wanted him or the people of Nottingham needed him, but because it was a better job, he would earn more money and he wouldn't have to live in Crystal Palace. Was there anything more to it than that?

3

1 February

London's cultural and creative sectors are central to the city's economic and social success.

— *The London Plan*, Section 4.32

It had taken James most of the week to write a reply to Graham Oakley – a long, friendly email that exaggerated all the things he was doing in Southwark, cautiously welcomed his offer and, while making it clear that he was very happy and not likely to consider leaving, made some off-hand enquiries about the role. Graham had replied almost immediately.

> Hi James,
>
> Great to hear from you, and thanks for getting back. Good to hear that everything is still going so well down in London – I always knew you'd make a success of it.
>
> Yes, the title would be Deputy Director, with full pay + conditions – I don't think I could lure you back here with anything less! The job's not completely in my gift (as ever, there's an open and competitive process!!) But I could get you in on an acting basis for six months without any bother, and assuming it all works ok it would be relatively easy for you to then

apply for the permanent role. Judith Davies has retired and HR are being a bit more cooperative these days.

Anyway, let me know. As I said, Guy isn't meant to be leaving for almost 3 months, so you've got time to think about it.

And there it was: an informative and sincere email, without any of the guile and ambiguity that James had become accustomed to. That was, James remembered, what Graham was like. He wasn't like Lionel: he hadn't kept his job through cunning, but by working hard and being good at it. There again, Nottingham wasn't like South London. People and planners there were straightforward and tended to speak the truth. They were, he supposed, nicer.

There was another mail in his inbox. It was from Felix Selwood, and it was much shorter. The message itself was blank and the subject title was just two words: 'Drink tonight?'

Eight hours later and James was in the Red Lion, around the corner from work. Nothing very unusual about that – it was, after all, a Friday night. But the big difference, the important innovation, was that he wasn't with anyone from the office and nor, thankfully, was he with any friends from university. He was with Felix.

Any wariness, and there had been plenty, had disappeared and James was almost starting to enjoy himself. They had had three pints of beer, that had helped, but there was more to it than that: they had formed a connection. They were allies and, as far as James could tell, it wasn't based on loneliness, a mutual enemy or shared feelings of inadequacy.

They had some significant things in common. They were both thirty-two years old, single, and yes – Felix was a planner too! It even said so on his business card. But he was a *brand* planner, an occupation that James had never previously known to exist but, as Felix explained to him, was central to how modern advertising, and therefore modern business, worked. There were some parallels: one of them made plans for consumers and one of them made plans for citizens. They both convened focus groups, and studied forecasts, and then had to write and implement strategies, which only rarely led to anything happening in the way they hoped.

Of course, there were some important differences. As Felix said, it was his job to understand what people thought they wanted, while James's job was more difficult – he had to understand what they ought to want. And one of them was much better paid than the other. James had a salary of £33,650 a year, with an extra £3,500 through his London weighting agreement; Felix earned £95,000 with a 20 per cent performance bonus and other benefits. But that didn't matter so very much, because Felix was quite wealthy anyway. And, of course, Felix didn't have a degree in geography.

'It was my good fortune,' he said, 'to have studied some economics. This really ought to be a sub-branch of sociology, but has ended up providing the only kinds of explanation that anyone is now interested in.'

James noticed that Felix spoke like this a lot of the time. He articulated bold and unusual opinions in full declarative sentences that caught the attention of people outside of his immediate group. Where had he come from? From London, obviously, but that could mean anything. He was Adam's friend, and he knew Carl, but it wasn't clear how. In fact, thrillingly, it wasn't even certain if he liked them all that much.

But the main thing they were discussing, and this really was unusual, was James. Felix was interested in James. Interested enough to email him, to come to this pub, and possibly even to help him. And despite having wise things to say on a range of important topics, he was also, just like James, a very good listener. He was attentive, he prompted with little nods and requests for information, and in no time at all James was speaking without inhibition. What did he have to lose? He talked about the night in the restaurant, and why he had run away to the washrooms, and how mysteriously his friends had become wealthy and Alice attractive. He talked about where he worked and where he lived, the difficulty of being a town planner in the modern world, the job offer in Nottingham and the fears and feelings that pulsed through him every day.

'So, I'm going to ask you a few questions now,' said Felix.

'Okay.'

'First of all, just to check. Are you still in love with Alice?'

'No.'

'Are you sure?' said Felix.

'I don't want to go out with her,' said James. 'But it would be nice if she wanted to go out with me.'

'Yes, I can see that. Next question: do you want a different career?'

'Well, there are some issues with the job I've got. But I like being a town planner. I trained to become one.'

'And the job you've been offered, the one in Nottingham. Presumably that would solve a lot of those issues? I mean, you'd be paid more, you could live in a nice place, that kind of thing.'

'Yes, all those things. I liked it there. Or at least, as I remember it, I do.'

'But if you did leave London now, it would feel like you've given up. As if you were running away.'

'Yes, that's exactly what it would feel like.'

'Okay, this is what I think the problem is – and excuse the pop psychology, but it is the best kind. What you're seeking is respect – some admiration and affection. Your hope is that having a better job, more money, a girlfriend, a house, high-quality material possessions will get you that.'

'Yes, well, they would. They would get me a lot of those things.'

'If that was the case, then the move to Nottingham is actually not a bad strategy. One of the most effective ways to find happiness is to spend your life around people who earn less than you.'

'But you don't think I should go back there, do you?'

James was, for a moment, suddenly anxious. What would happen now? What if Felix told him he should go to Nottingham? Did that mean he would just go? Was Felix rejecting him already, sending him out to spend his life with people on lower incomes? And why on earth should he take Felix's advice? He barely knew him. But there was no doubt that's what he was doing. No wonder he was so successful at advertising.

'No,' said Felix. 'No, I don't think you should. The problem you've got is not winning other people's respect, but your own. You've got a self-respect deficit.'

James took a gulp of beer. Felix seemed to have got to the root of the problem with unnerving precision and speed. Of course, there was always the chance that it was a different problem, or that he was completely wrong. But the swiftness of his reasoning was impressive.

'Don't worry, it's incredibly common. Among Western males, it's practically universal. In fact, it's the principal reason why the advertising industry exists. You just need some personal, rather than professional, development. You need self-respect, confidence, contentment, enlightenment.'

'But I can't just conjure up those things. I can't just become a different person.'

'Well, it's actually not that difficult. But for the time being, you'll need to be in London. Otherwise I can't help you.'

But now that Felix had decided he should stay, James wasn't sure if that was what he wanted either. Getting out of London meant a promotion and pay rise, the chance to own a property, no need to go to restaurants with friends from university. These were all real things.

'I think part of the problem is that you haven't yet developed a coherent vision. You've got some ethics, but they're just another source of confusion. What you need is a worldview. You need some kind of overarching belief about the nature of the universe and your place in it. That's where the self-respect will come from.'

Well, there was something in this – James could see that. He'd often, in fact, thought it himself. He needed to be anchored. He needed a philosophy, something to base himself around – a cornerstone to his personality that wasn't just his certificate in town planning.

'It doesn't even have to be true,' continued Felix. 'In fact, it's actually better if it's unverifiable – but it does have to work for you.

You have to be able to believe it enough so that a rich and fulfilling life can flow.'

'So I need a worldview. Okay, yes, I accept that. But how do I get one? It's too late to go back to university. Won't I have to read a load of books, or canoe down the Ganges or something?'

'Don't worry. None of that is necessary. That's the whole point of London: we've imported it all. You don't have to backpack across the southern hemisphere – you just get a train down to South London. Who needs Johannesburg and Calcutta when we've got Hackney and Southall? Some of the most spiritually powerful and economically dysfunctional places in the world are only a few miles away.'

'So I need to go and see the sights of Brixton and get mugged in Dalston?'

'Well, there's a bit more to it than that. Living in a modern city is an art form. What you need is some kind of plan to acquire and experience all the things in London that really matter. And curiously, you don't seem to have one.'

Felix was right. Planning worked – James believed in planning. Or at least, without a plan you're fucked. Even a bad plan, and they almost always were, had to be worth something. And James didn't just need any plan. What he needed was a *masterplan*: a comprehensive and all encompassing strategy for his own development. Christ, he was a *planner*. If he could draft plans for affordable housing provision and traffic calming measures, then he should be able to come up with a plan for himself.

'Perhaps it isn't so odd. It's certainly a familiar literary conceit – professional accomplishment belying personal incompetence. The distinguished chemist who doesn't know how to make an omelette; the Mafia boss unable to control his teenage daughter. We might have the same thing here.'

James knew hardly anything about London. He had studied it and worked on it – you could say it was his profession. But that was the problem with being a town planner. You spent your time describing a city, but not living in it. He had taken instruction in how to be as detached and objective as possible and in the process he had become self-detached: he knew a great deal about the city's air quality, but had no idea what to do with himself on a Saturday afternoon.

'Look, you really shouldn't go to Nottingham. Not until you're sure that you've done all you can here.'

'It's actually a good job offer. I know you don't think it's what my life needs, but professionally it would be a big step up.'

'All you need to do is make a plan and start implementing it. And if it doesn't work out then take the Nottingham job. How long did you say you have to decide?'

'About two months, I suppose.'

'Well, there you go. Two months – that's an enormous length of time in my sector. In two months products can undergo the most profound transformation.'

'In my sector, it takes two months to write an economic impact assessment. Nothing has ever happened in two months.'

'Believe me, in that time, all of London's treasures can be opened up to you. You're also good-looking – albeit in a not-very-exciting English way. That will make it easier.'

In all likelihood, thought James, Felix was a wanker. His name and profession were a giveaway. Plus, there was his appearance: the surly brown eyes, the unfriendly narrow nose and thin lips that seemed to be on the verge of breaking into a laugh but never did. He even smelt like a wanker – when he leaned in close, there was a zesty, menthol smell, as if he'd just that minute come out of one of his adverts for an upmarket brand of shower gel. And yet, for all that, there was no doubt that he wanted to help James, that he was being kind. Who knows, maybe he *was* kind.

'Do you want another drink?' said James.

'That would be good,' said Felix. 'But I don't think you should spend too much time in pubs like this. There aren't many personal development opportunities here.'

James looked around him. It was Lionel's favourite pub – a middle-manager's pub, a pub where he could sit, safe in the knowledge that, in here, he would always be the one on the highest pay grade. Even James could tell that it wasn't very nice. It wasn't unsafe or anything – it wasn't glamorously foul enough to attract thieves or drug dealers. It just didn't attract anyone – except for environmental officers and town planners. At lunchtime it served sausage and chips and pies with thick crusts that sometimes made Lionel's gums bleed. It had a dartboard and a fruit machine with a £4.80 maximum jackpot, which no living person had ever witnessed.

'I've been coming here for years,' said James. 'I've sort of come to like it.'

'That's the danger. You've ended up liking all kinds of things that aren't good for you.'

At the other end of the bar were numerous members of Southwark Council's Planning, Community and Environment Directorates. Not everyone of course, but enough – a representative sample of the profession. Neil Tuffnel was there, drinking beer and trying to dislodge a peanut that was stuck in his teeth. Rachel had a pint of Guinness and a packet of crisps. Rupinder was at a table with a glass of lemonade that would last her all night, a useless pillock called Shahid was telling jokes to a dimwit called Phil Struthers. None of them were bad people, some of them were even quite good at their jobs, but you'd never want to be one of them. And James was one of them.

'You're right,' said James. 'Let's go somewhere else.'

Just twenty minutes later and they *were* somewhere else. It wasn't very difficult, and James couldn't help be impressed again by Felix's speed and decision-making powers. It had taken no more than a swift, two-mile journey in a taxi, which Felix had put on expenses, and here they were – in a private members' club in Covent Garden. It was only after they arrived that it occurred to him that he hadn't even said goodbye to Rachel.

James wasn't sure if he approved of the concept or not – he almost certainly didn't, but he was prepared to gather the evidence. He knew that the first thing to do, always, was to make your survey. Survey before plan: the principle of Patrick Geddes, his second favourite town planner of all time. Whether it was the streets of nineteenth-century Edinburgh or a club in Covent Garden, you needed to observe, to study, to use the senses and understand how it functioned. It was only then that you were allowed to intervene and to ruin things.

He would have to accept that even on a preliminary viewing, it was a great deal better than being in the Red Lion. The lighting was sophisticated, with lamps strategically positioned in corners and above little round tables. Not too bright, nobody liked that, but not too gloomy either. The people here needed to be well lit, for they hadn't come to huddle in the shadows, to have too much to drink with nobody other than the person they had come with. They had come in the hope, in the expectation, of being noticed – of interacting in interesting ways with interesting people.

It helped as well that they weren't drinking pints of bitter. Felix had ordered two glasses of a new brand of whisky which he had spent much of last year preparing and planning for. The whisky was Scottish, but tasted as if it had been distilled in outer space. James could detect all the things that Felix had told him he should be aware of, plus some extra ones which he may have imagined all by himself: cinnamon, nutmeg, flavours with powerful propensities and exotic dangers. He was having, he realised, a brand experience, and it was a lot better than a normal one.

But the really important difference was not the quality of the interior design or whisky, but the other people. In places like this, you weren't even paying for the quality of service or better-looking bar staff. What you were paying for was a higher quality of fellow customers. Looking around, James was fairly confident that he was the only person there who worked in the public sector.

A woman strode over to join them at the bar. A tall woman with high, but not broad, shoulders and short dark hair. She had small, crinkled, black-olive eyes, which implied intelligence and an all-girls' school prettiness.

'Hello, lovely, I didn't think you were around today.'

'Ah, Erica – I'd like you to meet a friend of mine, this is James. He's new here.'

'Well, I'm sure he'll settle in well,' said Erica, looking at James carefully. 'He's tall and handsome, that's the main thing.'

'James is a planner as well,' said Felix. 'A really important one.'

'Oh, that's great,' said Erica. 'I'm just an account manager, so of course I'm totally in awe of all planners and their mighty brains. Where do you work?'

'Well, I'm based in South London, but I don't work for an advertising agency.'

'So you're an independent consultant?'

'Yes, I guess so. I tend to have public sector and not-for-profit clients.'

Technically, it wasn't clear to James whether he had just lied or not. It was something he didn't have much experience of, and wasn't very good at. He was wondering if he should try and start the whole conversation again, but Felix intervened at this point with a series of questions about what Erica was doing.

Once she'd left, Felix turned to James. 'I think it's encouraging that you lied just then.'

'I didn't mean to,' said James. 'It just sort of happened.'

'Don't worry. I think it shows potential. You just need to stay truthful to the big things, that's all. But first you need to decide what they are.'

They had some more whisky and Felix talked about Marxism. James went to the toilets and confirmed for himself that they were quite unlike the ones in the Red Lion. It was now eleven o'clock, but Felix, with his short, lean body, had a surprisingly hardy constitution, and was still dispensing high-quality advice.

'Of course, I'm flawed. I'm very glad of it. This is the era of the flawed hero. Think about it – think of the stories of our age. The maverick cop who infuriates his boss but solves the crime, the high school weirdo who beats the jocks and gets the girl. If you want to be a hero, then you need to be flawed. In fact, you've *got* to be – there is no other sort. Not any more.'

Where was James's flaw? He wasn't sure if he really had one. Instead he had professional development needs – skills gaps, limitations and weaknesses. He wasn't as good at Microsoft Access as he wanted to be, and his PowerPoint presentations weren't very compelling. At a push, he supposed he had insecurities – he often felt lonely and worried about money, but they hardly counted in the same way.

'So I need to get some flaws, is that what you're saying?'

'Well, to begin with, you could try to get yourself a bit more disliked by people. You need to stop fearing authority. In the end, they'll admire you more for it.'

'I don't fear authority, I just respect it,' said James.

Although actually, this wasn't true. James did fear authority. He was for instance frightened of pretty much every member of the senior management team at Southwark Council. God, he'd even been scared of *Lionel* for the first two months. It just so happened that he liked authority as well. That was okay, wasn't it – to both fear and like the same thing? It wasn't as if he liked people *because* he was frightened of them. He was reasonably certain on that point.

'Fear or – to put it more bluntly, cowardice – is, of course, the great inhibitor. The backbone of all conservative philosophies, the nourisher of suspicion and cynicism, the obstacle to progress, invention and improvement.'

Just then Erica returned with two other people, Camilla and Daniel. Camilla was an intimidating, antagonistic woman who immediately frightened him, but he was sure it was because of her anger rather than her status. It was partly deliberate, for while she could do little about the stern mouth, her chestnut hair had been tightly pulled back from her forehead, so the hairline was pre-emptively hostile. Daniel was compact, blond and savagely good-looking. He was twenty-seven years old and an international expert on social-media marketing.

'It could be said with some justification that Daniel is the most famous person in the room,' said Felix. 'He's got a blog that is actually read by people who aren't other bloggers, and a Twitter persona with more than forty thousand followers.'

'Oh, that's great,' said James. 'I don't really do Twitter or anything, but will definitely check it out. What's it called?'

'The recreational libertarian,' said Daniel. 'It's a semi-fictionalised account of modern urban living, aimed at high-income professionals who haven't been ensnared by the wrong kind of liberalism.'

At this point, Camilla initiated a discussion in a startling, creaking voice by declaring that advertising agencies would cease to exist in three years' time, a statement which Erica and Felix proceeded to accept, expand upon, challenge and refute. It was a strange conversation: Camilla appeared to have little mastery of her emotions, and she spoke with unfathomable grievances. Meanwhile, Daniel started explaining to James about a flamboyant business scheme, which was intended to convert his popularity on the Internet into a source of revenue through branded content arrangements with a number of commercial partners. James felt sure that it would succeed.

Camilla left to go to the bathroom, at which point everyone started talking about her. In that respect, at least, it was just like the Red Lion.

'Okay, everyone can stand down,' said Erica. 'We've got about ten minutes before I have to go and fish her out.'

'I'd forgotten what a hysterical disaster that woman is,' said Daniel. 'My God, I wouldn't want to be managing that one.'

'Camilla is the client, the brand manager,' explained Felix, 'and Erica is the account director. A large part of her job is therefore to keep Camilla feeling happy and loved.'

'Is that easy?' asked James.

'Christ, no – she's a nightmare,' said Erica. 'A twenty-four-hour walking psycho-drama. But in my own way, I've become fond of her. That's what happens. Now, what I really need is for one of you to give her an almighty fuck tonight. She hasn't had sex for six months. It's no wonder that the relaunch is going so badly.'

'Well don't look at me,' said Daniel. 'I've got my own brand to think about, remember.'

'I don't think the chemistry is there,' said James, who hadn't had sex for over a year, but didn't think he was ready to start with Camilla.

'Can't you get one of your account managers to do it?' said Felix. 'What about that beautiful boy Martin? He's got to be good for something.'

'Martin? He's fucking our Art Director. If I got him involved with Camilla that really would screw things up.'

This was more like it. James had spent enough time with urban planners and public servants, with people called Lionel and Neil. He needed to know more Felixes and Camillas. He needed to have drinks with people who worked in the glamorous parts of the private sector, and who could speak openly and cynically about sex and money, people with their own personal brands, complicated remuneration packages and opaque tax arrangements.

Camilla returned from the bathroom where it looked like she had been crying, and ordered an over-generous round of drinks and bar snacks. She then proceeded to be completely charming with everyone. In fact, James had just got to the point of wondering whether he ought to try and have sex with her after all, when she started to raise her voice again, and Erica immediately suggested that they go home.

'It's midnight,' said Felix. 'We should all probably go. One of the critical things with evenings like this is to demonstrate moderation and sound judgement. It's something Camilla has never managed.'

'Well, I didn't think she was too bad. In fact, all of your friends seemed very nice,' said James.

'They're really not, you know. Even Erica. They're just very skilled at their jobs, and they understand that in this profession you're always working.'

'Well, that's a good thing, isn't it?'

'Yes, I suppose so. After all, we are nothing more than what we pretend to be. I guess that goes for account directors as well as everyone else.'

James didn't get the night bus home that night. No – he got a taxi, all the way! He sat on his own in the deep leather seats luxuriating in the quiet, troubled by nothing more than his own thoughts – which were, unfortunately, so much worse than the students on the night bus. But it was still a good way to travel: going through South London at a constant speed, under bright but intermittent lights, even the shit parts, even the parts he was responsible for, didn't look so very bad. But the age of planning cities for the motorcar had long come to an end. It was a shame, in a way, for it had been a time when town planners had never had more power and prestige. Even Adam would have been impressed if James had demolished his house to make way for a dual carriageway.

So he needed a worldview – a doctrine, maybe a fierce modern one, or else something derived from ancient wisdoms. He needed to be theoretically willing to undertake great feats that would accelerate the direction of history or, failing that, help him to sleep peacefully at night and seduce women. His other friends had them, even if he wasn't entirely sure what they were. You could tell by the way that Alice became louder when someone was disagreeing with her, or in Adam's wry little smile – they knew something important about the world. Even Lionel probably had a worldview – a stoical acceptance of the hierarchies of incompetence, and his ineffective position among them.

He got out of the taxi. It had cost an exhilarating thirty pounds or, after income tax, about a third of what he'd earned that day. But the problem, of course, was that whichever method he travelled home by, however much he spent on the journey, he always ended up in the same place: Crystal Palace, SE19. James had a powerful understanding of his neighbourhood. The data was abundant, and extracting and analysing it was the kind of thing he did for a living. So he knew, for instance, that there were four times as many burglaries in his postcode than the national average and twice as many sexual offences. The proportion of homes with satellite television was unusually high and three-quarters of all residents received some form of income support benefit. It was, in short, a shithole. House prices had risen by 243 per cent in the last five years.

But the problems only magnified once you actually got inside his flat. James lived in a rented flat – it was the single greatest tragedy of his life. It would have been more acceptable, of course, if his friends hadn't all bought theirs at an eerily young age. It would also have been better if James didn't have flatmates, for he hadn't given anything like enough thought as to whom he would be sharing with. It was a characteristic error, exactly the kind of mistake that a town planner would make, and he had been living with the consequences for the last two years. He was living with them now. As he came in, long after midnight, he could hear the soft bangings and mutterings of Jane who was clumsy and inconsiderate, and of Matt, who was a massive berk, as they barged pointlessly around.

His bedroom was no refuge. He well knew how dismal it would look to a visitor, although that was something of a hypothetical concern. Everywhere he rested his eyes was another small monument to his lack of progress. The undergraduate textbooks on his shelves were an obvious giveaway, while the two science-fiction anthologies, although not in themselves a disaster, were accompanied by nothing more than some guides to planning regulations, *The Lord of the Rings* and the dictionary that his parents had given him for passing his A levels. And there were the same two prints, one by a famous impressionist and one by a famous surrealist, which he had owned for nearly ten years. It wasn't just that he didn't like them, he had never liked them, but now he wasn't even sure if he was supposed to – he wondered, for instance, what Alice would think of them. The items on his desk were also problematic: the rubber plant that he had thought was amusing at eighteen but which still hadn't died, the three pint glasses of silver and copper coins, which ought to have been taken to a charity shop but instead constituted his only financial savings, and a primitive computer, a discontinued line bought with enthusiasm just three years ago, but which now looked older than anything else in the room.

James was a young man – his bedroom was a testament to that – but there was plenty of other evidence. Every day his body produced high quantities of purposeless testosterone and troubling adrenalin. His spine was straight, his fat tissues low – possibly too low, for his diet was rudimentary and his meals irregular. He had stopped growing, but his short-sightedness had not yet stabilised and his wisdom teeth could still on occasion cause great sorrow. His collection of personal anecdotes and misadventures was small. He had no expertise in negotiating with drug dealers, nightclub bouncers or landlords. He would often wake in the middle of the night from sinister dreams. He had never owned a property, never bought a sofa and all of his personal possessions could fit into three suitcases. He was still attracted to women significantly older than him. He was over-sensitive – it was easy to hurt his feelings and he thought too much about what other people said about him. He worried about how the universe would end, and whether he had slept with enough women.

James was an old man. He paid more than the minimum into the staff pension scheme and he had multiple insurance policies. He fretted about utility bills and didn't like getting into debt. It was getting harder and harder to sleep soundly. He found it impossible to sustain a conversation with anyone under the age of twenty-five, though increasingly he found women much younger than him attractive. More and more, he tended to buy clothes on the basis of how comfortable they were. He had an unreasonable fear of dogs of any size, teenagers in hooded tops and beggars. He could no longer take his body for granted – for no good reason, he would experience an unpleasant stiffness in his back, often felt weary after lunch and his mouth hurt if he brushed his teeth vigorously. He worried about dying, and he knew that he hadn't slept with enough women.

James picked up his mobile phone and before getting into bed sent a text message to Felix: 'You're right. Need self-improvement, a worldview and much more. Will u help?'

It was half past two in the morning, but the reply came back immediately. 'Asking for help is 30 per cent of the solution. See you next week.'

4

5 February

London is a great city for night-time entertainment and socialising.

     – *The London Plan*, Section 4.36

'I'm not going to promise that you'll enjoy this,' said Felix.

'I know that,' said James.

'But it is necessary that you go through with it.'

'I know,' said James.

They were going to a book launch. It had been Felix's suggestion and James had immediately accepted. He knew that it was no longer sufficient to simply have professional and social interests: James needed a cultural life. He needed a *hobby*. He knew you could build entire friendships and personalities around such things, but it was important to choose the right one. Literature, theatre – these were perfectly reasonable choices. Crafts, contemporary dance, heritage – these were clearly dead ends, while going to the cinema every so often simply wouldn't cut it. And music? Well, you had to be careful. It was probably too late for him to be jumping up and down in front of long-haired guitarists in Camden, but then again he wasn't ready to sit down in a dinner jacket and come up with intelligent things to say at the end of an opera. So Felix had made the decision for him.

'It's my opinion,' said Felix, 'that even in 2013, a book launch is still a perfectly respectable way to spend a Tuesday night in London.'

James had his doubts, but he wasn't really in a position to nurture them, for while he understood the concept of a book launch, the format was almost completely unknown to him. It didn't help that he didn't know the geography either, for he was a long way from home. They were in a theatre bar off Islington High Street, a part of the city that filled him with foreboding.

'We better have another gin and tonic here. I warn you now: the quality of the wine at this thing will be outrageous. These are publishers, remember, not advertising agencies, and in certain important respects they haven't got a clue. Of course, these days they haven't got any money either.'

Earlier that day, James had spent almost an hour writing an email to Graham Oakley saying he would like to consider the job offer. As far as he could, he was going to keep his options open. There were good reasons for going back to Nottingham, even Felix had acknowledged that, and he didn't want to turn it down just because he now had a friend who took him to book launches. It had been, he thought, a pretty good email: positive, open, truthful, even, and the reply from Graham had been every bit as accommodating as he'd expected. So he had two months to make London work for him, to implement his self-development plan.

Felix ordered more drinks. The last time James had experienced gin and tonic was on a visit to his uncle's in the late 1990s. But since then the drink had undergone a significant repositioning in the market place. As Felix explained, following a successful brand-planning strategy, it was now a drink that was associated with affluence and good judgement. James had to acknowledge, it tasted much better than he remembered. More than that, he could feel it *making* him better, warming and strengthening him for the task ahead.

They left the bar, and turned away from the high street into a handsome, well-managed town square. Although James had never been here before it was unmistakably North London: smug, expensive and at a loss to explain its economic good fortune. Much of it looked like Crystal Palace, built at the height of Victorian prosperity and urban despair, when town planning was just getting started and everyone wanted to be at a safe distance from the thieves and typhoid carriers. Of course, it had been pretty much downhill ever since then, until unexpectedly, towards the end of the twentieth century, it had been rescued – made better by economic deregulation, the financial services industry, housing privatisation and a number of other things that James disliked.

The venue, too, was familiar. Islington Arts Centre was an early nineteenth-century town house on the corner of the square, converted into a cultural space, funded by the local authority and used exclusively by some of the wealthiest people in the country. There had been something very similar near where James lived, but which had fallen into disrepair and lost its funding.

Once inside, Felix went to get some drinks, and James quickly undertook his survey. They were in a large pastel-yellow reception room with some fold-up chairs against the wall and a carpet that needed replacing, but would have to wait many years for a spending review that would sanction it. There were about eighty people there, more women than men, with a level of ethnic diversity slightly higher than one would expect. James was one of the few people in a suit, and was also probably the tallest person there – but he knew that neither of these would be an advantage.

'Just as I feared,' said Felix. 'The wine is almost satirically bad. And look – it's being served in little plastic cups, as if we were on an aeroplane. I suspect that's a deliberate attempt to manage our expectations.'

James drank deeply, grateful that he had something to do with his hands. It probably was disgusting, but all those gin and tonics had deadened his palate and anyway James still wasn't old enough to tell the difference between good and bad wine.

'Are you okay?' said Felix.

'Yes, I'm fine. I'm just observing.'

'If you want a little confidence boost, then remember this: people in publishing earn fuck all. Believe it or not, a lot of the people here probably earn less than you.'

James nodded. He knew that in Islington, with its complex class ecology, that didn't necessarily count for much, but it was helpful to know this all the same. He went over to a table, refilled his beaker of wine and, not wanting Felix to have to introduce him to anyone, decided to take the initiative himself. Selecting the least attractive woman standing on her own, he strode over and began a conversation.

'Hello,' said James. 'Are you a writer as well?'

'Well, yes – that is how I earn my living, but I don't think I've got the patience to ever write a book.'

That seemed a reasonable reply, and allowed James to follow up with a series of supplementary questions. She in turn asked him things, quickly establishing that he had no connection with the cultural sector. Out of the corner of his eye he could see that Felix was thriving on the noise, drink and conversation of strangers. But James already needed assistance. It was clear that he had made a mistake. True, the woman he was talking to might have been unattractive if she worked in a pharmacy in Leicester, but she was actually a newspaper columnist, and arguably the most important person in the room. Her round cheeks weren't quite a camouflage, for doubtless she would prefer to be prettier, but they were an irrelevance and in any case, the key feature was her deep ferrous voice, with its connotations of private education and great sexual experience. For James, the grammar school boy with a geography degree, erotic excitement and social advancement went closely together, but in such circumstances there was always the danger of paralysis.

'Ah good,' said Felix, coming over to join them. 'I see you've met one another. Now Felicity happens to be an enormous admirer of your friend Alice Baum.'

'Oh, really? How do you know Alice?' said James.

'Oh I adore Alice! She is simply amazing. And what's your name? Sorry, you did tell me.'

'James. James Crawley. Alice and I went out together for a couple of years.'

'Gosh — really? Sex and everything? Lucky you! What fun that must have been. But that must have been a while ago?'

'Yes, I suppose. We were at university together. I suppose it was a long time ago,' said James. 'But she hasn't changed much.'

He went to refill their cups with another 175 ml of red wine. Now why, he wondered, would she say something like that? Why would it have been so long ago? It was, of course, but why would she think so? Another, related question was why it should bother him. After all, it wasn't as if trying to go back out with Alice was ever part of his plan. All that wine may have had something to do with it. By way of a remedy, he swallowed another mouthful and cultivated some destructive thoughts as he looked around the room again. It occurred to him that he would probably enjoy it more if Rachel was there.

Felix took him away, and steered him to the other side of the room.

'A useful tip at things like this is to avoid the journalists and writers, and instead go for the boys and girls who work in PR. They have particular expertise in being agreeable, and the good ones tend to be highly attractive.'

Sure enough, things were much better over here. In no time at all, James was welcomed into a pool of lightness and warmth. As Felix had said, the public relations women were genuinely skilled, with an uncanny gift for discovering a point of common interest, and then building an entertaining conversation around it. There was no nervous tension in the laughter, no debilitating intellectual chasms and none of the acute anxiety of being with someone who was his own age, but who had a much more prestigious job.

If James did have a gripe, it was that the PR women were terribly flighty, and wouldn't stay still. It might have been a strategy, as with herds of gazelles, for the constant movement made it very difficult to pick any one of them off. James would have liked to talk some more with Kate, who had a very pretty upturned nose and lived in a part of Southwark that James had particular knowledge of, but instead he found himself engrossed with Isabelle, who wore a turquoise ribbon in her hair and whose sister had been at the London School of Economics at the same time as him, but in fact he ended up drinking wine with Miranda who had bright pink lipstick and an old boyfriend who lived in Leicester.

But then, quite suddenly, Miranda disappeared, and he was back talking with Kate for a minute, before she abruptly left to do something critical to the functioning of the event, and he found himself alone with Felix. At that moment a grey-haired, small-faced man in a navy-blue suit strode into the middle of the room and people clapped their hands. He was the Managing Director of the publishing company and the host of the evening, though he seemed to be of little consequence and probably wasn't even that rich.

It appeared that two novels were getting launched that night, in order to maximise publicity and reduce costs. James tried to concentrate, but the gin and the red wine were now mingling unhappily in his blood, and he felt light-headed and hot-faced. There weren't even any crisps. Instead, Isabelle handed him a sheet of paper with biographical details of the writers, both of whom were now standing alongside the Managing Director, beaming out indiscriminate smiles and displaying approximately the right quantities of exuberance, humility and ironic detachment.

The first to be introduced was Amelia Zhang-Montel. James nodded in silent appreciation: she was an ethnic masterpiece, a perfect synthesis of the most physically attractive, culturally revered and economically dynamic nations in the world. She had a Chinese mother and Franco-Jewish father, and had been raised in New York and educated in Cambridge, Paris and Berkeley. Even at a distance, James could immediately see all of that. She was small and preposterously pretty, with honey skin, shiny dark hair, an impish nose and unnerving green eyes.

Lucian Woodward was more conventionally attractive – a large, dramatic young man with diabolical black hair and thick, tilted eyebrows. He was wearing crude jeans and an open-necked, white linen shirt. His father was a professor of philosophy with a logical paradox named after him, and his mother was the vice-president of an investment bank that had recently destabilised Indonesia's economy.

Standing at the back of the room, James felt himself becoming small-minded. As ever, the major problem was not so much where they had come from, their patronage, the cost of their education, or even their talents, but their *age*. Both of the writers were comfortably under thirty. What the fuck, thought James with a surprising amount of bitterness, could they possibly be writing about? Weren't novelists meant to possess a treasury of insights in matters relating to the needs and failings of human beings? Surely, for all their accomplishments, they hadn't had the time to accumulate this wisdom, to have experienced the necessary defeats and disappointments?

The answer became apparent once Amelia began reading from her novel, for the protagonists weren't actually humans. Instead, they were nymphs – magical woodland beings who lived in a mystical kingdom. Driven out of their forest by timber cutters, a group of them sought shelter in the nearest town where they were immediately hailed by some as angels to be worshipped, while others branded them as demons and demanded they be destroyed.

The crux of the problem was that the qualities for which they were most revered – their beauty, outlandish clothing, the affection they inspired in children and their warnings about the weather – were exactly the ones for which they were also reviled. Amelia read some extracts from the opening chapters, and wouldn't say what happened, though James suspected it ended very badly for the nymphs.

Amelia explained that it was based on a traditional Catalan fairy tale, but obviously it wasn't meant to be a children's story. Nor, as far as James could tell, did it seem particularly allegorical, which was as far as his powers of literary analysis and hard-won Grade B in A level English could stretch. Her book wasn't about the destruction of the environment or the banality of Western monotheism – it really did just seem to be about some nymphs.

Lucian's book, *Sexheads*, sounded more straightforward. It was about conjoined triplet brothers, who all survive a pioneering operation to separate them performed by a religious mystic, only for their minds to have miraculously fused, cursing them with a permanent psychic connection. As a result, all psycho-sexual experiences and ordeals were shared, however far apart they were. Their father, just before committing suicide, placed them across the world's continents, so they only knew one another through their respective sexual encounters, with the additional complication that one of the brothers was an unhappily married heterosexual, the second a promiscuous homosexual and the third a sado-masochist and convicted murderer.

James bought a copy of each book from Kate and Miranda, who were now managing a makeshift sales counter with very little efficiency but high spirits. It cost him thirty pounds, but if nothing else, he now had some books on his shelves other than *The Lord of the Rings* and the sixth edition of *Principles and Practice of Town Planning*. Felix called Lucian over, and at once he crossed the room to join them, his shirt cuffs flapping and his thick arms outstretched. He was tall, almost the same height as James, but with the volume and force of personality to go with it.

'James, this is Lucian. We used to work together, until he persuaded himself that his talents would be better applied elsewhere, and that what he really needed to do was reduce his annual income by three-quarters.'

Lucian smiled, a handsome, generous, smile. He was aggressively unshaven, with dark hair that seemed to be ripening across his jaw even as he spoke, craftily counter-balanced by long eyelashes and a chunky silver earring.

'And what do you do?' he said, turning to James. His voice was deep and stupendously upper class – he had not yet learnt to smudge his consonants or shorten his vowels.

'I'm a planner,' said James.

'Ah, like Felix. That's great,' said Lucian. 'Some of the most brilliant people I know are planners. Are you at the same agency?'

'No, sorry, I'm a different kind of planner. I'm a town planner.'

'Really? That's great,' said Lucian.

But Lucian's attention was now being taken by a woman who had approached them without any need for stealth or courtesy. She had small round glasses on the end of her nose and a tidy bob of dark hair, but was otherwise dressed like a prostitute, with a scarlet blouse, tiny lime-green skirt and spectacular red leather boots. She was called Louise, she was a literary critic for a national newspaper and, at this stage in Lucian's career, it was more significant if she liked him than if he liked her. They embraced without artifice, and with only a moment's hesitation. It was almost inconceivable that they hadn't slept together.

'Louise, I'm so pleased you came,' said Lucian. 'I was worried you wouldn't make it.'

'Of course! I wasn't going to miss this one. Sorry I got here so late. I had to show my face at some tedious awards thing.'

'Better leave him to it,' said Felix to James. 'He's made his career choice, and is now undertaking his professional responsibilities.'

Amelia joined them. Close up, her charms and talents were even greater than James had guessed. She looked, and she probably got this a lot, like one of her nymphs – a slender, precious being not of the material world. She had beautiful transnational manners, and made a point of introducing herself to each of them in turn, as if she really wanted to speak to everyone as much as she did to Louise. And so, by way of retaliation, James made a point of *not* talking to her or asking her to sign his book. It was a personal victory over her precocious success and beauty. Maybe, in years to come, after she had won the Booker Prize and become famous, he might be able to construct a memory in which he had snubbed her.

James turned to Felix. 'I can see that there is a literary scene,' he said, 'and that it works with its own structure and hierarchies. And I can also see that people might get into it. But I don't think it's really for me. And another thing: how does anyone make a living from it?'

'I agree, that is something of a mystery,' said Felix. 'People used to write books in order to make money. But now I think it is almost completely the other way round.'

Sensing that those with the highest status and net worth were coalescing into a single group, Felicity and the Managing Director came over. James, making the same observation, crossed to the other side of the room. But by now the public relations team had scattered for good. Their work was done, their objectives secured and the event would have to be considered a success, even James could see that. But without them, with nothing other than writers and journalists to speak to, it seemed a bit forlorn. Two South Asian women appeared and started to clear away the tables.

'Well,' said Felix, who also seemed to have given up. 'Mission accomplished. You have now spent an evening in the company of the metropolitan liberal elite. And what's interesting is how little you took to them.'

'Or them to me,' said James.

'Oh I wouldn't say that – the PR girls adored you,' said Felix. 'But at times like this, we should always remember the Dalai Lama: when you lose, don't lose the lesson.'

'The lesson. What's the lesson?'

'That you're not actually a liberal,' said Felix. 'I suspect your worldview is something quite different.'

'Well, I don't think I'm a conservative,' said James. 'Or a socialist for that matter.'

'Oh, I'm not so bothered about that. The crucial thing is not how good or bad the idea, but the extent to which you're prepared to live it. That's the fundamental problem with these people. Of course, it's a problem that liberals tend to have in general.'

'Well, I did really like the PR girls,' said James. 'They were great.'

The book launch was over, but Lucian was determined for the night to continue. He invited Felix and James on a North London safari: a group of them were going to play snooker and drink pints of bitter at a working man's club round the corner. The club had a formidable reputation, and was known for its violation of licensing regulations and historical association with criminal gangs, wholesale drug dealers and corrupt chiefs of police. The neighbourhood was full of highly regarded bars and restaurants, but James could see that for these people there were quite different requirements. They were assiduous social diggers, and actively sought out the company of the lower classes, the desperate and the dangerous. It wasn't really acceptable for Lucian to hang out with lawyers and hedge fund managers – he needed to develop friendships with retired bank robbers, former IRA commandos and trade union leaders from defunct economic sectors.

James didn't want to go with them, but he didn't want to go home either – or at least, not immediately – and he wasn't ready yet to enter London's public transport system. He may not have enjoyed being there very much, but he did, at least, feel intoxicated and over-energised – by the gin, the red wine, by Miranda, Kate and Isabelle, by Amelia Zhang-Montel and the glamour of post-structuralist fiction. And so, rashly, he decided to walk it off. After all, the bus station at London Bridge was directly due south and no more than two miles away.

He set off. It was a cold February evening, and on both practical and psychological grounds he needed to go very fast. He walked down the high street, past the bars and restaurants spurned by Lucian, the two hardback books in a plastic bag knocking awkwardly against his legs – even James was sure that was a metaphor. For no good reason, his mind working hard but not thinking, he took his phone from his pocket and sent a text message to Alice: 'Hey! Was at a book launch and met a friend of yours called Felicity'.

Outside Angel underground station, he saw Miranda, sitting on a bench in a coat that didn't look warm enough and crying into her mobile phone. He walked quickly past, and turned down the hill, away at last from Islington. But the problem, the problem he should have foreseen, was that he was now in the City.

The City of London. During his long and uneventful adolescence, James had sometimes liked to pretend that the whole world was his private joke. As jokes go, it had been a poor one, but it wasn't even that any more – he knew that now. For a truly private joke is a philosophical impossibility, meaningless and self-defeating unless there is someone to share it with. No, the world had ceased being a joke and was now something much worse: it was *reality*. It had to be reality, because no single solipsist could be so deranged. A fuck-up on this kind of scale needed a lot of manpower. Not even the most violently insane planner could have dreamt up the City in such detail, with such cruelty and indifference. No, nobody was responsible – that was the fundamental problem. This wasn't the work of planners, this wasn't 1970s Sweden. It was the work of humanity. Only humanity, in all of its raw, unprocessed energy and enthusiasm, could have produced this disaster.

He walked through it all, he saw through it all. The landscape was provisional and disposable, a thawing cacophony, and it wasn't clear if the city was unravelling in front of him, or being ambitiously rebuilt. That was the thing about economic crashes – they were indistinguishable from economic booms. Whatever the circumstances and financial constraints, whoever the developer or planning authority, the style was always the same: neo-apocalyptic, for every building was now made on the basis that the world was about to end, that however much it may have cost, however technologically innovative and courageous, it would need to be pulled down in the next business cycle.

The architects had got particularly carried away this time. Over-excited by the money from Asia and their new software packages, they had designed impossible shapes with computer-generated angles. Then along had come the civil engineers, the people who actually knew what they were doing, with their powerful machines and smart materials and deadly confidence, even when given the battiest of architectural plans. And the towers that they made soared above him, greedily penetrating the heavens, interfering with weather systems, communicating with satellites, oblivious to the fact that the ones who had granted planning permission all lived on earth.

Head bowed, still weighed down by the books but walking faster than ever, he continued past Moorgate. There were no skyscrapers in Nottingham, and probably not many book launches either, but maybe that was a good thing. The City, the whole of London, had detached itself from the rest of the country, and become instead a global capital for culture and commerce, for vanity and greed. You could only succeed here if you could forget everything you'd ever learnt in England. But he wasn't like Felix or Alice: he was essentially a provincial, with provincial aspirations and fears.

Another twenty minutes later and at last he came to the river, to the bridge, where London opened up to him and became three-dimensional. There was physical geography instead of all the other kinds. The entire wealth of the city had once been based on the waterway below, but now it was without economic significance, and humans had lost interest in it. Meanwhile, on the south side of the river, the new towers were coming, taller than ever, rising in clumps above the train stations, fracturing the skyline and heralding a new era of prosperity and ruin. He pulled out his phone. There was a text from Alice. It had taken an hour, but she had sent one: 'I love Felicity. She's fab. U at a book launch?!'

He stopped along the bridge and looked down into the darkness. If he smoked, he would have lit a cigarette at this point, but he was far too old to take it up now, and so instead he had little option but to send another text to Alice: 'She seemed very nice and is big fan of yours too. Hope all is good. Fancy going for a drink?'

This time, the answer was almost immediate. 'How nice. V busy at the moment in work + life. Will email you all soon to arrange something.'

So that was that – clearly she didn't want to meet. She was v busy and, he should have guessed this, not just with work. But it had never been the plan to go back out with Alice. He crossed the bridge, and went over the water to the train station.

5

9 February

Consultation and involvement activities should also seek to empower communities and neighbourhoods.

– The London Plan, Section 2.64

'Of course, the reason I'm still in this job is because of all the glamorous locations,' said Rachel.

It was a Saturday morning, and James was doing something that had to be taken seriously, but wasn't terribly important. He was consulting the public. It was something he had done many times before. For much of the wet summer and sullen autumn, he had spent his Tuesday evenings, his Thursday afternoons and not-particularly-precious Saturday mornings trying to meet the eyes of his fellow citizens, to ascertain the thoughts and feelings of the people he was supposed to be helping.

And this particular project really was going to help them. He had worked on it long enough to be certain. The masterplan for Sunbury Square would result in thirty new houses and 250 flats spread across six low-rise blocks, all compliant with energy-efficiency best-practice guidelines, and of which 35 per cent would be affordable for low-income families and a further 10 per cent reserved for designated key workers in the borough's health and education sectors. There would be eight retail units, ranging in size from 500 to 2,000 square feet, a nursery and new playground. Two existing doctors' surgeries would be merged into an improved health centre with paediatric facilities, and there would be a piece of public art commissioned by the Arts Council.

Although in practice it was quite straightforward, on paper it had been almost impossibly difficult. The masterplan crossed the boundaries of two local development frameworks and would need to be signed off by transport, housing, environmental and regeneration assessors and approved at council and city level, and possibly by the Secretary of State. And then the whole thing would have to be funded. There would need to be transport infrastructure investment, and there would need to be money from local, regional and national government. It probably wouldn't work without some match funding from the European Development Fund, and the developers would have to be persuaded to increase their costs and reduce their margins. In all likelihood, getting the planning consent and the funding package agreed would take longer than the Second World War. And before any of this happened, they had to complete the public consultation.

'It's very good of you to do this with me,' said James.

'Tell me about it. It's not even my project,' said Rachel.

So here he was again. This time he was in Clifford's, a once state-of-the-art shopping centre that had been admired by a group of highly influential but now generally despised planners in the late 1970s for its durable concrete-composite walkways, integrated multi-storey car park and smoked glass ceiling. He could at least see the point of holding a consultation here. There was little point in searching for the local residents of Sunbury Square in the public library, arts centre or any of the other things that the council provided for them. No, this was their natural habitat: if they weren't working in shops, then generally they were buying things in them.

But at least he wasn't alone. Rachel, deservedly the most popular member of Southwark Council's Planning Directorate, was with him as they stepped on to a raised platform in the very centre of Clifford's, directly under the glass atrium, at the intersection of four broad avenues of shopping units. Beside them was a coffee kiosk and a little grouping of indoor plants, which may have been natural – it was practically impossible to tell, let alone know what that meant. James unfolded the camping table he had brought with him, expertly assembled his plastic stand and unpacked two canvas chairs for them. He pulled out clipboards and felt-tip pens, and a neat pile of blank yellow cards, on which people were encouraged to submit opinions and ideas.

'Well, we've got four hours here. Let's see if anything happens.'

'Oh, I'm sure we'll learn something,' said Rachel. 'I'm quite excited. I haven't done one of these for ages.'

James had done this many times before, and what had he learnt? Well, nothing worth learning, nothing that would actually improve the masterplan, nothing that would make the building materials stronger or the houses less costly or the public realm more attractive. How could it? It wasn't as if anyone he ever consulted knew anything about these things. Felix had told him last week that he wasn't a liberal, but maybe he wasn't a democrat either. Rather, he was a technocrat: he believed in technical solutions to the city's problems, and he knew he wouldn't find them here.

'I wish we didn't have to be on this stage,' said Rachel. 'I don't like being so exposed. All those gormless people staring at my thighs.'

James gazed down the shopping alleys. As a rule, he wasn't comfortable about being on view like this either, but he didn't think they had much to worry about. It was a raised floor really rather than a stage, only one foot high, and it was unlikely that Alice, or anyone else he was at university with, was going to walk past.

'I wouldn't get bothered about that,' said James. 'The usual problem is trying to attract their attention.'

According to some measures, London was the most unequal city in the developed world, and hardly anyone gave a shit. That was one of the hazards of being a town planner. You ended up getting cross and anxious about things that no one cared about. You worried about the amount of nitrogen dioxide in the air, the target rates for domestic recycling and why more people didn't go to the theatre. You tried to absorb and articulate all of the city's problems, and you did this so that other people didn't have to. As a result, it was perhaps inevitable that you became fretful and unhappy.

There was another reason too. The night before he had spoken to his family on the telephone. He had mentioned the job offer in Nottingham and his mother, who even more than most mothers hated London, had spent an hour making compelling arguments why he should take it. And what reasons could he give for staying? To attend book launches, hang out in bars and seek enlightenment? His mother prided herself on never being influenced by television commercials and would not be impressed with anything Felix had to say. And yet . . . could he really go to Nottingham? It had, after all, just come joint runner-up as the British city with the highest quality of life. Why on earth would he want to live there?

The early morning shoppers walked past, curious only until they realised that they didn't have any gifts or product samples to give away. Rachel's enthusiasm had disappeared. There had been some spasms of disgruntlement, but that had gone too and now she was playing patience on her mobile phone. James was trying to read *Sexheads*, but was finding it hard to get into.

'When are you lot ever going to learn?'

James and Rachel looked up to see a short, middle-aged man. He was almost certainly the only person in the shopping centre apart from James wearing a tie, and he was shaking his head at them gravely.

'Can I help?' said James. 'Have you got a view on the new plan?'

James recognised the type all too well. Although he was dressed smartly, his suit could easily be second-hand. He had neat grey hair and a moustache. If you didn't know any better, you might have guessed that he had served in the army, but in fact it was likely that he had spent most of his adult life on some form of welfare benefit. James knew that he would be highly intelligent but economically incompetent and would have strongly held, wildly incoherent political opinions.

'This scheme you've been dreaming up. It just isn't going to work. None of it adds up.'

James could detect an unlikeable shrillness in his voice, the consequence of a lifetime of not being listened to.

'Ah, adding up. James, I think this is more your domain,' said Rachel. 'I need to go for a cigarette.'

'It simply isn't going to work. And it certainly isn't going to look like that,' said the man, pointing over James's shoulder.

James glanced back for a moment at his masterplan poster. He had overseen the design himself with a junior, and therefore less obnoxious, member of the council's communications team, and he regarded it as his greatest creative achievement. It was large, almost two metres high, laminated with a cotton backing, and Lionel had grumbled about how much it had cost. But it was well worth it, if only because the image was everything that planning could be, everything he had once been taught and which he still believed in.

In the top left of the poster, the morning sunshine slanted powerfully through a friendly blue sky. A handsome black man in a suit and glasses strode into the foreground, his briefcase swinging confidently. A white woman, equally attractive and well dressed, was at his side, speaking into a mobile phone while holding a take-away coffee. In the other direction, two boys on bikes with helmets and shoulder bags were hurtling towards school, while a grey-haired, fresh-faced woman walked her obedient Dalmatian dog. All of them were on a broad walkway lined with silver birch trees, which curved out from the new development behind them – a wonderfully bright and happy building, with rippled surfaces, undulating roofs bearing wind turbines, yellow bricks and green glass, irregular colour panels and rustic fittings. Just as important, of course, was what was missing: there were no cars, no clouds, no graffiti, no litter, no criminal damage or mental illness. They hadn't even had to airbrush anything out, for the entire poster had been made on a computer, an ingenious montage of photos that the council owned the copyright on, fanciful architectural images and shapes and textures rendered with Californian software tools.

'Do you want me to go through it with you?' said James.

'You don't have to. I've already studied it. You've got it all wrong.'

While the usual problem with the British public was that they tended not to know anything, the real troublemakers were the ones who actually did. The retired civil engineers with radical transport solutions, the autodidacts who spent their days in public libraries mastering European environment regulations. These were the ones who weren't just wrong, but were spectacularly, dangerously wrong – wrong in ways that must be discounted but couldn't necessarily be refuted.

'There are many problems with this plan, and I've outlined them in my written response. But the main one you've got is that it doesn't take any account at all of traffic. What about car parking? You seem to be under the impression that everyone who lives here is going to be travelling exclusively by bicycle.'

'Well, I think you're quite right to the raise the issue and it is an important one. We've actually given it quite a lot of thought. We did commission a feasibility study that looked specifically at this.'

'Oh, I'm well aware of that. But I haven't been able to read it. I've submitted a number of Freedom of Information requests, and am still waiting. You do know that you're obliged to reply in twenty-eight days to any request for information, unless it is pertains to the defence of the realm?'

James nodded sadly. Somebody like this couldn't be placated with a polite conversation or a perfectly friendly and meaningless letter. Like looking into the eyes of certain dogs, engagement meant escalation. Unless James left for Nottingham, it was likely that the two of them would now spend a great deal of time having lengthy telephone conversations, combative meetings and curt email exchanges. James may even come to like him by the end of it – that did sometimes happen.

Rachel returned half an hour later. She had been shopping, she had bought something, and she was happy. For many people, it really was that simple.

'I bought myself some new bed sheets,' she said. 'You know, it's a real shame we're knocking this shopping centre down.'

'We're not knocking it down. It's going to be refurbished. Have you even read the masterplan?'

'It's not my project – I'm just here for the moral support. Anyway, while you were dealing with the nutter, I've been doing some big thinking on your behalf. What you need is a girlfriend. It's actually quite urgent.'

'Do you think so? I mean, more than anyone else does?'

'Much more than most. It's practically an emergency. You need someone to organise your life for you.'

'But I am organised. I'm a town planner,' said James.

'Yes, but you're no good at making plans for yourself,' said Rachel. 'You're actually really bad at that.'

Rachel probably wasn't as clever as Felix. It had taken her longer but she had come to a similar conclusion. Should he now tell her about the job in Nottingham? No – she would only agree with his mother: tell him to take it, to leave London, to get promoted and earn more money. Ultimately, her worldview was far more hard-headed, far more than useful, than his would ever be.

'Look, it really is as simple as that. All you need to do is get a girlfriend and most of your problems will just disappear. It shouldn't be difficult – you look half-decent.'

James nodded. Yes, he was tall, that still helped a bit, but there were other, more substantial issues. There was where he lived, what he did for a living, how much he earned, the quality of his book collection and the prints on his bedroom wall.

'It's not hard,' said Rachel. 'There is a well-established format. All you need to do is take one out for a date, buy her a drink and a meal, try not to stoop too much, and take it from there.'

'Oh Christ – dates. I thought you might say that.'

'Oh, my dear boy,' said Rachel, who was actually the same age as James. 'What on earth has happened to your confidence? You know it's easier to date girls now than ever before in history.'

But James wasn't so sure. Yes, there was the Internet now and feminism and sexual liberation, but none of those things had done him much good. Women were better informed and could make more choices, but it didn't follow that they would choose him. In fact, what he could really do with was for the whole marketplace to become a bit less efficient, for people not to be able to see how many friends he had on Facebook, or find his job title and salary band on the Southwark Council website.

'I think,' said James, 'that the historical circumstances aren't necessarily to my advantage. I'm a town planner, remember. Most women I know have better paid jobs than me.'

'Well, that's true,' she said. 'It would probably help if you didn't work for a local authority. But not every girl wants to go out with an investment banker or architect. And at least you've got a proper job with a pension – you're not a poet or a skateboarder or anything.'

'Don't couples meet normally any more? Like at work or something?'

'It's all right. You'll be able to handle a date. They can't be any worse than all the other meetings you fill your life with. At least there won't be any PowerPoint.'

Just then two more people approached with a speed and purpose that James knew could only mean trouble. A couple – a bony white man and a larger, more classically unattractive woman. These were the authentic voice of the South London suburbs. They looked ten years older than they actually were, owned a house and a car, had incomes that had failed to keep up with the cost of living and were tremendously angry. Of course, everyone in London was angry, but the fact that they possessed things gave their rage a particular focus and power.

'Are you from the council?' said the man.

'Yes,' said James. 'We're from the planning department and we're here to talk about—'

'Then you're exactly the bloke I want to speak to.'

'Do you want me to talk through the development plan? Do you live in the local area?'

'I want to talk to you about our planning application, and why nobody in your office can be bothered to answer my phone calls.'

This was something that tended to happen at consultations. The problem was that planners spent a lot of time stopping things from happening. Up and down the country they were stopping people from turning their garden sheds into summerhouses and installing porches in conservation areas. And people hated them for it. It wasn't fair, but they did. And when they did allow people to do things, if they let someone build a mosque or a factory or a wind farm, well then everyone else hated them instead. Worst of all, whether they were allowing or stopping things, it took them an awful long time, for James, like all planners, worked calmly and methodically, he worked incredibly slowly.

'I'm sorry,' said James. 'Is this a specific planning issue? It's just that we're here to consult on a masterplan.'

'Do you work for the council or don't you?' said the man.

James looked at Rachel, who for a moment looked as if she was going to disappear for another cigarette.

'I'd be happy to talk to you about it,' said Rachel. 'James, why don't you go and get lunch for us. Residential developments are something I have responsibility for, and I'm sure we can sort this out.'

James hopped down and walked away as quickly as he could. But where was he going? The shopping centre, even one as old as this, hurt his eyes and he had no idea how he would ever be able to buy something as simple as a sandwich here. There were too many reflective surfaces, too much luminosity, too many adverts. Of course, what he really would have wanted was to start all over again. It was every planner's dream. Not to have to tweak deficient settlements, to accommodate narrow-minded residents or negotiate with selfish landowners. But, of course, you never did. Instead, you had to work with what you had. And what you had was always terrible.

It wasn't just Clifford's shopping centre or Sunbury Square or Southwark. It wasn't even London. For James had been born in 1980 and all the battles had been fought before he had turned ten years old. After a century of catastrophic utopian experiments, the Western world, James's world, the entire world, had settled on a system that best fitted human nature and was therefore, of course, the very worst of them all. A system of prohibitions and permissions, punishments and prizes, all constructed upon human faultlines and appetites, designed to provide an infinite variety of pleasures, and which had made people unhappy in ways that they could once only have dreamt of. And as a result, the shopping centre was unhappy, the city was unhappy. James could feel it, but he was unable to describe it, and all the town planning in the world wouldn't be able to cure it.

'I think I've just had a professional crisis,' said James. 'It's dawned on me that everything we do for a living is futile.'

It had taken forty minutes, he had got lost twice, but he was back with a plastic bag of sandwiches, crisps and orange juices. And, thankfully, in the meantime, Rachel seemed to have neutralised the couple with false promises and hopes.

'You're such a hilarious *novice*. All planners come to hate and despair of the job. I can't believe it's taken you so long. This is a real breakthrough. You might actually have a successful career in front of you now.'

'I don't hate all of it,' said James. 'I don't mind producing maps and plans. It's just that we never actually spend much time doing that. Instead, we spend most of our time talking to people who don't like us.'

'Of course, it would make the job so much easier if no one actually lived in London.'

He stared at the shopping centre crowds, the men in red tracksuits, the teenage boys in their shiny coats and the girls in their bubblegum pink skirts. This was his tribe – the people who he had vowed to help and to improve, whether they wanted him to or not.

'What can we do about it? We're only town planners,' said Rachel. 'We're not the city's parents. If you start thinking like that, if you start taking responsibility for everything and everyone, then you're doomed.'

James nodded calmly and sat back down on his canvas chair. They ate their sandwiches. The consultation continued, and lunchtime dissolved into Saturday afternoon. James and Rachel talked politely and listened carefully. James kept his spine bent, his shoulders hunched and tried as hard as he could not to be taller than the public. They asked people to write things down on cards and made a point of nodding their heads agreeably, asking helpful little questions and giving exaggerated thanks for each contribution. A man in a wheelchair was bothered about the safety of pedestrian crossings, but it wasn't clear if this was a problem with the masterplan or a more general concern. An Irish woman with a lovely voice was worried that the new development would bring more Muslims into the area. A Turkish man with sad eyes said that he was scared to go out at night because of all the black drug dealers. A handsome woman from Jamaica said that the area was being ruined by the Polish, who were always getting drunk.

'Now do you remember why you avoided doing public consultations for so long?' said James.

'At least when they're being racist, they're not behaving like customers. There's a bit of community sentiment going on. That's something.'

James went through the yellow comment cards. It was as he'd expected. There was a problem with the masterplan, and it had nothing to do with the building materials or traffic projections. It wasn't insurmountable, and once upon a time it wouldn't have counted for anything at all, but it was there – a gnawing, intangible, pervasive problem that made all the other ones much more difficult. *The project was unpopular.* It wasn't just the public art, it was the whole thing. True, it was difficult to get the public to express a cogent opinion – but when they did, it was unambiguous. People didn't like it.

In a way, this wasn't such a surprise. James knew that humans can get nostalgic for pretty much anything: brutalised childhoods, major wars, discredited education systems, uncomfortable and inefficient forms of transport. It was just the same with the houses they lived in. For, incredibly, most of the residents of Sunbury Square actually seemed to like where they lived. They *liked* the totalitarian housing units with their grey walls and poor insulation, they liked the cramped doctors' surgeries and the tarmac playground that their children were always breaking their arms on. Or, at least, they didn't want anyone to change it.

'You mustn't let it get to you. So what if they don't like what you're trying to do. It doesn't mean that you're wrong.'

James had stopped listening. He was looking at his poster again. Yes, it had been made on a computer and none of it was real and yes, he had spent so much time with it that what he saw were now largely his own projections. But did that matter? The main thing was that there existed a vision for London, or at least a small part of it, and they could always extrapolate from that. An orderly, sunny, energy-efficient vision of how things should be.

'You're doing that thing again,' said Rachel suddenly. 'You've been doing it all morning.'

'What thing? What am I doing?'

'That staring-into-space thing. You might think you're being mysterious, but it just makes you look gloomy. And women hate gloomy men. Moody and melancholy: yes. Gloomy and grumpy: no. If you're not careful, you'll succumb to self-pity, and then you'll really be fucked. It's only a shopping centre. It's not like we're working in an African coal mine.'

She was right, of course: it was only a shopping centre. Although James often thought that he'd be perfectly happy working down a coal mine provided Adam, Carl and everyone else he knew was working there too.

'You're right,' said James. 'It's only a shopping centre.'

James had a vision for Sunbury Square, but did he have one for himself? Well, yes – and it wasn't so very gloomy. He was thirty-five years old and he lived in a pleasant, if distant, suburb in West London, or possibly Nottingham. It was a Friday night and he had just gone with his pretty girlfriend, who looked a bit like Rachel, to the cinema. The film wasn't as good as they'd been led to expect but they'd quite enjoyed it all the same. Afterwards, they had had two drinks each at a pub and then they had travelled back on the last train, followed by a short walk to their flat, which they were able to afford because they had a joint income, and which had maintained its value despite the prevailing market conditions. It had, in short, been a satisfactory evening in what was generally a satisfactory life. And what was so wrong with that? His job wasn't as well paid as Carl's, his home wasn't as big as Adam's and his girlfriend was less socially confident than Alice. But that was only a problem if he made it one, and besides – nowadays, he rarely saw any of these people.

'All right,' he said. 'You're right. I need a girlfriend. And I also accept that in order to get one of those, I'll need to go on a date. Do you think you can get me one?'

'Don't worry,' said Rachel. 'I'll get you one.'

6

15 February

The 2,000-year history of London has been one of constant change. It has grown from a port and river crossing point into a bustling centre of national government.

– *The London Plan*, Section 1.2

'I suppose you must have chosen this place for its competitive pricing strategy,' said Laura.

James smiled bravely. The main thing was to concentrate on the positives, to learn lessons, improve his technique and not make a total fucking idiot of himself. This was, after all, the first date he had been on for some time and he shouldn't expect either of them to enjoy it.

It should have been quite manageable – he was thirty-two, it wasn't as if he could claim youthful inexperience. But the big challenge was that he hadn't been expecting Laura to be anything like this clever or pretty. This should have been a dry run, an evening in which he got to experiment on a guinea pig, someone with whom he could make mistakes, safe in the knowledge that he would be able to hurt her more than she could hurt him. On paper, on email, on the web, Laura had sounded ideal. She worked in economic policy for the public sector, she had a degree from nowhere to get worried about, and the only picture he'd seen, admittedly a small low-resolution image on Rachel's Facebook page, had given him no cause for anxiety. But the photo had been highly misleading, in fact he was now almost certain that it actually *had* been Rachel. Laura had a Masters from Cambridge, and although it was true that she did economic policy, she wasn't one of those well-meaning dumpy girls who worked in regeneration or international development or something. No, it turned out that Laura worked for the fucking Treasury.

In the light of all this, James had, he conceded, selected a poor venue. He had offered to meet round the corner from her office. That seemed to be a determining factor in why she'd agreed to this, and so his main consideration had been to choose a place that didn't run Friday evening drinks promotions and where sales teams wouldn't turn up and play drinking games. And so they were in the White Lion, one of those low-ceilinged Whitehall pubs with dark over-varnished furniture and a dun-coloured carpet that looked like it could keep secrets. It was a plotters' pub, a civil-servant pub, intended not for entertainment but rather to allow melancholy deliberation, the replaying of the day's events and for planning future ambushes and betrayals. It was a place where things – air, heat, light, words – could be relied upon to stay put, but not a place to take a highly attractive professional on a date. It was almost six years since cigarettes in pubs had been banned, but smoke still seemed to circle mysteriously around their heads.

'So Rachel tells me you're another town planner,' said Laura. 'One of those types that likes to go around distorting the market for his own opaque purposes?'

James looked at her anxiously. Something else that had become quickly apparent was that, as well as everything else, she was right wing. He should have guessed. It was well known that almost everyone who worked in government at a senior level didn't actually believe in government. That wouldn't make for an easy evening. All the right-wing people that James knew, and as he got older there seemed to be more and more of them, were so exhausting, so relentless and harassing to be around – in a way that, once upon a time, left-wing people probably were. The problem was, he was on a date. It was just the two of them. He could hardly *ignore* her. It wasn't as if someone else – Felix, for instance, would have been good – was going to pop up and answer questions on his behalf.

'Planning isn't about distorting the market. It's about bringing order, avoiding urban disruption, and ensuring that land resources are used as effectively as possible.'

As he said this, it occurred to him that he was quoting directly from the introductory chapter to one of his old textbooks, and that he almost certainly sounded like a moron.

'Land prices determine the most productive uses of land – is there really much more to it than that? And are you sure that what you call disruption is not just people getting on with their lives in enterprising ways that you don't happen to particularly like?'

'No, of course not. We don't just impose rules on people for the sake of it. We do things in order to make everyone's lives better. Better for everyone – we have to think about what's best for the whole community, the whole city.'

Laura paused to consider this. It was clear that she wasn't satisfied, and none of what he was saying actually sounded very plausible, even to him. Was that really what he did for a living? He couldn't remember Lionel ever saying that.

'I think that the problem with planning, as always with government, is incentives. Either they don't exist or else they're the wrong ones. You have strategies and targets and those are intended to motivate you to do certain things. But what you really need is customers.'

'Well, yes,' said James. 'But these things aren't arbitrary. Targets aren't just made up for no reason. They're intended to improve things, to do things like reduce pollution or traffic.'

'But those targets don't relate to people's lives in a direct way. For instance, you're incentivised by things like reducing traffic on the roads, but why? People want to drive to work. And you're told to put people close together, high up in small spaces, when in fact most people want the exact opposite. They want to live on the ground, in big houses and gardens.'

'Yes, but without some kind of order and planning, all you'll end up with is endless sprawl. You wouldn't want to live in a city like that.'

'Actually, I'm not especially snobbish about sprawl in the way that you lot are. Just because it doesn't meet your density targets it doesn't mean that people don't like living there. They can do their shopping, they can park their cars easily and have barbecues in their gardens. Those are things that people care about.'

Like everything else other than work, the evening was proving to be incredibly hard work. And yet, this was the strange thing, *she wasn't leaving*. He had been careful to give her plenty of opportunities, but no – she was still there, in fact, she was now going to the bar to buy some more drinks. Could it really be possible that she was having a good time? It was difficult to tell. Laura certainly didn't seem very happy. Then again, she wasn't going to hang around with him unless she wanted to. He'd met these Treasury maniacs before, he knew the kind of cost-benefit analysis they brought to every decision, every discretionary purchase and social interaction. But maybe she was lonely? After all, they lived in just about the loneliest city in the world.

Laura returned from the bar with two large glasses of white wine. There was no getting away from it – she was very pretty. She was tall and blond, but that was actually beside the point, and nor was she in the least what you'd call striking. Rather her face was an organisational triumph – the collective effect of a standard-shaped mouth with even teeth, set apart at a reasonable distance from a moderate nose, light-blue eyes and average-sized ears. As with her analytical reasoning, there were no mistakes or irregularities in her appearance.

'You're wrong,' he said, trying hard not to sound as if the argument had already been lost. 'About planning – I think you're totally wrong. There wouldn't even be a functioning market if it wasn't for planners. We're the ones that make things work, that tackle all the market failures.'

'Well, of course – it's not as if I'm an anarcho-libertarian or anything. I'm an economist and I think I understand the concept of market failure better than most. I'm just not sure how much we really benefit when people like you go around trying to fix them.'

'But the market failures in London are endemic. Congestion, poor housing, urban poverty, pollution, unemployment, crime. It's the job of planners to sort all of these things out. Imagine what it would be like if there wasn't any planning.'

James wasn't entirely sure if these were really market failures or not, but no matter – Laura was now beaming at him. That was the way with these Treasury types. They thrived on conflict, on being impertinently questioned and intellectually challenged – as long as in the end they won, which they almost always did. In fact, what he should probably do now, if he really wanted her to become affectionate, was to escalate, to manufacture an ill-tempered argument, and then try and insult her in some way.

'The problem isn't market failure,' said Laura. 'It's easy enough to identify those. The problem is *government* failure. Just because you're not pleased with something, it doesn't necessarily follow that the state's solution will make things any better. And, quite often, it ends up making something else much worse.'

'You're not a Conservative are you?' asked James.

'Oh God, probably, though of course I don't vote for them. I'm not like you anyway – I'm not a planner. I have a strong and healthy sense of the value of personal freedoms.'

James swallowed some of his pub white wine, and ate a handful of peanuts to moderate the aftertaste. Professionally he had been taught to distrust most types of freedom, and personal freedoms were usually the very worse. Developers, architects, graffiti artists – they were the champions of personal freedom, of economic liberty and self-expression, and they were all his enemies.

'Put it this way,' continued Laura, 'I trust the people to screw things up for themselves in ways that are more enjoyable and less costly than when people like you and me try and do it for them.'

'But that's not what I do at all. I—'

'I know it's not what you try to do. I'm not questioning your morals or anything. It's just what invariably happens. It's not even about economics. The way I see it is this: when people spend money on themselves, okay, it's not great – in my case I tend to buy books I'll never get round to reading. But when people spend money that belongs to somebody else, on behalf of other people, well, that's never going to work is it? Even if they're clever and well meaning it's unlikely to work. Never mind if they're stupid or venal. And let's be honest: almost everyone we work with is one or the other.'

'And what about the environment? You must worry about that? What happens when people do whatever selfish thing they like, and end up destroying the planet?'

'Oh God, yes – the environment. Don't worry – I'm not one of those mad old men who hasn't had sex for thirty years and is convinced that climate change is a plot invented by communists. It's just that, somehow, I can't bring myself to worry all that much about it. And, of course, I can't stand woolly headed environment-alists, who do seem to be the only type there are.'

James stared across the room. He couldn't be sure if it was Laura's worldview or the pub that was making him so dispirited. There were two young men in duffel coats drinking lemonade and push-ing buttons on a quiz machine, a red-faced man at the bar reading a tabloid newspaper and four middle-aged North American tour-ists sipping half pints of bitter and consulting their guidebooks, wondering if they had the right to feel let down or not. The barwoman, a young Ukrainian with poor skin, was playing a game on her mobile phone. He decided to go to the bathroom.

'It's not true,' he said, as he got up. 'About everyone we work with being so awful and so useless.'

Although actually it was. He might not be prepared to admit it, but he would accept that it was at least partly true. For even now, he was still dismayed by his colleagues. Okay, Graham in Nottingham hadn't been so bad and Rachel was good at her job, but where were all the highly competent taciturn professionals with specialist technical skills and for whom service was its own reward? Why weren't they more like him or, failing that, why weren't they more like nobody at all? Why were they so much like themselves? Why were they so much like *Lionel?*

They were unmistakably inner-London pub toilets: small and ancient with inadequate ventilation, the damp walls had been coated comprehensively but unreassuringly with a dark red paint, and a urinous tang was still perceptible beneath the carbolic acid. But at least they were empty, and there was no danger of anyone else trying to wash his hands for him. James checked his phone. There were three text messages from Rachel: The first one said: 'Are u still with L or have you bored her already?' The second, sent two hours later said: 'I thought you'd get on. U owe me for this' and the third, sent an hour after that said: 'OMG! Your most probably having sex right now'. Although probably impossible, maybe he should have gone on a date with Rachel instead. He would, in as much as this counted for anything, have enjoyed it more.

He tried to order two small white wines, but it seemed that such a concept no longer really existed, and he returned to the table with two unhelpfully large glasses, which he knew could determine the trajectory of the evening if he didn't keep his wits about him. By now they had had so much to drink and so little to eat that it didn't really matter what they talked about. They discussed Rachel for a while – James was sure she wouldn't have minded – and speculated as to why she didn't have a boyfriend. And then Laura embarked on a long account of how the Treasury worked and all the things she did there, which seemed to centre around the fact that they had better mathematical models and more robust data than the economists at the Department of Work and Pensions whom, as far as James could tell, were sort of her rivals. In turn James told her what it was like working in local government, and she gamely asked lots of questions about his job and shook her head solemnly whenever James admitted to inefficiencies or organisational failings.

'You know, I've never really got local government,' she said. 'I know it's fashionable these days for everyone in central government to say how important it is. But it just seems to be full of busybodies who don't know anything about economics.'

'Yes,' said James. 'It largely is. That's probably why I like it.'

Anyway, the good news was that Laura wanted very much to kiss him. She'd probably had too much to drink, but that didn't account for the manner in which she was leaning across the table and reaching out to hold his hand. No longer combative, she was now attempting to be amorous. But of course she was far less good at this. Laura's talents were of a higher level than James's: she was accomplished at scrutinising spreadsheets, identifying flaws in public policy arguments and being disagreeable in meetings whenever someone wanted to spend money. But she had no talent at all for being friendly, let alone for seduction. She was, thought James and it rather impressed him that this had occurred to him, bound to be terrible in bed.

'So what do you want to do next?' said Laura. 'Shall I get another drink? Or we could get some food if you like?'

He had never expected this to happen, but it was clear that, however much wine they drank, James was now in control of the evening, and what happened next would depend on how he felt about it. And how did he feel about it? Well, many things, but above all he felt *tired*. He was tired of the small dark pub with its prints of Victorian London and illustrations from Charles Dickens imported from the Philippines, he was tired of eating roasted peanuts and salt and vinegar crisps, and he was even tired of them being the most attractive people there. But changing the venue, which he could easily do if he wanted, wasn't going to help, for most of all, he was tired of Laura.

'Let's go,' said James. 'I think we've had all the fun we can out of this place.'

Laura sprung up to leave, with an over-eagerness and willingness to please that her professional conditioning was meant to have suppressed.

'Yes, good idea. I think if we stay any longer we'll soon reach the point of negative marginal utility.'

As she said this, she urged a chuckle into her voice, to make it clear she was attempting a joke.

Outside, it was quiet, as the streets often were in the very centre of London, as if the entire ruling class had left for a cocktail party. All around them were substantial square buildings made of Portland Stone, set back from the road and protected by cast-iron railings. It was here that plans were drawn up and instructions issued for the rest of the country by public servants who were far better paid than James and enrolled on to different pension schemes. But it was Friday night, and the lights were all out. Nor was it clear that anyone was listening anyway. And maybe Laura was right, maybe it was for the best if no one in government did anything other than come up with compelling reasons for not doing anything. It wasn't as if anyone seemed to like what James did. That was another problem with spending an evening in the company of somebody who was right-wing: you often ended up agreeing with them.

'So whereabouts in London do you live?' said James.

'I'm in Balham,' said Laura.

James nodded. He could have guessed that.

'Yes, it's nice there,' he said, absent-mindedly.

He wondered what Alice was doing that evening. She wouldn't be in a pub in Whitehall, that was for sure. Primrose Hill, Notting Hill, Islington, Farringdon – even James knew that no one who lived in London, who really *lived* in London, spent their evenings in the town centre. At any rate, it was a consolation that Laura was better looking than her.

'Yes, I really like it. It's got everything really. And fortunately my brother and I bought our flat there a while ago, just as prices really started to rocket.'

'Oh, that's great,' said James. 'What does your brother do?'

'He's an economist too,' said Laura. 'But he works for a bank.'

They walked together down the road in the direction of the Tube station – it seemed to suit them both not to specify a plan for the moment. Laura lurched heavily into him and put an arm over his shoulder but, again, she was no good at this sort of thing and it wasn't clear if she was trying to be intimate or had clumsy ankles. James tried to think of something to say, something about her brother or Balham or the global economy, but it was difficult. It was difficult because he wasn't interested. He already knew what her flat would be like, that it would have a glass coffee table, stainless steel kitchenware and blonde wood furniture, and he knew approximately how much it was worth, and the kinds of things her brother would have to say.

And so James left *her* outside the station. They had kissed goodbye at the entrance – on the cheek to begin with, and then, as she had turned her face into his, he had stepped back and used his height to neatly kiss her on the forehead.

'Well, goodnight,' he said. 'It was really great meeting you.'

'Yes,' said Laura, confused and suddenly uneasy. 'Yes, I really enjoyed it. Aren't you getting on the Tube too?'

'No, I think I'll get a bus home.'

'Really? Are you sure? That sounds a bit arduous.'

'It's probably the best way to get home at this time,' he said.

'Oh, okay. Well, goodnight. It was nice meeting you.'

'Yes, goodnight,' and as he said this, she was already moving smartly away from him, attempting, at the very end of the evening, to reassert her status. James knew it was important that he let her do this.

It had been simply done, but it was a massive victory nonetheless. True, she had been gruelling company and he was glad to be rid of her, but still, the fact remained: she was a very attractive woman and he could have kissed her a great deal more if he'd wanted. He could have taken her for another drink, escorted her back home, let the night continue in all sorts of ways, but he had decided not to. And the reasons for doing so had only been partly based on fear.

Okay, he had probably hurt Laura's feelings a bit. But he reasoned that his self-esteem had risen more than hers had fallen. Plus, she almost certainly still had a lot more of it than he had. Laura herself could hardly object to his reasoning: it was the kind of analysis she did all the time, and, besides, the main thing was *she'd be absolutely fine*. There was very little point worrying about the Lauras of this world. She was, after all, Civil Service Fast Stream. Before too long she'd be going out with a special advisor, or engaged to someone in the Bank of England. It was only a matter of time. Ultimately, she was a much better prospect than he was.

Well, whatever the evening had meant for Laura, for him it had been a major confidence boost – a triumph he'd have to call it, even if nothing much had actually happened and he hadn't really enjoyed it. He reached for his phone and sent a text message to Rachel: 'Thanks for fixing me up with Laura. She was good, but not good enough.' He regretted doing it immediately afterwards. But no matter – it wasn't a time in his life to be nurturing regrets. It was a time to be doing things. And now it was obvious what he needed to do next. He needed to go on another date as soon as possible.

7

19 February

Decisions will have to be made at global, national and regional levels
that will have profound consequences.

– The London Plan, Section 1.36

James didn't believe in conspiracy theories – they were too good to
be true. If only the world *was* being run by a cabal of highly intelligent Jews from Yale University. But no: the sad truth was that no
one really was in control of all this. No secret organisation in Oregon
was responsible for global warming or the crisis in the Middle East,
which meant that no secret organisation was ever going to sort them
out. Instead, there were seven billion people stumbling around doing
shit things to one another and wondering why shit things kept
happening to them. And the only people trying to help them were
people like him – the planners. The regulators, busybodies and
do-gooders. But there weren't very many of them, not really, and
most of them were so bad at it that they just made things worse.

He was with them now, on the fourth floor of Southwark
Council, sitting at his desk in the middle of the Planning and
Environment Directorates. It was, indisputably and reassuringly, an
office. He was well aware that nowadays they weren't all like this.

He had been to other ones, architects' mainly, where things were done differently with a colourful collection of conflicting objects and furniture – plasma screens, red sofas, leather beanbags, table-football machines. But there was no such ambiguity here where every desk, filing cabinet and patterned carpet had come from a single supplier, carefully selected from a national procurement roster on the basis of a wide range of factors, none of which had anything to do with the attractiveness of its products.

The most important feature of the room was directly in front of his desk – the fourth floor kitchenette, a monument to the failings of collective responsibility. From where James sat, he could see the white plastic kettle and the counter coated in hardened sugar and spilt coffee granules. Below was a cupboard of mugs with slogans from health promotion campaigns, and the communal fridge, long ago rendered unusable by the stack of unclaimed Tupperware boxes with their pasta salads and tuna bakes. How many rounds of tea had he made here? And how many hours at the end of the day had he spent at the sink washing up mugs in lukewarm water, rubbing away at tannin stains, or trying to dislodge the insoluble remains of instant soup mixture?

James turned back to his screen. There was a long email from his sister, a letter really, with observations on her teacher-training course, news from home, which wasn't significant enough to be considered good or bad, and enthusiasm about the job offer in Nottingham. James hadn't even finished it before he turned to read another email, from Felix.

In person, Felix liked to speak at length, making eloquent pronouncements in complete sentences. But when it came to electronic communications he was curt and brutally to the point. His emails were businesslike, forcefully punctuated and demanded action. To James, who had only ever worked in the public sector with colleagues who were well mannered and socially unconfident, this inevitably meant that they came across as menacing.

Subject: The Date
What happened? Need a full report.

Without delay, James started to write a detailed reply, describing his evening with Laura and what had and hadn't happened. He was meant to be drafting a briefing for Lionel, which should have taken him three hours, but so far had taken two days. This wasn't for any of the usual reasons: he hadn't been interrupted by a crisis generated by the communications team, he hadn't had to deal with an aggrieved planning applicant, and it wasn't because his computer had broken down. He just couldn't be bothered. It was barely two o'clock and he felt fatigued, uninterested, mildly unhappy and unappreciated. He felt like someone who worked in the public sector.

Rachel came over to his desk. 'Have you done that baseline briefing on Sunbury?'

'The meeting isn't until Friday.'

'I think Lionel wants it before then. I wouldn't mind seeing it either. I've got a meeting with the community housing lot tomorrow. Would be good to be able to tell them about a project that isn't fucking up.'

'Well, I haven't done it yet.'

They looked into each other's eyes for a moment. Rachel was wearing a long dark coat with a red scarf over her shoulders. Her black hair was flat and she looked unusually professional and unfriendly.

'Come outside and sit with me while I have a cigarette,' she said. 'I want to give you some grief.'

Without saying a word, he got up and followed Rachel out of the office and into the lift, in which they stood in careful silence alongside the Deputy Chief Executive while it bumped its way down to reception. It was only after they had got outside and Rachel had lit a cigarette that she spoke.

'So. The date with Laura. Given the lovely text you sent me, I gather you didn't think very much of her.'

'Oh God, yes – sorry about that. I'd had too much to drink. Have you spoken to her?'

'She rang me last night. She says you're a weirdo.'

'Well, I don't think that's fair. And I did like her.'

'Really? Tell me the truth. I know what a useless liar you are.'

'I did like her. She's very clever. We just weren't very compatible. You know what these Whitehall types are like. I felt as if she didn't have any time for what I do.'

'Really? That doesn't sound like her. She's never been like that to me. What did you talk about?'

'Planning policy and market failure, mainly.'

'Christ, you really know how to give a girl a good time.'

'Well, believe it or not, she did most of the talking. I'm surprised she's a friend of yours actually – she's pretty right wing.'

'She isn't really. She's just an economist, that's all. She's smart and she likes to challenge people. She's always been like that – it's one of the reasons I like her.'

Rachel blew a thick cloud of smoke into the cold air. James felt the need to defend himself further.

'Okay, but you must admit – she is a bit snobbish and superior.'

'She's really not, you know. She's from Stoke, for starters. There aren't many snobs up there.'

'She didn't sound like she was from Stoke. She just sounded like someone from the Treasury.'

'Did you even ask where she was from?'

James looked away and across the road. It had gone lunchtime, but the traffic was still heavy.

Rachel lit another cigarette. 'Anyway, I don't know why I'm even talking to you, given some of the things you said to Laura about me.'

Christ – what on earth had he said to Laura? Pretty much anything she'd wanted to hear, given that they were in the early stages of a date.

'I didn't say anything about you.'

'That's not what she said.'

'That's rubbish,' said James.

Rachel shrugged. 'Maybe. Laura can't be completely trusted, I will grant you that.'

'Well, she's talking rubbish. I didn't say anything.'

'Fuck it,' said Rachel. 'I'm not bothered.'

'Well, I didn't.'

'Like I said, I'm not bothered,' said Rachel.

But she was bothered. They both were. Rachel stubbed out her cigarette after just two drags and wrapped her scarf around her neck, and James tried to think of something that would end the conversation on a better note.

'Are you going back upstairs?'

'No,' said Rachel. 'I haven't eaten yet. I'm going to get a sandwich. See you up there.'

James nodded and looked over the street that he knew so well. One of the problems was that it was too narrow for them all. The cyclists and drivers and bus passengers and pedestrians and pet dogs, all with their pointless preoccupations and over-heating minds. Every interaction required negotiation and tolerance, eye contact and a mature approach to shared space. It wasn't like this in Nottingham. Yes, there were people, of course, and they were probably just as bad, but there were far fewer of them. They weren't always banging into each other. He shivered in the cold and hostility. He had to get back inside. If nothing else, the public sector could still be good for shelter.

Back at his desk, James stared at the screen, but he still didn't feel like doing any work. Now would probably be a good time to start writing a novel or maybe get into social media, but all the websites were blocked. Nor did he have the strength to reply to his sister. He thought about offering to make a round of tea for everyone, having a conversation with Rupinder about her holiday or perhaps going over to chat with Neil Tuffnel about traffic forecasts.

At that moment, Lionel emerged from his office. It was something he liked to do once every afternoon – a proprietary walk around the part of the fourth floor that was still under his command.

Walking with great purpose and a full bladder, he came to the kitchenette and ate a flapjack. He looked up at a flickering light, made a remark about the weather and talked to Neil about the fortunes of the England football team.

Slowly, he made his way over to James. He gave an egalitarian smile and perched at the edge of the desk, his short soft legs dangling down.

'Ah James. How's things? Everything all right with everything?'

'Yes,' said James. 'How was the members' meeting?'

'Yes, fine, thanks. No real need for me to be there. But you know how they like to see my face at these things.'

Lionel was at least half a foot shorter than him. It was a challenge that James had worked hard to overcome and now he was barely even aware that, as he spoke to his manager, he crouched forward, lowered his neck and looked upwards. Although he did sometimes wonder if it might be having a detrimental impact on his spine and his personality.

'So all good here? Lots going on, I know. Have you managed to do that briefing for me yet?'

'Yes, sorry – just starting it now.'

'Hmm, I really wanted it earlier today. I think I did say that.'

'I know – sorry. I didn't think the meeting was until the end of the week.'

'No, it isn't. But I'd like to have it today. I'm seeing Duncan Banister tomorrow for a one-to-one, and I'd like to share some thoughts with him ahead of the meeting.'

As James well knew, the one essential quality that every town planner must have is industriousness. Analytical reasoning was a plus, imagination was neither here nor there, and you didn't need to be particularly charming. But you absolutely couldn't be lazy. There was too much information to absorb and too many reports to write and meetings to sit through. Lionel knew that too – partly because he *was* lazy.

'Don't worry. I'll crack on with it. I'll definitely have it for you by the end of the day.'

'Great stuff, appreciate it.'

'No problem.'

'We should catch up for a drink sometime. Maybe in the Red Lion this Friday? I haven't seen you there for a while.'

'Yes, that sounds good.'

James had just experienced that rarest of things: a managerial moment, an interaction in which Lionel had asserted his authority, set a task with a specific deadline and attempted to incentivise him. He hopped off the desk, clearly energised by what he had achieved, and continued his walk around the office. James watched him go: the very essence of dynamic public administration, artificial sweetener, instant coffee and anti-depressants coursing through his veins. Lionel inspected a pot plant, walked over to Rupinder and initiated a conversation about asthma. James turned back to his computer. But he wasn't going to start doing any work yet, certainly not now that Lionel had tried to make him. Instead, he opened up his personal email again. There was a reply from Felix.

Can't understand why you didn't try to fuck her. She was pretty. She liked you. You were drunk. You didn't like her. Four reasons: one of those ought to have been enough.

Perhaps this was what he was really like – it wasn't just Felix on email, it was Felix distilled. Stripped of the good manners and social generosity, the expensive drinks, nice smell and ironic thin lips, he wasn't just a clever wanker who worked in advertising, but something more dangerous. Undaunted by obscenity-checking firewalls, economic downturns or the English class system, he lived without fear and was therefore capable of doing great harm.

There was also an email from Carl. It was, and James could have really done without this, good news. He hadn't got promoted – his career didn't have those kinds of progression routes, but he had just made a large amount of money. It was what he did: he did deals and made trades, fucked people over, went short on social-democratic economies and long on despotic governments with oil reserves. It seemed he had done something particularly lucrative this time – he had paid far too little for some bonds from a Russian bank, and then sold them for far too much to the Mexican government, and now he wanted to celebrate. In fact, he already was celebrating – he had sent the email from a champagne bar near Bond Street requesting that everyone drop everything and come to join him.

It hadn't always been like this. Carl had been a most under-whelming teenager and an immediate confidence boost when James had met him, his next-door neighbour at the halls of resi-dence, on their very first day at university. His fluttering hands and mumbling speech, which was now put down to high intelligence and drug use, had back then signified only nervousness and a provincial childhood. No one would have guessed that ten years later he would be bullying small nations and making idiotic spend-ing decisions with a corporate credit card.

Adam, who had the room across the corridor, had been very different. His upbringing in Chiswick and year off in Vietnam had given him a head start and he had arrived at the London School of Economics not to make friends and smoke cannabis, he'd already done all of that, but to study and improve his prospects. Alice, of course, had been much the same, albeit she had been brought up in North London, had spent her year off in Tanzania, and had come to study so that she could improve Sub-Saharan Africa. And James? Had he really studied and worked so hard, harder than any of them, that he could be sitting here, on the fourth floor of Southwark Council?

The responses came quickly. Adam was up for it, and so it seemed was everyone else: that unfriendly woman called Olivia who inexplicably got invited to things these days; Adam's fiancée Justine, who was bound to ask James why he didn't have a girlfriend; Helen, who had studied geography with him but now worked in the pharmaceutical industry; and a little fucker called Stuart, who had done maths with Carl and was partly responsible for his damaged worldview. Yes, everyone was coming – everyone except for Alice:

Darlings – of course I would have loved to join you, drunk champagne at the expense of a bank and helped celebrate another of young Carl's triumphs on behalf of international capital. But . . . I've got to be at a film gala and so alas will be in Shoreditch rather than Mayfair tonight and suspect will be drinking white wine (if I'm lucky) rather than Bollinger. Have fun and try not to behave yourselves xx

So Alice wasn't coming. And in refusing the invitation, she was maintaining the moral high ground while also making it clear that she had something much better to do that evening. Well, in that case, James wouldn't go either. He'd find something better to do himself. He'd go for a drink with Rachel. She was, after all, better company than any of them. He could make amends for the fuck up with Laura, and talk about planning and Lionel.

He waited thirty minutes and then spent another ten writing a suitably carefree and rushed email, with carefully re-engineered spelling mistakes and grammatical errors.

> Sorry, can't make it either. I've already something got on this evening (though not a film gala, whatever that is) and too much work to do to get away early.Have a greatt time.

Almost immediately there was another email from Alice and, for the first time in months, this one was sent exclusively to him.

> Well, it's nice to see that at least someone from our generation is using his talents for the common good rather than personal gain. Hope you're not working too hard, and still getting to book launches xx

Alice was headed for great things. You could tell that by the way she dressed, the savageness of her fringe and the style and speed of her emails. And James? Where was he headed? To do things for the common good, to be a *good guy*? That sounded an awful lot like middle-management.

In need of a distraction, he opened up some files and started to do some work. It was, after all, what he was meant to be doing. But it didn't provide any comfort, it just heightened his sense of responsibility and anxiety. The idea was to make Sunbury Square look like his poster, but at the moment it looked like it did in his spreadsheet. Row after row of failure: statistical outliers, dismaying trends, figures that were high when they should be low, and low when they should be high. On the multiple deprivation index, it was the poorest ward in one of London's poorest boroughs. The violent crime rate had doubled in the last five years. It had the highest number of teenage pregnancies in the south of England, and fewer than one in ten residents had any A levels. And the fact that the people here were so much poorer than him was no consolation – after all, he hadn't gone to university with any of them.

James worked through it slowly, calculating averages and variance and extracting headline figures. His ancient desktop computer whirred unhappily as he opened up multiple files and programs and carefully constructed the briefing paper, marshalling evidence and putting forward rationales for intervention that had been used many times before. He wondered what Laura would have made of them. And then he had to write a long email explaining to Lionel what the briefing actually meant, and the things he should and shouldn't say in his meeting.

He closed down the programs and opened up a news website. The government was promising to make more cuts to local authorities and an opinion poll showed that 70 per cent of people thought this was a good idea. It had gone five o'clock, it was dark outside and the building was starting to empty. Rachel had left without saying goodbye.

If this was it, if this was what he was going to do for a living, then shouldn't he do it somewhere else, somewhere where he was more senior and better paid? Of course, even then it wouldn't be enough. What he needed was not to earn money but to *make* money, like Carl. But that was going to be difficult for, as he well knew, there was no such thing as a rich town planner. You could no more make money from town planning than you could from being a tax inspector or a football referee. True, you could take a certain satisfaction in stopping other people from making money, but that wasn't the same thing at all. No, the only way to make any money from planning was to be crooked. You could take bribes, pass on intelligence, help property developers make large amounts of money and take a portion along the way. But who on earth was ever going to bribe James? The only person he had any influence over was Lionel.

James put on his coat and, for the last time that day, checked his email before he turned off the computer. There was a note from Rachel, saying she was sorry she had to run off, and that it would be nice to go for a drink soon. There was also a message from Felix:

Okay, you're going on a date this Friday. Her name is Harriet. More details to follow. Be brave and you'll enjoy it, be afraid and you won't. She's a lot of fun.

8

22 February

The physical character of a place can help reinforce a sense of meaning and civility.

– *The London Plan*, Section 7.14

It was Friday night, exactly a week after his date with Laura. But this time it was very different. For one thing, James wasn't in a pub. London was full of pubs, they were one of its distinctive characteristics, and they were mainly disgusting. They were, as he knew all too well, places where the city's administrators went to drink beer, eat packets of crisps and talk about all the people they worked with who weren't with them. No, instead of a pub in Whitehall he was in a theme bar in Soho, which in a crowded marketplace had had to compete through specialisation and stocked two hundred types of vodka. And it wasn't small and atmospheric and two hundred years old – it had only been open for six months, and would very likely be a Japanese noodle restaurant in a year's time.

More importantly, the girl he was with was different as well. Harriet was twenty-eight years old, put undue emphasis on star signs and worked at a commercials production company that did things on behalf of Felix's advertising agency. James had only vaguely understood, but whatever – it was enough to know that he had some kind of hold over her, and that it was in the interests of her career that James didn't have a completely miserable evening.

Although it had soon become apparent that Harriet didn't worry very much about her career. Nor did she seem to have any interest in his. This was obviously a good thing – there would be no need to justify town planning to her on the grounds of market failure. Instead, and helpfully, they had talked almost exclusively about her. And what they had talked about was not what she did for a living, but all the things she liked doing. So they had talked about bars, cocktails, India, dance music and famous people she fancied. They had also talked quite a bit about Felix – after all, he was the only person they both knew – and they agreed how peculiar he was. James was sure that he wouldn't mind. And after no more than an hour or so of this, she had started to share confidences, reveal endearing vulnerabilities and to become mildly amorous. Already, her feet were gently but purposefully knocking against his.

Was dating girls really this easy? James was sure it never used to be this straightforward. But now it seemed all you had to do was turn up in a dark suit, speak pleasantly and with good manners, listen attentively and get them drunk. It was a big help that they were in a bar that only sold spirits. They didn't have to sit there sipping drinks thoughtfully and maintain structured conversations for any length of time. Whenever James didn't know what to say next, which happened quite often to begin with, all he had to do was swallow his drink and go to the bar to buy them something else. And, of course, the drinks were a good talking point them-selves. Already they had drunk a Vodka Pistachio, Vodka Chilli,

Vodka Snickers and Vodka Seroxat. They had also had a Vodka Oxygen, which had been a bit disappointing, and a Vodka Vodka, which was a great deal more expensive than just a double vodka, but neither of them had been able to work out why. He couldn't remember ever going to a bar like this in Nottingham.

Another good thing was that Harriet was at approximately the right level of attractiveness. She didn't, for instance, look anything like Laura. She wasn't tall and blond, and she didn't have the kind of aristocratic good looks that made you feel conscious of the fact that you had an A level in Business Studies. Her hair was a reassuring, nothing-special dark brown and her eyes weren't a calculating blue but an unreliable green, with a cluster of small freckles naively arranged around her nose. But her most important feature, the thing that had probably always, and only slightly inaccurately, defined her, was her mouth. A wide, entertaining mouth that was too big to be pretty, too big for her small, disorderly teeth, and which was often getting her into trouble – not for the things it said, but for the things it did.

And thankfully, of course, she wasn't an economist. She had about two-thirds of a degree in Art History from a higher education institution that he had never heard of, and which she was meaning to get back to one day but for the moment had too much else going on. She took pride in her rudimentary arithmetic and limited powers of logical reasoning. She read widely, however, and dressed with an erotic crudeness and primary-colour stupidity that could only mean one thing: she was highly intelligent. So James would have to be a little bit careful.

'Do you know what your problem is? You've got square glasses,' said Harriet.

'Is that a big problem?'

'Oh, it's a *massive* problem. Because you've got a long face. I've got a lovely round face, and so I should wear square glasses to give me some gravitas, but you need to wear round glasses to stop yourself looking like a grumpy horse.'

'So I should get new glasses?'

'Yes, or maybe just take those ones off,' and with that she reached over and snatched them from him. This was, without question, a flirtatious act. An aggressive one as well, but the two usually went together – James knew that much.

'There – now we both look better,' she said, placing the glasses in the folds of her blouse and essentially making it impossible for him to retrieve them.

There was, he could appreciate, a certain irony here. After all, he had gone on a blind date and as a consequence he had effectively been blinded. And there was a reason why James wore glasses instead of contact lenses and for once it wasn't just the expense – he actually looked much better with them on. Without glasses, he didn't look fresh and handsome, but exposed and vulnerable, as if his face had fallen off. But this was no time to get distracted by what he looked like. His main concern, and now that he had drunk all those vodkas he could see what it was with great clarity, was that he badly needed to sleep with Harriet. It was really important. In the medium-term, at least, his well-being and self-respect largely depended on it.

How many girls had he ever slept with? Not enough, obviously, but also, and this was the point – *not enough*. Fewer than ten, which he understood to be a standard benchmark, but also, more troublingly, fewer than six. And how many girls had he slept with just the once, on a first meeting, and then never seen again? How many – and he was aware how quaint the expression was in twenty-first-century London – how many *one-night stands* had he had? The answer was zero. He'd never done it before. Every one of the girls he had ever slept with he had known for some time and it had been achieved through the geographic processes he was so comfortable with, through attrition and erosion, the wearing down of surfaces and defences. Well, none of those techniques were going to work here. Instead, he would need to be quick-witted and possibly a bit duplicitous. Plus, as was so often the case, he would almost certainly have to throw money at it.

Harriet returned from the bar with two more glasses. This time they were twice the size, brightly coloured and ominously thick-looking, like little portions of pumpkin soup.

'I got combinations this time. Vodka Aniseed and Vodka Custard. Apparently if you mix them, then they *really* fuck you up.'

They held the drinks together and leaning across the table looked closely at one another before swiftly and courageously drinking them. James spluttered for a bit, and she affectionately put his glasses back over his face. He smiled at her amateurishly, she stared into his eyes expertly, and with an impressive lack of ambiguity. He carefully extended his leg forward, so that it brushed against the inside of one of hers. She brought her legs together, cheerfully squeezing his knee. She reached out her hands and he good-humouredly held them – surprisingly, they were almost exactly the same size. There was no doubt it was going really well. He was doing all of the right things, perhaps not all that skilfully, but they were definitely the right ones.

'I'm going to the bathroom for a bit,' she said. 'I think I've drunk too much vodka.'

It was pretty clear that Harriet was someone who didn't believe in planning. It wasn't as if she had ideological objections like Laura, it just wasn't what she did. How then *did* she function? She was probably upper class, that always helped, but it was more than that. There was something else there: she had a worldview. It was difficult to be sure what it was, but she had one – a set of values and personal beliefs that existed outside of Western religion or the free market. Maybe she was a Zen Buddhist, or more likely it was just hedonism – the increasingly uncontroversial belief that the pursuit of personal pleasure should be the underlying rationale for all actions and ethical choices. It also partly explained why she was so attractive.

All of this was instructive and worth discussing with Felix at some point, but for the moment James had more logistical concerns. The principal one was that he lived in Crystal Palace. This was something of a double-edged sword. On the one hand, who in their right mind would agree to go there for the night? Even if you lived there, you'd think twice about it, but to travel all the way out there with someone you'd just met that evening? Surely no sensible girl would consider that – although good sense wasn't Harriet's most obvious quality. On the other hand, if he did manage to get her there, she wouldn't be able to go anywhere else, except possibly Kent. It also occurred to him that taking her home via two night buses wasn't really going to work either.

He was still considering his strategy when Harriet returned from the bathroom. It was entirely possible that she'd been sick, but she didn't appear to be in the least bit wounded or weakened.

'Come on,' she said. 'Let's get a cab back to my place.'

Outside, on the street, in the back of the taxi, Harriet was in control – everything she did was quick and authoritative. She removed his glasses again but this time it was done more gently, looked into his eyes for a full second, and then kissed him firmly and comprehensively. It was the most accomplished kiss that James had ever had in his life. She pushed him into the corner of the leather seating and held his face with both hands. There could be no doubt that she was highly trained in all of this. Meanwhile, they were travelling north at great speed. James wasn't sure exactly where, his vision was obscured, but he knew that it was further and further from home.

'Let's get out here,' said Harriet, suddenly pulling herself away. 'I need some air and some cigarettes. I need some chocolate.'

The taxi stopped at her prompting, but Harriet had neglected to negotiate a price beforehand, and so James had to hand over an incredible amount of money to the driver before they could climb out. He looked warily around him – he hadn't been here for some time, but he knew exactly where they were. Some years ago, James had chosen to live in South London. It had almost certainly been the wrong decision, but he had self-identified and there was little he could do about it now. But that was okay, because he had studied Camden Town in depth for his planning certificate and knew exactly how it worked. He had read its strategy documents, gone over its numbers and written a high-scoring essay about it.

So he knew that the planning framework for Camden Town had for many years been predicated on the development of its night-time economy. It had been a pioneering and influential approach. You didn't need factories any more, everyone knew that, but it had turned out you didn't need business parks or offices either. You didn't even need prize-winning shopping centres and generous car parking, and you certainly didn't have to spend millions of pounds on arts centres and museums. All you really needed was lots of young people getting drunk and spending money in foolish ways. It was a winning strategy, and for years now Camden had had one of the fastest-growing economies in the country.

James had to acknowledge that it was all very dynamic and entrepreneurial. Everywhere he looked, in the bars and on the streets, in the shops which never closed, outside the churches that never opened, older people were making money by selling younger people things that they shouldn't have but very much wanted: strong European lager, spirits mixed with caffeine and sugar, a wide variety of recreational drugs, fried food with high levels of fat and salt, contraband cigarettes and unlicensed forms of transport. James had never been to West Africa, but he imagined that the cities there looked a lot like Camden Town.

'God, I love it here,' said Harriet. 'I'm feeling much better now.'

As a result of its wildly successful local economy the public realm was ruined. It looked the very opposite of James's master-plan poster: the street furniture was broken, the pavements were littered with bin bags, soggy cardboard boxes, broken glass and polystyrene cartons, and the signage had been vandalised. The frontage of the bars, cafes and restaurants were strikingly unattractive, shrewdly designed to disorganise the senses and encourage sub-optimal decision-making. The pollution was post-industrial but nonetheless immense, for it was a product rather than merely a by-product of all the activity. All around were light, noise and misdirected energy, and the thinness of anything that tried to contain them.

It seemed to have been raining in North London, for the neon and sodium lighting of Camden's night-time economy was reflected in shiny roads and dirty puddles. There was a stiff, cold breeze. Cars, buses, taxis, minicabs, scooters, and intoxicated young pedestrians were inharmoniously sharing a badly designed junction. Horns honked, pub doors opened sending out pub noise. Lost male undergraduates, young and new to the city, blundered across the road with their bottles of beer, recklessly trusting the traffic to stop for them. Girls with too much make-up and not enough clothes walked behind them. There were teenagers here too – white ones huddled together, brave enough to come to Camden on a Friday night, but not to do anything else. And there was at least one authentic lunatic – a man whose age was impossible to calculate, and who sat on a traffic island pulling menacing faces at anyone who dared to catch his eye. It occurred to James that for an economy dedicated entirely to pleasure, it was striking how unhappy everyone looked. The only people who seemed to be really enjoying themselves were a pair of alcoholic tramps, laughing manically in a supermarket shop front.

Harriet guided James through it all, holding him tightly towards her as they continued their journey north, away from the noise and the crowds. She was a native, in the way that hardly anyone in London ever was, and she feared nothing. People in Camden were always getting drunk and fighting, and it had one of the highest homicide rates in the country, but she walked its backstreets with the strength of character and misplaced confidence of a sex worker. And luckily for James, he had drunk all of that vodka – he was protected not just by Harriet, but by his own diminished sense of danger. They crossed a canal full of poorly concealed secrets and headed to the east, where it was quieter and darker, but by no means safer.

And then suddenly it was light again – there was light everywhere. Not the whites, reds and violets of Camden Town in a late capitalist bloom, but a deep, totalitarian yellow. It was something of a surprise, but it served James right for not concentrating. For they had gone down an unpromising narrow footpath, and it had abruptly opened, as footpaths in London often do, into the middle of a gigantic housing estate.

'This is where I live,' said Harriet.

Harriet had clearly chosen her accommodation on different criteria from himself, for these were, indisputably, London council flats with all that that entailed. It was very unusual for James to be somewhere like this in anything other than a professional capacity. Even if the estate was no longer owned by the local authority, and they hardly ever were any more, it would at least have been built by one, constructed in an age when town planners ruled the world and architects had to do what they were told, and when buildings looked dreadful but cities were magnificent.

All the textbook design faults were here: the indefensible space, the communal garden that everyone was meant to care for but no one ever did, the flat roofs with their primitive drainage, the high unbroken walls which failed to make anyone feel safe, the uniform facades and fittings that suggested oppression rather than cohesion, and the laborious steps, elevated walkways and treacherous ramps that intimidated visitors and exhausted the residents. As it had been made before the 1990s, no one had tried to make it more cheerful with wooden cladding or dashes of pink brickwork. The graffiti, like the architecture, was also lacking in irony. It wasn't humorous or even especially offensive – just a half-hearted attempt to make the rippled concrete walls uglier than they already were.

'Okay, I know, it's probably not what you were expecting, and it does look pretty foul, but the rent is really low and – you'll see – the flat is great.'

'I really like it,' said James.

'You're so sweet,' she said. 'I actually think you're telling the truth.'

As she said this, she stopped suddenly, besides a well-meaning but badly damaged notice board and, pulling him roughly towards her, she started to kiss him again. And now it seemed to James that she even kissed like a housing estate – open but unyielding, her over-sized, poorly designed mouth firmly held his. Above their heads was a mural of smiling farm animals standing under a lumpy rainbow, painted twenty years ago by delinquent teenagers before the local youth club lost its funding. The light, or maybe something else, started to make a loud buzzing noise. Abruptly, Harriet stopped kissing him and took his hand. They continued up the stairwell.

But as soon as she opened the front door, it was clear things were going to be more complicated. Harriet hadn't really explained to him beforehand, but there were at least a dozen people in her flat, though it was difficult to tell for sure because they kept moving around so much. Apart from a strange, horrible man with tattoos on his hands, who sat at a table constructing and distributing cannabis joints, James was certain that he was the oldest person there. Many of the girls were pretty, but it was difficult to be certain exactly which ones, and there were lots of men there too – some of whom would have to be classed as rivals, but others who were simply colourful distractions and tremendously gay, with exaggerated mannerisms and squeaky voices. There was an elegant black stereo system in the middle of the room playing low-frequency dance music at a volume that James estimated to be significantly higher than the 85-decibel threshold admissible in an inner-London residential area.

Harriet introduced him without any great skill or attention to detail to a group sitting on cushions, and immediately disappeared. James, who was determined at this stage not to be disheartened, sat down and attempted to join in. It wasn't easy. The problem wasn't just that there were so many of them or that he wasn't terribly good at this kind of thing, it was that they were all so incredibly young. They didn't argue about the government's macroeconomic policies, they didn't even talk about music and clothes shops. What they talked about was each other. It was a difficult conversation to contribute to – a group of people he'd never met before, all of them several inches shorter than him, were talking about other people he'd never met.

James gave up trying to participate, and decided instead to watch them with an ironic detachment. He was older than his companions and so he would act older. He would be *calmer* than them. It wasn't very difficult, for it was striking how excitable they all were. It was something of a puzzle: why weren't they more anxious and deflated? Hadn't everyone agreed that this was a terrible time to be young? But instead of worrying about global warming and the economic crash and debt and house prices, they just made an amazing amount of noise. Everything seemed to delight or surprise them. They laughed at things that weren't in the least bit funny, and squealed at things that weren't frightening, and then laughed some more. It was like being on the night bus.

James got up and tried to find Harriet, but it was surprisingly difficult. The flat was much larger than had first seemed, that was one of the features of post-war social housing, and the long narrow hallway, with its row of white wooden doors, was unpromising. He was very keen not to burst into anyone's bedroom unwanted, while the bathroom, which James knew might well be a focus for activity, was empty. He tried the kitchen, but there was nothing going on there except a woman sitting at the table on her own, sobbing loudly, with her head in her hands.

James had little direct experience of weeping young women. He had never been sufficiently successful with girls to make it happen very often, and Alice had never felt the need to get tearful about anything, except injustices in the developing world. But he knew that it was a mysterious phenomenon, and that their motives were almost always unfathomable. Women really did weep with joy, for instance, or after reading a nineteenth-century novel. And at other times they were capable of doing it on purpose.

So he could easily get this badly wrong, and it was unlikely to be straightforward – he could be certain that the girl wasn't crying because her ankle was sprained or her pet cat had died. It was tempting to slip back out, but he knew that wouldn't be possible. Although almost always the best thing to do, he was unable to watch another human being crying without doing something about it.

With immense caution, he said, 'Are you okay?'

She paused for a moment and then continued crying, without making a meaningful reply. But at least she wasn't doing it with any greater intensity, so he could be confident that he wasn't making things worse.

'Can I get you a glass of water or something?'

That was even better. She looked up at him and gently shook her head. She was pretty with chaotic black hair, big eyes and dramatic lips, but that may have just been an effect of the crying. It didn't always come off, but James knew that if done correctly, it could be an ingenious way for a woman to become more attractive.

'Do you live here?' said James.

The girl nodded, and then rested her head back down on her arms.

'So, do you live with Harriet?' asked James.

'Who are you?' she said.

'I'm James. I'm a friend of Harriet's.'

'She's a fucking bitchface,' said the girl.

James nodded calmly. She was probably right, even if she wasn't being very grammatical about it. It was the best explanation for why he was now in a flat in Camden and why they had drunk so many vodkas, almost all of which he had paid for. Of course, she was a bitchface. What did he expect – she was young. That was the whole problem with London: there were too many young people there.

He went over to a handsome red fridge in the corner of the room and helped himself to a can of beer. Maybe he should try to sleep with this girl instead? She was attractive, it was practically certain that Harriet wouldn't mind much, and the fact that she was so distressed ought to make it a great deal easier. He sat down next to her at the table and put a comforting hand on her shoulder. He tried to speak as softly as he could.

'Are you okay? Do you want me to do anything?'

'I really want you to fuck off,' said the girl.

James realised that in no way was he going to be able to seduce this girl. Yes, she was distressed, but it was the wrong kind of distress. He needed self-pity, defeat and despair to work with, but she was just dysfunctionally angry and there was plenty of venom, but very little sorrow in her sobbing. What on earth had Harriet done to her? In truth, it could be almost anything – slept with her boyfriend, taken her drugs, stolen her money. After all, they lived on a housing estate in Camden, a place where other people's property was rarely respected, and they weren't old enough to know any better. Or maybe Harriet hadn't done anything much at all – that was so often the problem with weeping young women. He took some reflective gulps from his can of beer and returned to the living room.

It was actually even worse now. A few people had left, but many more had turned up, and he couldn't at first see where he would be able to sit. It had got much noisier, and the average age seemed to have fallen even further. There was still no sign of Harriet. He sat down in front of a peculiar-looking girl who didn't seem to be talking to anyone else. Maybe she was lonely? She had a wide nose and big gums, and if they had been at school together in the East Midlands, she would be the sort of girl you would safely befriend. But this was Camden, and a different set of aesthetic criteria, criteria that he didn't fully understand, had to be applied. And so James decided that he would try to sleep with her instead.

'Hi, I'm James,' he said.

'I'm Cordelia,' she said. 'What are you?'

'I work in planning,' said James.

'Oh, like in advertising. That's really cool.'

'No, a different type of planning. I'm a town planner.'

Cordelia looked at him blankly. It was clear that she had terrible manners.

'What do you do? Do you work? Are you a student?'

'I'm a jewellery designer,' she said.

James looked at her unhappily. He should have guessed – she was wearing the biggest and ugliest bracelet he had ever seen. A lump of red plastic, possibly a melted Lego block, with another yellow block screwed on top.

'Oh, that's really great. I was actually admiring your bracelet. Did you make it yourself?'

'Yes, that's right, and this necklace as well, and these rings.'

James hadn't noticed before, but now that he looked more carefully he saw that everything she was wearing was preposterous. She looked like the housing estate mural, a childish arrangement of primitive objects and bright colours. She looked mentally ill. Was it just that she was hopeless at jewellery design or was he missing something important? After all, he was probably at least four years older than her.

'So, did you study jewellery at college?'

'No, I taught myself. I just seem to have a flair for it.'

'Yes, I can really see that.'

It was a shame, but they had run out of things to say. What, after all, could a jeweller and a town planner talk about? The scale was all wrong, and neither of them had the charm or imaginative powers to overcome their predicament. And now James was certain, absolutely certain, that she wasn't in the least bit attractive.

There was still no sign of Harriet, but he hadn't entirely given up. He took another gulp of beer and this time he went over to the other side of the room, as far away from the music as he could, where a young man was sitting on his own with his back against the wall. James sat alongside him and leant over.

'Hi,' said James, 'I'm James.'

'I'm Felix.'

'Oh really? That's funny. One of my best friends is called Felix.'

But this Felix didn't seem particularly interested by the news.

'So do you know Harriet?' said James.

'Yes, of course,' said Felix. 'Everyone knows Harriet. She's a fabulous public asset.'

James realised that he had made another mistake. Young men were always so much worse than young women, but it wasn't just that. There were several clues that James should have spotted before he even went near him. There were the formidable black-framed glasses and the feminine good looks, the crisp black clothing and neat dark hair. Most of all there was the way he sat, composed and impressively at ease with himself. He wasn't squealing like any of the others – he was under thirty years old, but he was on his own, and didn't look in the least as if he minded. He wasn't even smoking or playing with his mobile phone.

'So, are you a designer?' said James.

'I'm an architect,' said Felix.

'Oh really? I work in town planning. At Southwark Council.'

Felix nodded, but didn't say anything.

'So I expect you deal with planners?'

'No, not really – I try to avoid them if I can help it. I like to keep more focused on the creative side of things.'

'So who do you work for?'

Felix worked for an architecture company that even people who weren't architects had heard of, and which was responsible for some of the most expensive and unnecessary buildings in the world. He was creating the future, rather than merely trying to improve it. He was designing museums and contemporary art galleries, international conference centres and retail complexes. Above all, he was designing hotels, which were now the most important buildings of them all.

'Have you ever done anything in Southwark?'

'No,' said Felix. 'South of the river isn't really my thing.'

'What about the rest of London?'

'We have done, of course, but not much now. All the action is elsewhere. London is dying. The whole country is, and Europe's no better. Dubai, Abu Dhabi, Shanghai, Singapore. That's where the money and talent is. That's where the ambition is. I'll probably relocate in a few months. There's not enough going on here.'

'So are all the architects leaving?' asked James hopefully.

'The good ones,' said Felix. 'But I'm sure there will still be more than enough left to do conservatories in Basingstoke.'

James didn't say anything. They sat together in silence for a while.

'I don't suppose you've got any stimulating drugs?' said Felix.

James shook his head. He got to his feet, at least that way he got to end the conversation, and looked over the room. It was louder and more colourful than ever. He suddenly felt very tired. That was the problem with being thirty-two. You were so old. Who wants to be old? Nobody ever wants to be old. But nobody should ever want to be young either. Nobody should ever wish to be so witless, so fearful and so fucking irritating.

It was no good – he would have to go home. That was obvious. The question was how. It was the eternal problem. In all his years of living in London, he still hadn't found a satisfactory solution. How did anyone ever get home at night? When you thought about it, it was rather extraordinary that they did. Tonight his options were particularly bleak. It was either forty pounds in a taxi, a complicated series of night buses or else a three-hour existential walk. Either way, he would have to head back out into Camden alone, and the effects of the novelty vodka had long worn off. Perhaps, he should have just spent the night with Rachel and the others in the Red Lion.

There was little point in saying goodbye to anyone. Harriet was missing, it was technically impossible to have a conversation with Cordelia, the girl in the kitchen was still crying, and Felix was an amazing bastard. No, it would be better if he just quietly left. He got to his feet and tiptoed around the bodies, the burgundy rugs and maroon cushions, the wine bottles and cans of beer. Young people were so untidy, so careless, so irresponsible, so *dirty*, and this was their own flat – this was the private realm. No wonder the housing estate had failed and Camden was fucked.

But then, just as he reached the hallway, Harriet reappeared. That was of course yet another thing about young people – they were so inconsistent. She had bare feet, and looked at him affectionately and with a kindly smile. She was twenty-eight years old, she had a precarious job in a time of great economic uncertainty, and for many more years the most valuable things she would own would be her fridge and digital music system. But she was sexually adventurous, brave, wiser than she looked, and improbably happy. She was also almost certainly off her head on drugs.

'There you are! I do hope you're not trying to leave. I've been looking for you everywhere!' she said.

That was highly unlikely – the flat wasn't *that* big. Of course, the question was what had she been doing for the last hour, and who with? But the important thing was not to ask or worry about it. It was worrying about things that caused all the problems, and which made people so unattractive and unsuccessful, which made them so old. And James had made up his mind not to worry. It was the crucial lesson. Harriet took his hand, and led him away from the front door and back down the hallway.

'Now, because I don't really know you all that well, I'm not going to have sex with you,' she said.

'Okay,' said James.

'But,' she continued, 'depending on how we get on, I might suck you off.'

'Okay,' said James, and he followed her into a bedroom.

9

1 March

A growing London population is likely in itself to support an expanding economy, with growing demand for leisure and personal services.

– *The London Plan*, Section 1.18

James needed to be on drugs – proper drugs. It had been obvious that at some point this would have to happen, this would be something that he would just have to do. It was 2013 and everyone was taking them, unless they had a very cool reason why they shouldn't – a conviction for smuggling, or else if they'd already fucked up their livers and hearts by taking too many. But James had no such excuses.

Once upon a time, of course, it had only been slum-dwellers and the aristocracy who took them. The class system still counted for something, it always did, but now the distinction was only really in the type and quality of the drugs they took. James, of course, was a lower-middle-class drug user, and as a result he had never got any further than boasting that he'd smoked some particularly potent cannabis. But that was hopeless – he wasn't seventeen any more. He needed to be able to look people squarely in the eye and tell them how dismal their cocaine was. And that meant having some drugs of his own to consume and allocate. Not all the time, of course – it wasn't part of the plan to become an addict, and apparently that never happened anyway. But he did need to take enough of them to know better.

It was here that, once again, Felix came in, for it seemed he was on very good terms with a professional drug dealer. It was much easier for Felix, who didn't reside in the English class system, who wasn't bound up in the conventions and fears that ruled other people's lives. He was class-blind, as comfortable hanging out with thieves and criminals as he was with advertising executives and aspiring politicians. It was almost certainly, of course, because he was so upper class.

So it was only to be expected that Felix had access to a supply of cocaine. The real surprise was where they had to go to get it. Lacking both personal knowledge and a sound economic model of spatial distribution for the sector, James had assumed that you either bought drugs on the streets of Hackney or the salons of Mayfair. But no – instead they would have to head out west, out to the very ends of the suburbs. For it was here, it seemed, that all the serious drug dealers lived and worked.

'There are many advantages to suburban living if you're a drug dealer of any significance,' explained Felix. 'A low crime rate, easy parking, good access to national road networks, neighbours who mind their own business. It's only the small-time crooks, the ones who peddle to students and get caught all the time, who actually live near their customer base.'

They were in a cafe in Notting Hill, round the corner from where Felix lived. James knew its heritage, had studied it, for the entire area had once been a battleground in the class war. But that was a long time ago, and it was now principally a site of historic and cultural interest, a successful node in London's leisure economy popular with the sons and daughters of internationally famous businessmen.

And where was James meant to be? Well, it was Friday morning and right about now the surface transport meeting was about to start, but courageously James had *pulled a sickie*. It was his first one ever, another small but significant milestone. And, after all, why the fucking hell not? He worked in the public sector. The average British employee took 7.5 days' sick leave each year, and he didn't have to check the figures to know that it was bound to be higher in government where everyone was always so weak and ill. But in six years he had never taken a single one. He had even come into work when he was sick. He had sat feverish and unhappy, watching PowerPoint presentations that made extensive use of Clipart and saying nothing in meetings where nothing happened. That meant he was owed at least forty backdated days. And the really instructive thing was that no one seemed to be interested in the slightest. He'd spoken briefly on the phone to an unquestioning colleague and he didn't have to put on a croaky voice or pretend that he had a chest infection or that his knob had turned blue. And, anyway, if it came to it, he *was* sick. He was, almost certainly, mentally ill. Of course, he should really have rung Rachel, but they still hadn't gone for their drink together and, besides, she was different – she *would* have suspected something.

Felix, who hadn't even bothered to ring his advertising agency, was eating a cooked breakfast.

'We have a long and challenging day ahead of us,' he said. 'It is important to stock up on all the food groups now. You're unlikely to eat much later.'

'Yes, I know that,' said James, who had undertaken some desk research. 'I know it suppresses the appetite. Is that breakfast any good?'

'It's magnificent. I try to come here at least once a week. This is the best cafe in Notting Hill, and it's our duty as citizens to protect it when consumers won't. I'm worried that it's going to get destroyed by capitalism – all the rents are going up. You know about this stuff. Maybe the council could save it?'

James shook his head. 'I don't think so. It's not a listed building, or a school or anything.'

'That's the problem with planners – you're always protecting the wrong things, the things that no one actually likes.'

'Legally, we can't protect this as a cafe. I expect it's got A3 usage, so you don't need permission to turn it into any other restaurant or coffee bar.'

'So you can't stop the landlord from shutting it down and doing something else with it?'

'Well, it wouldn't be straightforward to turn it into a chemicals factory or a bank or make it residential. I'd have to check the borough's local development framework. That's the crucial thing.'

Felix shook his head. 'No, that's not the crucial thing at all. The crucial thing is that it stays exactly like it is and continues to be run by the same inbred Armenian family, who know how to make decent all-day breakfasts.'

'You're mixing use with ownership. Planners can't make a judgement on who owns buildings, only the different uses they put them to.'

'Well, what about if the government owns them?'

'We don't really own all that many buildings any more. We certainly wouldn't own the lease on a cafe like this.'

'In that case, your whole profession is fucked. Ownership is everything. If you don't own anything then you're nothing.'

They walked to Felix's car. It was, and James should have guessed this, elderly, French and battered – the smallest and least expensive car on the street. It was like the pieces of public art that accompanied new shopping centres: an expression of non-market values, paid for out of the proceeds of consumerism. James was not necessarily any closer to having his own worldview, but he was at least getting better at understanding Felix.

They drove off and left the knowing streets of Notting Hill with its pink and blue houses, dark velvet bars and retail follies run by the wives of investment bankers. They crossed the West Way and continued north-west, beyond the Georgian terraces and Victorian villages. They travelled between the disputed territories of Kilburn and Kensal Rise and into Willesden with its food wholesalers and less fashionable ethnic minorities. They went on, passing Cricklewood, which James had always found difficult to interpret, and through Wembley's uncompetitive light-industrial base.

Further still they went, until the roads widened out, the speed limits rose, the cars got bigger and they were somewhere else altogether: they were in Metroland. James knew it well – not from direct experience, but from the books he'd read, and the things his lecturers had told him. Terrible things. For this was London's Wild West – unplanned, unregulated, manically constructed by speculators before Patrick Abercrombie and his men at the County Council had tamed the city, bound it with Green Belt and stopped it from eating England. But what had been done couldn't be undone: Uxbridge, Stoneybridge, Ruislip, Harrow Town, Ickenham – they would be here for ever now. The permasuburbs, more enduring and solid than the city they had come from, as if it was London itself that was the afterthought, the shanty town in the centre that wouldn't stay still.

As James knew, it had happened very quickly – no more than twenty years – for private investors can do bad things so much faster than public investors can do good things. And everything had been set-up for them, largely of course *by* the public sector, who had constructed an Underground line, new arterial roads, energy supply lines and beautiful train stations – everything the developers had needed. In no time at all they had built tens of thousands of semi-detached houses that were perfectly designed to make money. Beloved by house buyers, estate agents, mortgage lenders. Beloved by *Laura*, and all those people who didn't know anything about town planning.

And ever since then, all those new families on moderate incomes and long-term fixed-rate mortgages had come here with their pet goldfish and made decisions entirely on the basis of their own desires, unconstrained by planning restrictions and with the sole purpose of increasing their individual happiness. They had built porches, bought plastic window frames, decorated facades with replica Tudor beams, covered their brickwork in stone cladding, poured concrete over their front gardens and stuck satellite dishes on their roofs.

'I can't bear this part of London,' said James. 'The way it just goes on and on, and with all these bloody awful people.'

'I won't hear anything against them,' said Felix. 'These are my tribe. I may not interact with them on a personal level, but these are the people whom I am paid to relate to. There wasn't really even an advertising industry until they came into being.'

But it was more difficult for James to take an objective perspective. Largely because he was one of them, James couldn't abide the lower-middle classes. It had taken a long time and quite a lot of money for him to learn this, and to learn to be suspicious of his own tastes and values. But now he knew better. He was a planner, and one of the things he was paid to do was to have opinions and make judgements on how horrible other people's houses were. Although, the strange thing was, driving at forty-five miles per hour on a dual carriageway in the sunshine, it didn't actually look all that bad.

'I think part of the problem,' said Felix, 'is that cities are never finished, like works of art, and they don't die like humans. There's no shape or dignity. London is two thousand years old, and it's still an unruly adolescent.'

On they went, on and on – across monumental roundabouts, over the mega-junctions, through the town centres that could only be recognised by their one-way systems and beneath road bridges of strategic importance to the national economy. They travelled past lucrative car dealerships, docile industrial parks and under-used public facilities until the air thinned and they were at the very edge. They had gone beyond Harrow, the capital of Metroland, they had gone beyond Pinner and Northwood and, at last, after nearly two hours, they had run out of city.

Now, if there was anything James feared more than the suburbs, then it was the countryside. And if there was anything worse than the countryside, then it was where the two met. A coming together of town and country, but there was no synergy here, no collision even, just a dismal petering out, a leakage of urban waste into the reservoir of England. Ahead, there was space – miles and miles of it – but it was the wrong type. This wasn't planned space, like the squares or parks that he tried to design and protect. This was bad space, crude space, the kind that lets blasts of wind gather momentum on cold March days, that makes the sky bigger, the earth browner and humans so much smaller. And it was here, in the very last house in London, that Felix's drug dealer lived. A two-storey, brown-brick house on the end of a terrace, with an untidy front yard and an unvarnished wooden gate that didn't shut properly.

Felix knocked firmly on the peeling, poignant white door, and they waited for two minutes. There were no more street lights, but in the distance James could see all the ingredients for another metropolitan fuck-up: Portacabins and breeze-block huts, skips half full of rain water and rudimentarily stacked pallet towers, portents of car parks and supermarkets, bowling alleys and multiplex cinemas.

The man who finally appeared looked much like his front door – an unhappy white 35-year old, but his skin was so worn out, it was difficult to precisely guess his age or income. It was likely that he took many of the drugs he sold for a living and that these were accelerating the ageing process. James understood that this was a common occurrence.

'Marcus – good to see you,' said Felix. 'This is my friend James.'

Marcus nodded and, without saying anything, they followed him down a hallway. The house was unnecessarily warm, and Marcus wasn't wearing nearly enough clothes. All he had on was a large orange T-shirt, ill-disciplined tracksuit bottoms and woollen socks. It was likely that he'd slept in them. Unwisely, Marcus was clean-shaven, for his face was without mystery and didn't stand up well to scrutiny. It looked soft and in need of protection, made for the indoors, and his eyes were wet. It was not, James would have said, the face of someone who was ever meant to be a drug dealer. And the name Marcus didn't seem right either. Perhaps he had only got into it after making some fundamental and irrecoverable mistake, like a degree in geography.

Marcus sat back down on a green sofa, not far from an enormous television. There was a duvet in the corner of the room. James wondered how much of the house he ever occupied. At his feet were mugs and spoons, an electric kettle, tea leaves, two jars of instant coffee, opened packets of biscuits, spilt sugar granules, a variety of herbal tea bags and cartons of milk. Collectively, it was the most important feature of the room, possibly the whole house, but there was no offer to make them anything to drink.

'What would you like then?' said Marcus.

'The usual, of course, but it needs to be of the highest quality.'

Marcus shrugged. 'It is what it is,' he said.

'Then we might have a difficulty. The last stuff was particularly useless.'

'I can't do much about that,' said Marcus. 'I only sell the shit.'

'I fear that what we have here,' said Felix, 'is a particularly striking instance of market failure through information asymmetry.'

'Is that going to be a problem?' said Marcus.

'It was the American economist Keith Arrow, who formulated the concept of information asymmetries,' said Felix. 'These are transactions in which one party, almost always the vendor, has more information about the product than the buyer. In such circumstances, there exist opportunities for the vendor to cheat. For while the buyer knows the price of a product, it is only the vendor who knows its true value – its scarcity, efficacy, durability.'

There was a glum silence. If Felix had wanted to do some high-concept sparring over the course of negotiations then he needed to get another drug dealer. Marcus sniffed, he clearly suffered from colds pretty much all of the time, and looked bored. He reached for the remote control and started to flick through some television channels. But it wasn't, James thought, a negotiating tactic – he just was bored. It was, he could see, probably something of an occupational hazard.

Not in the least discouraged, Felix continued.

'There are a variety of solutions – regulation, consumer warranties. One could say that my own profession, advertising, is nothing but an attempt to address information asymmetries, or I suppose one could equally argue that the industry exists in order to perpetuate them. But none of these easily apply to the sale of illegal drugs. If your stuff is unsatisfactory or makes me ill I can hardly complain to the government or wave a receipt at you, and it's not as if you have much in the way of a brand to protect.'

'So do you want to buy some gear or what?'

'Yes, but my point is – is it any good?'

'Well, why don't you just try some now? I'm not really in the mood for this shit.'

Felix nodded his head. That did seem the obvious answer. Without getting up, Marcus reached down under the sofa and pulled out a wooden box. He rummaged around and handed something to Felix, who went upstairs to the bathroom. In theory, being alone with a drug dealer was a new and socially challenging situation, but James didn't feel the slightest bit nervous or intimidated. A sign of progress, but also a sign of just how physically unimpressive Marcus was. If anything, James might have been intimidating *him*. Being a cocaine dealer seemed to be as unglamorous and poorly paid as local government. Marcus turned the volume up, and they watched some television together.

'How long have you lived here?' asked James.

'About four years. It's pretty convenient.'

'It must be nice and quiet,' said James.

'It's okay. The landlord is an arsehole, but he doesn't bother me.'

'Is it expensive?'

'He charges a fortune, and doesn't do anything. But the housing benefit covers the rent.'

As he said this, he scratched his scalp and his belly, under his arms and between his legs. In his own house, at least, he made very little effort to seem what he was not. His wrists were thin, but he had a surprising amount of dark hair on his forearms. It was almost certain that he had head lice, a vitamin-D deficiency and fungal skin infections. He was a barbarian, but a weak one – not so much an affront to civilisation as a minor, long-standing problem, something that democratic society would just have to tolerate along with everything else.

'Have you known Felix for long?'

'Oh yeah – years. We were at school together for a bit,' said Marcus.

'Oh, did you know him well? What was he like at school?'

'Not really. He was a dayboy, so we didn't mix much. Anyway, I didn't stay there very long.'

They watched some more television. It was the lunchtime news. There had been floods in rural India, food riots in Jakarta and an especially significant assassination in Mexico. But here, in this little terraced house somewhere on the outskirts of Watford, it was safe and warm.

Felix came down the stairs. He was moving swiftly and with great purpose. He didn't look like someone on drugs, but like a man who needed things around him to happen as quickly and decisively as possible. For the first time since James had known him, he looked exactly like an executive in an advertising agency.

'Uneventful,' said Felix, 'but it will have to do. You're very fortunate to be operating in such an inefficient market. It better not give us dysentery.'

'So how much do you want?'

'I'll take six grams. That should save me the bother of coming out here for a while. Although, of course, it's always very good to see you.'

Marcus shrugged. He didn't seem especially interested one way or another.

'So I'm expecting a discount on the basis of the size of my order and our long-standing friendship,' said Felix.

'Not for six grams,' said Marcus. 'That's not enough.'

'Well, I'm not buying any more than that.'

There was a silence for thirty seconds or so, but it didn't feel especially uncomfortable. Marcus lived most of his life not necessarily in peace, but certainly in pauses, during the commercial breaks, or while the tea leaves stewed. While Felix and James stood waiting, he seemed content to sit on his sofa thinking about any number of things, or perhaps nothing at all.

'Come on, Marcus. Let's do the deal.'

Marcus shrugged again. 'Fuck it. Okay. Call it three hundred quid.'

'Good man,' said Felix. 'I'm fine with that.'

'Okay, wait here.'

Marcus left the room. He went up the stairs and came down again a minute later. It might well have been the only piece of work he would do all day. If it wasn't for his central heating, thought James, Marcus's carbon footprint would be impressively low. He returned with a small paper bag, which he handed to Felix, and then sat back down on the sofa. Felix gave him some money, and Marcus put it in his wooden box.

'See you around,' said Marcus. 'Oh wait, I better see you out.'

He walked them to the door, back through the hallway and into the open. The sky had darkened and a breeze had picked up. A day much like any other was coming to a close. James found himself suddenly shivering in the cold air, no longer warmed by Marcus's overactive, welfare-subsidised radiators.

'Goodbye,' said Felix.

Marcus nodded, James nodded back. There were no secret messages in their nods and sighs, just a tacit understanding that communicating in this way was less wearisome. It occurred to James that it was unlikely that he would ever meet Marcus again and, on balance, that this was probably a good thing.

★

And now, six hours later, James had taken his drugs and was dealing with the consequences. One of the most important was that he had had loads and loads to drink. Overexcited by the drug deal and who knows, maybe even the drugs themselves, James had proceeded to drink five pints of strong lager, brewed by Slovakian monks to a secret fourteenth-century recipe. It had seemed the obvious thing to do. They were in a pub in Clerkenwell with wooden floors. James wasn't able to say much more than that – it wasn't his territory and his powers of reasoning were diminished. All he could say for certain was that he was in North, arguably East, London. Disturbingly, and this was something which hardly ever happened, he didn't even know which borough he was in.

There were seven of them, and although Felix and Carl had jointly coordinated the group for a specific purpose, there didn't seem to have been any thematic criteria to their selection. There was Olivia, who had been in the restaurant that night with Adam, and who seemed a great deal friendlier than he remembered – but he couldn't be sure if that was because she was on drugs, or he was. There was Erica, the advertising woman James had met at Felix's club, and who looked exactly the same as he remembered, except she was wearing trainers. Perhaps, just like the other evening, she regarded this as work.

Carl had brought along two colleagues from the bank: a beautiful boy called Rafael, with dramatic black hair and amber-brown skin, who hardly spoke and may have been intended as a sex offering for one of the women; and Rick who was a terrible little man with dirty fingernails, teeth that were close to ruin and cunning red eyes. He had his own source of drugs and, unlike Marcus, Rick really did look like a cocaine dealer, but he was actually a commod-ities trader. James had tried to invite Harriet, but she had abruptly left her job and gone to Marrakesh for four weeks.

'I think,' said Felix, 'that all the ingredients are here for a success-ful evening. The preparation has been thorough. James and I, in particular, need to be congratulated for crossing the entire city region today on everyone's behalf.'

'You've both done very well,' said Erica.

'This is fucking brilliant,' said Rick.

'I am so very excited,' said Olivia. 'I haven't been out like this for ages.'

'I'm *too* excited. Let's go outside and smoke some weed,' said Carl. 'I need to self-medicate a bit.'

James, Felix and some of the others followed him outside, through a side door to the back of the pub, from where there was an alley leading into a small, closed yard set against the walls of a Roman Catholic church, and which didn't appear on any maps. As James knew, in this part of London history always trumped geog-raphy. Five hundred years ago it would have been a designated site for burying religious heretics, witches and plague victims, but it now seemed purpose-built for taking drugs.

Carl produced a joint from his jacket pocket and lit it with a happy flourish. He looked like someone who had taken exactly the right amount of stimulants and narcotics: overconfident, expansive with his thoughts and generous with his cannabis.

'Do you know why, at some point in the 1990s, London defini-tively overtook Frankfurt as Europe's financial centre?'

James shook his head. He didn't really know what Carl was talk-ing about, and he'd never been to Germany.

'I'll tell you why,' continued Carl, with an extravagant inhalation of the joint. 'Have you ever been stuck in Frankfurt on a Friday night?'

'Fuck – yeah,' said Rick. 'I defy anyone to find a single good line of coke there.'

Carl handed the joint to James. He looked at it unconfidently, raised it quickly to his lips and inhaled deeply and incompetently – so incompetently that it would either be entirely ineffectual or else leave him comprehensively intoxicated.

'It's not just the drugs. It's *everything*,' continued Carl. 'I've had to spend whole weeks of my life there. It's the lack of high-quality bars, the crummy football team, the piss-poor modern art gallery and the fact that everyone is so fucking white. No Jews, obviously, but no blacks or South Americans either. All they've got are Turks, who I admit aren't white, and Poles.'

'And what's your point?' said Erica.

'My point is, London is the best place to do business, because it's the best place to do things like this.'

'You don't have to tell this to James,' said Felix. 'It's his job – he's the town planner, remember. If you want to thank anyone for London's premier position as the world capital of neo-liberalism then it's him. He's our great wealth creator. It's why we mustn't let him run away to Nottingham.'

'That's actually sort of right,' said James.

'Fuck – respect, man,' said Rick, nodding his head gravely.

Felix took the joint and breathed in deeply. There was a moment of peaceful reflection. James felt fairly confident that, despite everything he had done and all the money he had spent, he wasn't having a bad time.

'Personally, I was always led to believe that the best place to live in the world was Norway,' said Felix.

'Norway? What the fuck are you talking about,' said Carl.

'There's actually a little-known philosophical proof,' continued Felix. 'Ludwig Wittgenstein once said that Norway is the greatest country in the world. Wittgenstein only spoke truth. Therefore . . .'

'That's right,' said Erica, unexpectedly. 'Wittgenstein did say that. The syllogism holds.'

'So do you think I need to worry about capital and labour moving to Norway?' said James.

'Christ no,' said Felix. 'Do you know how much tax they pay over there?'

Carl looked at them all grimly. 'That's the thing about cocaine,' he said. 'It makes everyone so fucking *clever*. At this rate, Rick will start speaking in symbolic logic. Come on, let's go back inside. I need another drink.'

But having come out, James wasn't now sure if he wanted to go back in. Something had happened to him, something to do with the cannabis, which had cancelled out the cocaine, and suddenly made him question what exactly he thought he was doing here. He wasn't the great wealth creator at all. He was James Crawley, he worked in town planning at Southwark Council, and he didn't even know which borough he was in.

He peered anxiously through the doorway. Felix had already made it back to the bar, but James was stuck. He wasn't sure what he should do next, and the necessary journeys ahead of him – to the bar, to the toilet, to the others – appeared treacherous, with untold obstacles and dangers. But thankfully, he wasn't alone. Erica was there with him too.

'I think we may have overdone it,' she said. 'That joint was very strong. Let's just wait here for a minute, until the head rush stops.'

She stood with him in the alleyway. Even wearing trainers she was tall, but of course not too tall for him. She held his hand, and looked at him as affectionately as her small black eyes would allow.

'Don't worry, it will soon pass,' she said.

James nodded. She was right – already he was starting to feel better. The alleys of Clerkenwell were bright but soft in the moonlight. He could hear Erica breathing unnaturally loudly, but he was sure he would have done without any drugs, and anyway it was a nice sound.

'So is Felix a good friend of yours?' said James.

'Well, I thought so once. But now I'm not sure if Felix really has any friends.'

'I don't know. He seems to have lots of friends.'

'He has projects. He has people who interest him. But it's not the same thing.'

'I like him. He's been good to me.'

'I'm not saying he isn't kind,' said Erica. 'If anything, he's too kind. For a while, at least. And then, quite suddenly, he isn't.'

'That sounds ominous. What happens?'

'Oh, nothing really. Nothing happens.'

James nodded. He didn't understand, but that was all right for now. For now, he wanted to think about other things.

'When we met before, I thought you worked with Felix. But you don't, do you? You work for the government or something.'

'No, sorry – that was a misunderstanding. I'm not a brand planner, I'm a town planner.'

'You should have told me. I think that's so much more interesting. I hate advertising.'

As she said this, Erica squeezed his hand. He squeezed hers. They stood for another minute, maybe two, without saying anything.

'Okay?' she said.

'Yes, I'm fine. Are you okay?'

'It's fine. To be honest, I'm just glad to get away from Rick. He's such a creep. He's been harassing me all night.'

James nodded, determined to protect her – if nothing else, it would be his mission for the night. They squeezed each other's hands again and went back inside, where the others were making more noise than ever. The conversation had become worryingly unstructured and was in danger of breaking down completely. People were still saying things, sometimes even good things, but the narrative had been lost, and the only person listening to what was being said was probably now James.

'Drugs are not sufficient for a successful night out,' said Felix, 'but they are becoming increasingly necessary. I think it's because we're all getting older.'

'We're going to need them for where we're going,' said Carl.

'I'm sick of this place. I need to be dancing,' said Olivia.

'I need to take a fuck-load more,' said Rick.

'I agree,' said Rafael.

'My mouth is completely numb,' said Olivia. 'It's like being at the dentist's.'

'The problem,' said Carl, 'is that you always need so much of it.'

'Come on, let's go,' said Olivia.

'None of it's any good any more, that's the problem,' said Rick. 'It's all just shit.'

'The lesson, as ever, is to be happy with what you have, rather than to have what makes you happy,' said Felix.

It was now 11 p.m. and the pub was closing, but James had only got through about 40 per cent of the evening, for next they had to go to a nightclub. Again, he understood that this was something that would have to be done. There was even, now that he had held hands with Erica, a chance he might enjoy it.

Displaying a wide range of professional skills, Carl singlehandedly organised the transport. He telephoned a local firm and agreed a fee for a seven-seat taxi, reopening negotiations with the driver as soon as it arrived and reducing the price by a quarter. He marshalled the group in a good-humoured but firm manner out of the pub, and oversaw operations closely as they all incompetently and theatrically climbed in, for by now they were bringing out hysterical tendencies in each other. The journey itself, however, was uneventful and largely unnecessary, lasting slightly less than four minutes. It seemed that Olivia had refused to walk.

And now here they were – outside a nightclub in approximately the same part of Clerkenwell. The entrance, of course, gave little away. There were no illuminated signs, just a long, well-behaved queue trailing back from some large, unpainted wooden doors. What James hadn't expected was that it would cost thirty-two pounds to get in but, as Felix explained, that was essential and actually to be welcomed. Ideally, you only wanted to take Class-A drugs with Class-A people. Just like a private members' bar or boarding school, what you were paying for was the other customers, and if you didn't pay enough then you ended up in a room full of fuckheads from north Kent. Although, of course, if it was *too* expensive then you risked finding yourself exclusively with tall girls from Chelsea and corporate lawyers who lived in Clapham – Felix did acknowledge that.

The demographic mix was important too. Ideally, you didn't want that many black men there, but you did want enough to be able to buy drugs, and you certainly wanted plenty of black women. You also wanted Japanese, of either sex, but it had to be the kooky architecture students rather than the dippy tourists. Scandinavians were hugely welcome, though southern Europeans less so. Australians weren't always as bad as everyone said, but South Africans and Israelis were, and it was a given that everything was significantly better if at least 20 per cent of the dance floor was homosexual. Above all, though, what you really wanted to avoid was a club full of white British people.

But the main thing was that, whoever was going tonight, James and his companions weren't actually in the queue with them. Or at least, they were in another, smaller and better one. They were on a guest list. Not the list of famous people, but they were definitely on a list, which was, James recognised, an important achievement. It was one of the perks of buying your drugs from Marcus, who had a long-standing commercial association with a doorman. Felix described it as an ingenious piece of cross-selling that helped to differentiate him in the marketplace but, having now met Marcus, James wondered if it was really as thought through as that. But whatever the reason, it was to be welcomed – even James knew that the better the quality of the queue, the more quickly it moved and, in no more than ten minutes, they were inside the nightclub. Things were just as speedy in here as well: they paid with debit cards, they were briskly searched for concealed weapons, the women and Rafael went to the cloakroom, and then they were gently pushed through some heavy black doors.

Now there was no turning back, they had stepped out of London into a world that was alien and dangerous. Dazzled by laser beams, humbled by the noise, his lungs filling with purple smoke, James stumbled forward like an explorer on Jupiter. The music was so loud he feared that it would interfere with the functioning of his heart, but there was nothing to do but keep going. At the end of the room was an entrance to another, almost identical room, and then another after that. Everyone James had come with had scattered immediately, as if it was an adventure game. He wondered where Erica was, but didn't know how he could find her, for the nightclub was enormous, in some ways as big as London, with tunnels, steps, vaults and secret chambers that went deep into the ancient heart of Clerkenwell.

By the time he had got to the fourth room, he had started to acclimatise. It was a fundamentally hostile environment, but he could see that it was possible to function. The music no longer crushed him, and his eyes had adapted to the irregular flashes of light. There was little nervousness, the drugs had at least helped with that, but the problem was he now felt restless and manically dissatisfied, with no sensible idea of what it was that he wanted. Just because you're wandering it doesn't mean that you're lost, but in this case it was fair to say that he probably was, and although he was still looking for Erica, he was no longer sure why.

After half an hour, he at least managed to find Carl, who was standing on the edge of a dance floor, drinking a bottle of Coke and with a curious, sinister expression as if some great but unwelcome truth had just been revealed to him.

'Hi Carl,' he said. 'I don't know where anyone is.'

'Hi,' said Carl. 'Neither do I.'

Carl walked abruptly on, out into another room. That was actually to be expected, for one of the things James had learnt was that sociopathic behaviour was standard here. The music was too loud to do anything else, and there was no reward system for good manners. You banged into people who were in your way, you ordered drinks with hand gestures, and if you wanted to display affection to someone then you danced very closely to them until either something happened or they moved away. And as a result, muted, you ended up feeling lonely and alienated, unless you had taken enough drinks and drugs not to know any better. He thought about sending a text message to Rachel, but didn't know what to say and, besides, she would be asleep.

James had tried his hardest, but it was no good – he was feeling old again. Worse than that, he was feeling *young* again. He was surrounded by lovely, frail faces with lean bodies, but there was a seasoned competence to them. They were veterans of London's night-time economy, and were highly experienced at having a very good time. True, they weren't obviously enjoying themselves like in other bars and clubs – they weren't shouting or laughing or fighting, and no one was getting off with anyone else – instead, they were methodical and sombre, focused on the task of dancing to the music as truthfully as possible. And if they weren't dancing they were resting. Like athletes, they were being careful with their bodies. They drank bottles of mineral water and replenished their blood sugar levels with sucrose bars and energy drinks.

Eventually, he was back in the first room, where some of the others had regrouped. He could see that Felix was dancing brilliantly. Or, at least, and this was the key thing, he looked exactly like he knew what he was doing. He was probably dancing with little technical skill, but that didn't matter. He was dancing with great strength of character, expressively and in perfect harmony with his worldview. At the same time, and James wasn't sure how, he was dancing with irony. Rafael and Olivia were dancing nearby, but slowly moving away together. It was inevitable that they would have sex later that night. Erica was nowhere to be seen.

'Felix, what time is it? We've been here for hours.'

'Alas, young James, I fear you've made the mistake of confusing the ontological with the phenomenological. We actually only got here forty minutes ago.'

'Oh Christ, really?'

'Don't look so disheartened, my friend, you're here to have a good time remember?'

James nodded, and bought a bottle of beer for a bewildering amount of money, but the fact that this would deter poor people from coming was no longer any consolation. At least there was no need to feel self-conscious about things, because no one was taking much interest in anyone else. It was quite possible to look at someone at length without anyone minding, so he did that for a while.

There was a woman dancing flamboyantly not far from the bar, and so he watched her. He stared at her for so long, and so intently, that eventually she looked back at him.

'Hello,' she mouthed, waving her hand.

'Hello,' he said, waving his hand back.

She moved closer to hm. She was a talented dancer and if there were any significant defects in her appearance, then they weren't picked up by the club lighting. He was almost a foot taller than her. She asked him something, but the music was too loud to be sure what, and she was unlikely to be interested in town planning. It was clear that English wasn't her first language. They both smiled, but not at the same time. It was no good. He might as well have been trying to have a conversation with a zebra. He would have to give up.

'Where's Carl? Where's Erica?' said James, but Felix couldn't hear him.

James went into another room, and then went through a door he hadn't noticed before. He walked down a long, narrow corridor and found himself in a smaller room in which no one was dancing. Instead, people were sitting on the floor and staring at a wall on to which was being projected a series of images. It wasn't particularly orderly, but it felt very calm. Either everyone here had taken different drugs from him, or else they had taken the same drug at different times. The images were abstract and senseless: shapes, colours and lines, the kinds of things that opticians test you with, but they didn't hurt his eyes or his thoughts, and after a while he started to think they might even be good for him. Maybe they could heal his mind. There was music here, but it was of a different sort – gentle, melodic and, best of all, it wasn't that loud.

James wondered if he could just stay here for the rest of the night, or even the whole weekend. It would be nice if Erica found him here, and they could see it through together. But then, to his surprise and dismay, it suddenly became apparent that he couldn't, that he would have to go somewhere else as quickly as he could.

'James! Fucking hell! It's James Crawley.'

James had been assured that cocaine had no hallucinogenic properties, otherwise he may have wondered if his mind had manufactured some ghastly phantom. Ian Benson, rising star of Southwark Council's IT Services department, was grinning at him.

'Oh, hi Ian,' said James. 'Good to see you.'

'I didn't expect to see you here. Didn't think this was your sort of thing.'

Was Ian on drugs as well? Probably, although he was such a haphazard creature, such a strange and obtuse personality, that it was impossible to tell. He had an unusually large head, too big for his body but not for his brain, which was known to be powerful, if often misapplied. He had a degree in physics, was in charge of the office intranet, and the only person who could be relied upon to mend James's computer, though it was almost always him who broke it in the first place.

'I'm with Alex,' said Ian. 'Alex Coleman from work. We're on a proper night out. I don't know where he's gone. He'll be chuffed to see you.'

Now that was even worse. Wasn't the club's pricing policy designed to exclude these kinds of berks? Alex from Comms and Ian from IT – junior local authority employees, exactly who shouldn't be able to afford the entrance fee, and who you didn't want to meet at two in the morning when you were feeling at your most defenceless.

'It's magic here, isn't it,' said Ian. 'Great atmosphere. Properly buzzing.'

'Yes,' agreed James. 'It's really great. Do you come here a lot?'

'No, mate, not often. Too expensive. But when I do, I like to really go for it.'

'Totally,' said James. 'I'm with some other people, so I better go and find them. I'll come back and see you in a minute.'

'Cool,' said Ian. 'See you in a bit. I'll be here.'

James went to the toilets, but they were a refuge from the music only. The lighting here was merciless, with the kind of luminosity normally associated with medical interventions, but the real problem was that they were so busy. The main reason for this was that it was full of women. It wasn't that he had blundered into the wrong ones, and it wasn't even as if they were designated as unisex. Rather, and as a planner he should have understood this, it was simply an out-of-date regulation that was being widely ignored. Women wanted to go into men's toilets and so they did, and the men didn't seem to mind. But James minded, for he wanted to be alone for a while, and that was impossible. All of the toilet cubicles were in medium- to long-term use, while a variety of sex and drugs crimes were being committed. Standing over a sink, the only calm he could construct came from looking deeply into himself in a mirror, but after no more than thirty seconds of this he became saturated with horror.

A door banged open, and James turned to see Rick and Erica come out of a cubicle, their faces flushed and overheated, their clothes disorganised and their bodies entangled.

'That was the best fucking shit I've ever had,' announced Rick.

James smiled at them. It was a tremendous feat – the greatest smile he had ever produced in his life, a smile strong enough to forgive Erica and to neutralise Rick's evil cackle. But they walked straight past – either they hadn't seen him or maybe the parts of their prefrontal lobes responsible for facial pattern recognition had been disabled. James often wished that he had studied biology at university, but he had taken the wrong A levels. The cubicle was taken by two blond women in black leather trousers.

It wasn't long afterwards that the solution came to him. *He would go home*. It was the only, the obvious, thing to do – why on earth hadn't it occurred to him before? A unilateral, and not even that bold, decision – it was all that was required. He didn't know where everyone else was, and he didn't care: he felt far too preoccupied to bother about his companions who were, after all, largely wankers. Who knows, maybe they had all done the same thing hours ago. But once the decision had been made, it had to be acted upon at once.

He walked quickly, he ran, all the way back through the club, determined not to meet anyone – particularly anyone from work, particularly not Rick or Erica. He didn't want anyone to slow him down, or make him have to explain. His head lowered, he crossed the floors as directly as possible, barging youths aside, knocking over drinks and disrupting the dancers. He was, just like everyone else there, behaving badly. He went through dance rooms and bars and chambers and cloakrooms, passed doormen and barmen and drug dealers, and heaved open the wooden doors until finally he had left the noise and the heat behind him.

He now had to face a new set of challenges which were less drastic but more intractable. For, if the cocaine had ever worked at all, its effect was to leave him unable to sleep and feeling sad and self-absorbed. It had made him *modern,* and there was little he could do about it. Outside the club there was a market that was either under- or over-regulated, he couldn't decide which, but it was clear that doormen were allocating people to taxi cabs and destinations on an anti-competitive basis. Unable to negotiate, unwilling to be humiliated, James instead walked off. If this was a night for anything at all, then it was a night to walk home. A cold, dry night. No stars, of course, there never were in London, but there was three-quarters of a moon and the drink and drugs would at least keep him warm.

He headed off in what was, he knew, only approximately the right direction. Earlier he had been lost in the nightclub, and now he was lost on the streets. That was Clerkenwell for you, but did anyone really know where they were going in this city? It was still difficult to understand how it had happened. An obscure Anglo-Saxon riverside settlement in an abandoned Roman military camp that had, like Anglo-Saxons everywhere, got wildly out of control. It was the least-planned city in the developed world. No invading power had drained its marshlands and founded a city state, no tyrant had ever razed it to the ground and rebuilt it on more orderly principles. Some Victorian engineers had done their best to clean things up, but the really big opportunities, the Great Fire and the Blitz, had been wasted. It had been two thousand years before Patrick Abercrombie had got round to producing a plan, and by then it was all much too late.

There was no grid system, and no wide boulevards elegantly radiating out from the city centre. In fact, there wasn't even a centre. Apparently there had been once, but it had got lost, buried and hidden along with everything else. There was a plaque on a wall somewhere near Charing Cross Station, there was a pipe under Blackfriars Bridge where the River Fleet trickled into the River Thames, and there was a piece of stone in Cannon Street, which had once meant something important, but no one now could remember what. And on top of these were Modernism and capitalism and the twentieth century, and all the things that the heritage organisations and conservation societies, the environmentalists and town planners had failed to stop happening. There were no city walls or gates or guards left either. There was nothing to keep them in and the others out, no one to keep them safe. And as a result of all this James, the town planner, was lost along with everyone else.

He had walked for no more than fifteen minutes, but already he was prepared to surrender. His serotonin depleted, his legs aching, London had defeated him yet again. He was developing what he knew would be a debilitating headache, but it was hard to tell if that was due to the legacy of the drugs, all those pints of Slovakian lager, the cannabis, the after-shock of the music or just the city he lived in. It had hardly been a controlled experiment. A car passed by very slowly, James raised his hand and it stopped. The driver offered to take James home for an extraordinary amount of money, almost twice as much as he had been quoted outside the nightclub. James accepted without a word and climbed in.

6 March

It is worth remembering that change presents opportunities for London, as well as challenges.

– The London Plan, Section 1.50

'Yes, of course. That would be really nice.'

'Yes, it was a real shame I couldn't come up. I've just been so busy with work.'

'Don't worry – of course, I have been thinking about it. I've been thinking about it a lot.'

James was speaking to his mother. Even in 2013, these kinds of mistakes still happened from time to time. His mobile phone had rung, the number hadn't appeared, and he had thought it was someone else, maybe Harriet calling from Morocco, for instance. And now, here he was, outside a bar on the King's Road in Chelsea, having a conversation he didn't want to have for at least another week, while Felix was inside drinking a bottle of white wine.

'I know it's a very good opportunity, but I'm not sure if it's the right time in my career.'

'Yes, I know. It would only be an hour away. But you know, that's not much further than where I am now.'

What was the news from Leicester? It was much the same as it had been two weeks ago. His father wasn't well, but nobody really knew why, his sister was enjoying her teacher training, the weather was wet, the economy was contracting, the garden wall needed repairing, the hospital where she worked wasn't, after all, going to get its neo-natal units.

'I've got to get going. My friend is waiting for me.'

Not so long ago, James had been on the verge of going back. Not quite back to Leicester, but certainly back to the Midlands. It was still an option. There was, for a few weeks longer, a job waiting for him. Deputy Director of Planning at Nottingham City Council – the man he would be replacing was at least ten years older than him. From a certain perspective, by local government standards, James would be a success. But would anyone else ever know that? Would it feel like success?

'Yes, don't worry – I'm definitely coming for that weekend.'

'I've got to get going. Speak soon. I love you lots.'

James put the phone back in his pocket. He had just told his mother that he loved her on the King's Road in Chelsea. Because of her poor hearing, because of the phone reception and the noise from the street, he had said it quite loudly. Not with great pride, but certainly with volume. Enough for a good-looking young man with ruthless blond hair, expertly smoking a cigarette and drinking a bottle of beer, to look up at him with an amused smile.

Well, it was true. He did love his mother. Just as he felt sorry for his father and worried a bit about his sister. But that, surely, wasn't enough to leave London. What about the life plan? He was, after all, only halfway through. Okay, he hadn't enjoyed the nightclub or the drugs much but he was, he felt sure, developing. He was moving, jerkily and expensively, in the right direction and he was still committed to the process. It was why he was here on the King's Road.

'If you really want to understand London,' Felix had told him earlier that week, 'then you have to hang out with some rich people. It's what this city is all about.'

'Yes, I can see that. But does it have to be football?'

It seemed that it did. Just as in the salons of nineteenth-century Europe, a gentleman was expected to be able to speak knowledge-ably about warfare, so in 2013 a young man of any standing had to be able to hold his own in a discussion about football. The prob-lem, of course, was that James didn't know anything about it: football was yet another of those things that he had never been educated in. No one had ever talked about it when he'd been a student and while it was true that his school had had a strong tradi-tion of team sports, they were all the wrong ones. Like most grammar schools, James's had made a point of competing with great seriousness at cricket and rugby, of beating comprehensives with ease and losing valiantly to schools that had much more money. But that was no use now when all that anyone was inter-ested in was football and anyway – he had never even been any good at rugby or cricket. The only thing he had ever been good at was the long jump.

But here they were. It was a Wednesday night and James was now back inside the wine bar with Felix, round the corner from Stamford Bridge football stadium in the Royal Borough of Kensington and Chelsea. James hardly ever came here, but he knew its statistical profile all too well. The figures were formidable, and everyone working in London government was meant to be trying to make their part of the city more like this one. It was the borough with the highest life expectancy, the highest average income and the lowest unemployment. More people participated in cultural activities than anywhere else and fewer people got run over or murdered.

Sitting in the bar, some other things struck him – things that didn't come up in the data, but which weren't actually that surprising. For instance, people were generally taller here than they were in pubs in South London – for reasons not fully understood, the positive correlation between income and height had been maintained, even though poorer people now ate more than rich people. Being around tall people was never something James had to worry about, but more troubling was the fact that everyone was good-looking. It wasn't like being in East London – you didn't have to study people closely in order to work out whether they were attractive or not, and what the strategy behind their choice of personal disfigurement was. Everyone was just good-looking – it was as simple as that. The men had thick arms and well-structured faces and could only really be described as handsome, while the women had long, sternly combed hair, nimble features and clever mouths. And what with being so tall and good-looking and wealthy, they were also unusually loud.

'What are you getting so grumpy about? It's not so bad in here,' said Felix.

'It's not really my kind of place,' said James. 'It's far too noisy.'

'The key thing is to judge people by your value system, rather than to judge yourself by theirs.'

'Well, okay. I don't really like the people here.'

'You've got to learn to enjoy London,' said Felix. 'And it's largely because it's brimming with appalling people that it's so enjoyable. The half-witted celebrities, the venal politicians, the pretentious artists, the oikish footballers – all paid for by the cretinous bankers. Imagine how impoverished the city would be without its monsters. Anyway, let's go. I promise you'll enjoy it more than the nightclub.'

They left the bar, and joined the thickening stream of Chelsea fans walking conspicuously towards the stadium. It was, James noted with satisfaction, a stupendously poor piece of town planning. Or rather, and this cheered him all the more, there hadn't *been* any planning. It was a welcome reminder of why cities needed long-sighted, over-officious professionals like him, why everything would be so much better if only it looked like it did in his master-plan poster. There were railway lines here, but no mainline station to service the stadium. The pavements weren't wide enough, there were coaches stuck in traffic, insufficient parking spaces and unlicensed stalls selling scarves and football shirts. And through all of this marched forty thousand men.

Even if Felix had promised him that they would be watching the match exclusively with people on very high incomes, they still had to get there along with everyone else. They had to wait in lines, to squeeze through ticket gates, walk up stairwells and get given directions by men in their sixties who were supplementing their state pensions. All of this gave James the opportunity to have a good look at the football fans. Rich, well-educated people now went to football, he knew that, but what was more surprising was that working-class people still went as well. Almost certainly, these were the affluent working classes, who had travelled here from across southern England. This was the socio-demographic group who decided general election results and drove saloon cars, and who were deeply suspicious of government but wildly susceptible to Felix's advertising campaigns.

'I know, I know. It's not what you were expecting,' said Felix. 'But we'll enjoy the private box all the more for having to go through this.'

James had been brought up to fear all crowds, but there was, he soon realised, no need to be worried. They weren't in the least bit violent and even though they supported the same team, they didn't have enough sense of common purpose to act as a mob. It was no more than a dense concentration of moderately unpleasant men. They had drunk just enough alcohol to raise their voices without embarrassment and to swear a great deal, but not enough to sing songs or get into fights. Instead, most of them were eating hot dogs and playing with their mobile phones.

But the higher Felix and James climbed, the fewer of these people there were, the fewer there was of anyone. On the upper floor of the stadium were the executive suites, and a pleasing sense of well-managed calm, as if they were in a conference centre in an unspecified northern European city. They walked past a row of identical wood finish doors, each with a name plaque belonging to companies that James knew he ought to have heard of.

'Everyone thinks that London is the world centre for capitalism,' said Felix. 'But, in truth it actually functions more like a tribal gift economy. It's composed of business people giving things to other business people. And the trick is to give them enough that they then give you something back which turns out to be of greater value – like a contract or profile in a newspaper. And the wider and more generous the giving, the better chance that you'll hit upon someone who will one day repay you.'

They stopped outside a door just like all of the others, with the name Galbraith & Erskine sombrely engraved on a copper plaque. Felix boldly pushed it open and they came into what looked much like the room of a hotel in the vicinity of Heathrow airport. It was a square room, with a colour-flecked carpet. The lighting was bright and uncomplicated and the brass wall fixtures shiny. Adam, who was still arguably his best friend, was there.

'Adam,' said James. 'I didn't know you were going to be here.'

'Well, I think the bigger surprise is that you're here. I didn't think football was your thing at all.'

'Oh, well – you know. Like a lot of people, I'm sort of interested.'

Adam nodded. 'What do you think of our chances then?'

James paused uncertainly. It wasn't enough to have come to the match, he should really have done some preparation. After all, he would have done for a meeting at work, and this was going to be far more challenging.

'Well, it could go either way,' he said.

Adam smiled. He was looking at him in a way that wasn't quite unkind, but was certainly unwelcome. James hurried along to a table where there was a tray of pale yellow lagers. There didn't seem any choice but to take one and start drinking.

'Here,' said Felix. 'Come and meet our hosts and fellow guests.'

Every single person in the room was white and male. James had expected that, but on being introduced he realised something else, something Felix hadn't warned him about – almost all of them were property developers. They were his greatest professional enemy. These were the landowners, speculators and spivs, the people determined to shape the way London would look for the next ten years, but had no interest in what happened after that, and who had completely different kinds of ambition and money from James. It was the developers who paid for all the architects and lawyers and construction companies, and who fucked cities up. And it was his job to stop them from doing all the things they wanted to do – wrecking skylines, spoiling conservation areas, building on green spaces and breaking affordable housing commitments. And the peculiar thing was, now that he was actually meeting them in person, he couldn't help but like them. They were well mannered and friendly, they were generous hosts and hard-working conversationalists. They were, in fact, much nicer than any of the town planners.

'Everyone here basically works in property,' said James.

'What did you expect?' said Adam. 'That's how anyone makes money in this city. It's how I make my money. It's not as if we have any manufacturers I can sue or write contracts for.'

'Listen,' said Felix, 'the very best brand consultancy is also management consultancy, or in your case, career guidance. So here goes: you work in property as well. Stop thinking of yourself as a town planner, and start thinking of yourself as a professional who works in the property sector with specific, highly sought after expertise in public policy.'

Adam nodded. 'That's actually quite good advice. And also try not to say anything completely stupid about football.'

A man called Robert came over to talk to James. To use one of those football idioms that James had always disliked, his was a face of two halves. He had wide-spaced, boyish teeth and soft vertical grooves beneath his nostrils. But his eyes were small, fast-moving and treacherous, while his narrow, worn brow suggested that he had hosted many evenings like this one – he had given many things away in exchange for others.

'So it must be tough down in Southwark at the moment, what with the new social-housing targets,' said Robert.

'Yes, it is difficult. We've got some sites going through assessment at the moment, but not enough and everyone's worried that to make them work they're going to be too tall.'

And they then proceeded to have an interesting and productive conversation about housing densities, building specifications and the property market in South London. Robert clearly knew what he was talking about, and thought that the development framework for Southwark was too restrictive and risked inhibiting private investment. And James, who had actually helped draft the development framework, warmly agreed with him. For one thing, it was so much easier than disagreeing.

'You know,' said Robert, 'it's really good to meet someone from Southwark. We've got a lot of interests there, but have always struggled with the council. It's good to have a friendly face on the planning side for a change.'

'Well, it's true, planners can be rather hard work.'

'God, yes – what's the name of your director there? Leo whatsit?'

'You mean Lionel Rogers?'

'Yes, that's the chap – Lionel. He's a bit of an old sod, isn't he?'

'Yes,' said James. 'He is a bit.'

'Been there for years, won't let anything happen. Typical old-school planner – still believes in zones, thinks he owns the place. No wonder you're struggling to get enough investment.'

'I know, I know. He's holding Southwark back.'

This was, James knew, largely untrue and unfair. Lionel was, after all, his mentor and friend, the person who hired him, who taught him how planning in London works. But how else do you grow up in this world? The generations don't replace one another; they displace one another. If they have to, if they're able to, they murder one another. It wasn't progress exactly, but it was how things happened. He swallowed a large mouthful of lager. It was fresh and strong and hurt his lips.

'Come on,' said Adam. 'It's starting.'

They filed out of the back of the corporate box and on to a narrow balcony. James had only been to one football match in his life before, and that had been in Leicester in the 1990s – a misconceived day out with his father and sister, neither of whom knew anything more about football than he did. It definitely looked a lot better this time. That surely was because of the light and perspective and money. They were very high up. The Chelsea players' blue shirts and white shorts shimmered under the powerful beams of the floodlights, while the other team's red shirts and black shorts glowed menacingly. And the pitch itself was lovely: a rich, luminous green, so bright and flawless that it looked as if it had been made on a computer. It shone, and not just from the floodlights beaming down, but as if there was a light pulsing up through it. James thought it would have been quite enjoyable just to drink beer and stare down at that all evening.

It was a European Cup match, and the red team had a name that was difficult to pronounce and was from an East European country with a poor human rights record. That made it slightly easier to support Chelsea, which wasn't something that came naturally to James who, despite being a believer in the merits of collective endeavour, distrusted all tribes and teams.

'There you go,' said Felix. 'This is one of London's great spectacles and industrial sectors. People travel from across the world to see our football. It is also, by the way, the only hope left for European integration, the only thing that dock workers in Hamburg and computer programmers in Reading can successfully hold a conversation about.'

James nodded. He didn't quite know what Felix was talking about, but there was no doubt that the footballers themselves were beautiful. You could tell that even at a distance. No wonder young women were always wanting to have sex with them in nightclubs. Unlike other athletes, they were gracefully proportioned, their bodies adapted for a range of different tasks. They had marvellous strong legs, counter-balanced by high shoulders, and topped with thick long hair. Many of them had glorious tattoos. And, after all, maybe there was something heroic about them. Anyone paid that much money had to be admirable in some ways, just as contemporary novelists surely warranted at least some contempt for being paid so little.

'We better win this,' said Adam.

'Oh I'm sure we will,' said Felix.

'We ought to beat them,' said Robert. 'Their entire team cost less than our goalie.'

But now the match had actually got going, things were more problematic. All the things that James disliked, which he was paid to eradicate, were happening on the pitch in front of him. There were too many players and they weren't evenly distributed. There was congestion and along with this there were collisions and conflict. Perhaps, he wondered, if the teams were playing better it would be different, but he suspected not – there were simply too many people moving quickly in a limited space, and they were playing with just a single ball.

James looked at the clock. To his surprise, no more than nine minutes had passed. Despite his best efforts, his interest was in danger of waning. It wasn't just him – already some of the others were talking about property prices again. Was this really what all the fuss was about? Yes, the players all looked great, but he didn't know any of them or care what they were doing. Plus, he now recalled that many of them tended to avoid paying tax. He started to feel sorry for the referee, the official who had regulatory authority over them, but hardly any money or respect, and who was getting shouted at by the crowd.

He went back into the executive box and drank some more beer. Inside, a couple of people were watching the game on a large television screen. James sat and watched with them for a while – it actually looked a bit more exciting and comprehensible. After a few minutes, some others came inside to join them.

'I really don't like the way we're playing,' said Robert. 'It's far too crowded in the middle and far too deep at the back.'

'It's appalling,' agreed Adam. 'There's no width there at all, and the strikers are totally disconnected. It's like they're playing for a different team.'

James stared at his friend in admiration and, therefore, anxiety. So it seemed that Adam knew about football too! How on earth had he ever managed that? Along with becoming a successful commercial lawyer and buying a house in West London and getting engaged and running half-marathons and everything else, he had somehow found the time to learn about football – to make perfectly intelligible, albeit unverifiable, statements which other people would agree with.

'You're right. This is total fucking dogshit,' said someone else, shaking his head menacingly.

'We're playing like bastards,' said a man called Angus. 'We're playing like fucking gay bastards.'

Angus was a retail developer, and had a number of features which would normally be considered defects in a modern male, but in fact only added to his overall impressiveness. He was in his mid-fifties, overweight, unambiguously bald and had an alarming West Country accent. His big white shirt flapped in the evening breeze, and was difficult to distinguish from his skin.

James turned to Felix. 'Is this standard? Everyone seemed so pleasant until the football started.'

'Yes, this is generally what tends to happen. As they say, those who waste their youth attaining wealth are doomed to waste their wealth trying to attain youth. Football is one of the main ways in which men do that now.'

James watched some more of the match, alternating every few minutes from going outside, where it was authentic, chilly and confusing, and looking at the television screen inside, where things were warmer and more atmospheric. Either way, it seemed to James that Chelsea were doing badly. The red team had control of the ball more often, and the Chelsea players looked cross and were committing more fouls. The really interesting thing was that he actually minded – he was, he realised, worried about the outcome. He wasn't necessarily enjoying the match, but he was at least absorbed, which was very nearly the same thing. To be concerned about something you have no control over was, he knew, psychologically ruinous, but it was starting to happen.

'Do you think we're going to win this?' said James. 'It seems very close. I thought we'd have scored by now.'

'Well, I think it's good that you're taking an interest,' said Felix.

It was half-time and, without anyone asking, a Korean girl brought in another tray of lagers. Some plates of food had also appeared, and people were eating high-quality proletariat food: mini hamburgers, short beef sausages, large potato chips and pork pies. Everyone was having a brilliant time and James could see why – they were all being intelligently looked after and cared for, they were being given the things they wanted, things that gave them pleasure, were perfectly legal and wouldn't do them all that much harm.

'Here, James,' said Felix, calling him over. 'This is Simon Galbraith. I think you two especially need to meet. You're respected figures in the same field, and you both have a shared interest in growing the economy of South London.'

James shook hands with Simon. He was approximately the best-looking man that James had ever met – a graceful, youthful-at-fifty executive with tightly curled, lightly greying hair, a boyish but by no means flimsy nose, and science-fiction blue eyes that dazzled and disorientated. He wore a calm black linen suit, which didn't reflect any light at all, and his top shirt button was undone, revealing a pale and slender neck above a dark tie.

'I should also say,' said Felix, 'that it's Simon's hospitality we have all been enjoying tonight.'

'Oh, of course – thanks ever so much,' said James. 'It's really been a fantastic evening.'

'So you're the planning wizard that I've been hearing about,' said Simon.

'Well I don't know about that. But yes – I am a planner.'

'Well, I think you're behaving very well given that you're stuck in a roomful of property developers. I hope my colleagues haven't been bothering you too much.'

James was being flattered, and not just by anyone. He was being flattered by the host, the richest and most important person there. He wanted very badly to please him, to do something to make his handsome face smile.

'Not at all! It's actually really good to meet them. Planners can be rather an insular bunch – it's good to get out with the people we should be working with.'

'Well, that's a very healthy attitude,' said Simon. 'It's refreshing to meet a planner who thinks that way. As you've probably heard, Southwark is a particular interest of ours, but we've not always found it as straightforward as it should be.'

'We ought to do something about that,' said Felix. 'Maybe you can talk again after the evening's entertainment.'

But when they went back out, the mood was sombre. The match had started again, and already the red team were winning 1–0. It wasn't obvious to James when or how this had happened, but the fact was incontrovertible and, apparently, not even that surprising.

'Well, I was afraid something like that was coming,' said Felix.

'It's no good defending as deep as this if we can't even get the basics right,' said Robert.

'Hopeless,' said Adam. 'If we can't deal with set pieces then we might as well go home now.'

Angus shook his head and swore with great effort but very little imagination. It was remarkable how cross he was about what was happening down below on the pitch. Although, James himself was also far more dismayed than he'd ever expected to be. Everything else – the lager, the property developers, the sausages – had been so good, it seemed a shame that the evening was now being ruined by something as arbitrary and pointless as a football match. It just didn't seem very *fair* – after all, everyone had agreed that the other team weren't very good, and that Chelsea ought to win. Clearly, it was necessary for there to be some element of uncertainty in football, James could see that, but did it have to be this evening?

Sensing that there was nothing he could say or do to improve the situation, James went back inside to have another beer and eat some more chips. Having a lot to drink was essential in these circumstances. Inside, people were gloomily sipping their drinks and shaking their heads at the screen. It felt, for the first time that evening, as if the country was in the midst of an economic depression.

'I'm sorry that the game is proving to be a disappointment,' said Simon. 'I was promised that we were going to win this comfortably.'

James realised that his host cared very little for football. Nor did he seem particularly interested in the hospitality he was providing – he held a glass of beer like everyone else, but made no sign of drinking from it. He spent much of his life surrounded by the highest quality food and drink, but was a master of deferred gratification, and foregoing pleasures in return for greater rewards.

'So, do you think we're going to be able to work together?'

'Yes,' said James. 'I think that's a very good idea.'

Simon held out his hand, and James gave it a good shake. It wasn't entirely clear what they had agreed to, but it was nice that they had. At that moment, Robert came through to join them, as if he had been called over on a sub-audio frequency.

'Now, Robert, you've been chatting to James, and it sounds like we've got an ally in Southwark at last.'

'Yes, I think James is the kind of man we can do business with.'

'As Robert probably told you, we've got a number of potential projects in your patch. Sunbury Square is a particular interest – we submitted at the EOI stage, of course, but haven't quite decided what to do next. I think the team had a few issues which we couldn't make work.'

James could see that Simon had a worldview, and there was a wonderful purity, maybe even a naivety to it. He just wanted to make as much money as he possibly could. He didn't necessarily want to spend it, he just wanted to accumulate it. It was touching, in a way, while at the same time it gave him a strong sense of purpose and competitive edge.

'Well, I'd be very happy to talk those through with you. Is it a problem with the density targets?'

There was a huge and startling roar outside, which half a second later was repeated on the television. Felix came back into the room.

'Okay, you'll be pleased to hear that we've equalised. There isn't long to go now, so you need to come out and get a bit Nuremburg with the rest of us.'

James allowed a flicker of irritation to pass over his face. He would have liked to have continued the conversation with Simon, to drink some more beer and say something helpful and clever.

'Ah yes, of course, the football. We mustn't forget what we all came here for,' said Simon.

'You have to be careful,' said Felix, leading James out. 'They've realised you could be valuable to them.'

'I think I can handle myself,' said James. 'We were just talking business. Don't worry, I know what these evenings are for.'

'Yes, but remember what I told you? Never forget that they're capitalist swine and you mustn't give anything away too easily. You've made a good impression; I saw that. But you need to make the most of it. Anyway, you can always talk to them later. You should really watch some football now.'

Back out on the balcony, James could see that things were more exciting. More importantly, he had drunk a great deal of lager, and was now prepared to annihilate himself for the common cause, to forego his ability to reason effectively and make sound judgements. For the rest of the match, he would enthusiastically defer to the wisdom of the crowd. He would risk his happiness on something he had no control over, identify with one group of immensely wealthy footballers whom he had never met, and develop an intense hostility for another. In short, he was going to be a *fan*.

'Come on,' shouted Adam. 'Come on, come on, you arseholes.'

'The referee doesn't have a fucking clue,' said James, for no particular reason.

Adam shook his head approvingly. 'Too fucking right,' he said. 'Where is he from, anyway?'

'He's a fucking *Austrian*,' said Angus.

Even James could tell that Chelsea were playing well now. They had much greater possession of the ball and were kicking it forward more often. They were running faster than the red team and seemed to be trying harder. There was a reason for all this urgency. It seemed that Chelsea had to win the game. For reasons James accepted but didn't quite understand, a draw would mean expulsion from the competition, and nobody would regard such a thing as any more satisfactory than actually losing.

'Ten minutes left,' said Angus. 'Come on, you fuckers. *Come on.*'

James was now incredibly anxious. The red team didn't look in the least like scoring, everyone was agreed on that point, but the big problem was that Chelsea had to score and there was nothing he could do about it except watch and shout. Harmful chemicals were building up in his bloodstream.

'I'm not enjoying this in the least bit,' said Adam.

'These overpaid homosexual fuckers are going to fuck it up for us,' said Angus.

James went back inside and swiftly drank some more beer. He had now drunk six pints of lager and was, to all intents and purposes, drunk. Adam and Felix came with him.

'Jesus Christ, we better win this,' said Adam.

'Do you think we can?' said James. 'I think we're going to fuck this up. I can't see us scoring.'

There was a weighty pause, and then Felix spoke. 'Don't worry,' he said. 'We're going to win this.'

Adam and James nodded. No wonder Felix was so professionally successful. He was a leader and radiated assurance, good faith, fearlessness and a lack of moral scruple. He was very different from James. He was the very opposite of Lionel. No wonder people bought all those hair products and chocolate bars he marketed.

They went back out on to the balcony, and sure enough, eight minutes later, Chelsea had won the match, just as Felix had said they would. Although James had been watching intently, he still had little idea how it happened. There had been a corner kick, and a jumble of bodies and thrashing arms and legs as red and blue players jumped around and, essentially, fought one another. After five seconds of this, the ball bounced into the net. He was pretty sure that the scorer had been black and that he had meant to do it.

The euphoria was comprehensive. Adam and James and Angus were clutching each other tightly and swearing joyously. Robert the developer and James the planner embraced. He was the poorest person there, but it didn't matter. He still didn't like football and could barely name two members of the Chelsea team, and that didn't matter either.

'We've fucking done it,' shouted Adam. 'We've fucking done it.'

The referee ended the match immediately afterwards as if, just like the girl serving drinks, he too was under instruction, and they marched triumphantly back inside. Adam was right — *they* had done it, they had made the emotional investment and it had paid off.

'Thank fucking Christ for that,' said Angus. 'We need to celebrate this one properly.'

'Well that's easily done. Come on through,' said Robert. 'James – let's speak again very soon. Why don't you come over to visit at the office? Something tells me we're not going to talk business again tonight.'

The hospitality was as relentless and indiscriminate as ever. More trays of lager and new bowls of chips were being brought in, even as people were starting to leave. But James had no intention of going just yet. They each reached for a glass and held it upwards, clashed them together like Viking warriors and took long, deep gulps

'Well done, everyone,' said Robert. 'It was close, but a mightily deserved victory.'

'Yes, thanks Robert, that was immensely enjoyable,' said Felix. 'And all the more so for conforming so beautifully to Aristotle's first principle of drama.'

'Too fucking right,' said Angus.

'Fucking cheers,' said Adam. 'We've fucking done it.'

They brought their glasses together again, and drank some more. Adam did some more swearing, he was getting better and better at it, while Angus made some homophobic remarks, which Felix in particular seemed to enjoy. Out of the corner of his eye, James could see the Korean girl, who was looking prettier than ever, arriving with a tray of brandies.

'James, I'm going to leave you to your festivities,' said Simon, handing him a business card. 'But you're very welcome here anytime. Just give me a call. And do fix something up with Robert – there's plenty for us to talk about.'

James took the card. It hadn't just been a good evening, it had been a highly successful one, and in this world the two were indistinguishable. Felix was right: he wasn't a town planner, he was a planning professional – it was a crucial distinction. He might not be leaving the public sector just yet, but it looked like his years of public service were coming to an end.

11

12 March

London is an increasingly polarised city.

– *The London Plan*, Section 1.27

It was just as James had suspected. Alice had a boyfriend. Not just a lover, but a partner. He dreaded to think what he did for a living or how she'd met him, but the substantive fact was that she was in a structured sexual relationship – probably highly sexual, given it was Alice. He'd emailed her suggesting they go for a drink and, two days later, she'd replied in a hastily written email full of heartless typing errors, saying that she was going to be away with Sam for a week, as if he ought by now to be well aware who Sam was, and that she'd be sure to get in touch soon.

Well, that was fine. He was really fucked off about it, but it was fine. After all, it had never been his intention to go back out with Alice. Not now, not after all these years. It wasn't part of the plan: it wasn't what he wanted and it clearly wasn't what she wanted. So what did he want? It was one of the first things Felix had asked him and he still wasn't sure. On balance, what he would probably settle for was for her to be *impressed* with him. If it was his name she could be mentioning in dinner-party conversation, instead of all the writers and broadcasters she'd slept with. If she could be irritating and undermining her current boyfriend by continually banging on about James and all the astounding things he was up to – well, that would probably do.

All of this was unlikely to happen because, and there was no getting away from this, he was a town planner. Who on earth was going to talk about him at a dinner party? In all of history, how many famous town planners had there been? There was Baron Haussmann in Paris but he was controversial at best, there was Robert Moses in New York, who turned out to be wrong about everything, Albert Speer, who was only famous because he worked for Hitler, and then there was Abercrombie, who was indisputably great and good, but whom no one apart from other planners had ever heard of. And if there were any monuments to planners, then it came only after forty years of public service followed by a short fatal illness, and never amounted to anything more than a plaque on a park bench or, maybe, just maybe, having a Town Hall committee room named after you.

'James, are you confident the average housing densities are compliant with the LDF?'

James looked around, and wondered for a moment where he was. In a meeting, obviously, but it was difficult to be certain which one. Lionel was speaking, Rachel wasn't there, Kemal from Finance was – although that meant nothing and there was every chance that he wasn't actually supposed to be. But the silly cow Jane who looked after the website was there, and so was that cocksure bastard Alex Coleman and Henry, a research officer who nobody knew much about and looked too old for his job title. So there was a good chance it was one of those entirely useless monthly planning-communications matrix meetings that Andrew Metcalfe had initiated six months ago, shortly before losing his job, but which no one had ever got round to cancelling. The truth was, James didn't know. He had got into the office with an incredible hangover, turned on his computer, read his emails, noticed that a meeting had just started, and hurried to the room. All he had done since then was eat biscuits and drink tea and think about Alice.

'I'm sorry,' said James. 'What was that?'

'The policy commitment on densities – are you sure that these are okay for the report?'

'Oh yes, yes – this isn't a problem. We're comfortably over the target on the other sites in any case.'

'Okay,' said Alex. 'Because you know, we don't want to get this wrong.'

'Well, we won't,' said James.

'Good,' said Alex. 'Because, as I said, we don't want to get it wrong.'

James sunk back down in his chair and ate another biscuit. In as much as this meeting was going anywhere, it was moving on to other matters – something to do with the community engagement initiative or a new online discussion forum. This morning, he didn't really care. Maybe that was another sign of progress? He had spent far too much of his adult life caring about such things.

No, he had to face facts: Alice was never going to boast about her glamorous ex-boyfriend who worked as a town planner and sat in meetings discussing community engagement. It wasn't just that planning was difficult, it wasn't even important any more. He'd been born two generations too late. The Second World War – now *that* was the time to be in public administration. And afterwards it had got even better: rebuilding East London, designing the welfare state, running airports and coalmines. Those had been the heroic days – mainly because there hadn't been any heroes. There hadn't been any internationally famous architects or Asian billionaire property developers. Instead, there had been committees with long titles and opaque processes, and men in dark suits who had sat in chilly wood-panelled rooms in town halls and been respected by the working classes.

But at least there were other options now, even for town planners. No one these days was expected to do the same thing all their life. Felix was right: he worked in the property sector, it was just a matter of positioning and presentation. He had valuable skills and knowledge, he just hadn't realised it before. All he needed was the contacts to make the most of them.

'James?'

He looked up with a start. God – had he managed to drift off again? Yes, he had a hangover, but really, this was inexcusable. He'd never done this before. Thank God he worked in the public sector.

'I'm sorry. Could you just repeat that?'

'I just did,' said Lionel. 'But again: James could you tell us whether the key-worker targets are going to apply to all of the sectors?'

'This is important,' said Alex. 'Lionel, the Strategy Delivery Assessment is going to publication next month, and I need your team to be on top of this.'

James stiffened and Lionel looked hurt, his pink, crustacean face retreating, his plump body shifting. The Director of Planning hurt by Alex fucking Coleman, who was nothing more than a twenty-eight-year-old junior public affairs officer with a degree in media studies.

'Yes, I'm sorry about this,' said Lionel. 'James could you briefly talk us all through it – I know you've got the details.'

James couldn't stand Alex Coleman. It wasn't just that Alex worked in Communications, the eternal foe of the Planning Directorate. It was even worse than that – he *believed* in Communications. It was quite possibly all he did believe in. Post-ideological and post-literate, it had been his ambition to work in advertising, but he had graduated at a time of great expansion in the public sector, and never found a way to get back out. It didn't help that by local authority standards he was unusually good-looking – he had a well-crafted, modern face with sceptical lips and metallic blue eyes. At last year's office Christmas party Rachel had given him a handjob in the stationary room.

'Sorry, I'll explain,' said James. 'All of the priority key sectors outlined in the draft strategy are subject to our overarching targets, but it allows for a certain degree of flexibility across different sites – I can give you the exact figures if needed – and also includes, for new developments only, dedicated, sector-specific housing. This means that, once the new nursing sites open in 2014, we should be able to manage the allocations so that all of the other targets are met.'

There was a wary silence. There was no getting away from this but, even wounded, he was good at his job, far better than Jane the web editor and, more importantly, than Alex, who was unlikely to have understood more than a fraction of what James had just said.

'Okay,' said Alex. 'I'll probably follow up with you by email, but I guess that will have to do for now.'

'Great,' said Jane. 'Could you copy me in on that?'

'And me please,' said Henry.

The meeting ended, as all meetings must. There was a series of action points that Alex had noted, almost all of which were assigned to James. The others left, but Lionel signalled with two stubby fingers for James to wait behind.

'God,' said James, 'that Alex Coleman is such an irritating little shit.'

'Never mind him,' said Lionel. 'He's just the latest young know-nothing from Comms. He won't be the last.'

They sat together in silence for a minute. James looked carefully at his manager and mentor, looked into his small mild eyes. Erosion wasn't always a gradual process. Cracks happen. Things break. You can unravel in so many ways. Synapses fizzle out, cell walls disintegrate, organs stop. Bones calcify, the juices drain drop by drop and then, one day, they snap. Was something similar happening to Lionel? Had he suddenly started dying faster? His hands looked smaller than ever.

'Are you all right?' said Lionel at last, in his soft, fat-weakened voice. 'I've been a bit worried about you.'

'Yes, I'm fine,' said James. 'What's up?'

'You seemed more than a little absent-minded just then. And you've not really been on it these past few weeks, not like you usually are. You don't look great now, to be honest. Is everything okay?'

The reason James had a hangover was because he had drunk five pints of lager in a pub while watching a football match on the television. He had done this with Matt, his foolish, clumsy flatmate who had short hair and big ears and worked in marketing and whom James had never had a fully successful conversation with until last night. It was a revelation but, as Felix had told him, once you knew about football, once you knew enough to talk about football, which wasn't actually all that much, vast social opportunities opened up. James had taken conversations he'd heard about the Chelsea midfield, reapplied them to an analysis of the Arsenal defence, and sat back as Matt had vigorously nodded his head and warmly expanded on his theories. It was a lot like drafting a masterplan.

'I've got quite a lot on my mind at the moment, but don't worry: everything is okay,' said James. 'There's just a lot going on, that's all. You know – with work, Sunbury Square, housing commitments and everything else.'

Lionel looked at him carefully, his eyes ponderously scanning James, like an analogue security system in a domestic airport. He was getting scrutinised, possibly even disciplined. It was difficult to tell for sure – it had never happened before, and it was coming from Lionel who had little emotional range and was a poor communicator, reluctant to speak directly but with no mastery of subtext.

'And I noticed you were away for a couple of days – you missed a Friday and then a Monday the other week. That's not like you.'

'No, I know – I had that bug that was going around.'

'So you weren't just gadding about town then?' said Lionel, forcing a stunted laugh into his voice.

James flinched. That wasn't a joke. It was the type of joke Lionel would make, but in this case it wasn't one – he *knew*. Surely Ian Benson hadn't said anything? No, he was a fucker, but not that kind of fucker. Maybe he or Alex had been blathering about it in the office? It didn't sound very likely – but there again, what else did those goons talk about? And would Lionel really have overheard them? More likely, someone else would have told him. After all, he worked in government, he had enemies everywhere.

'God no, I felt awful. It's not like me at all – I think it's the first time I've ever missed work since I've been here.'

Lionel nodded. 'Yes, that's what I thought. Not like you at all.'

The only sickie he had ever taken and somehow he'd been caught out. There was probably a lesson in there.

'I'm fine. It was just a bad bug, that's all. I actually thought I'd shaken it off by Friday evening, but I was laid up all weekend.'

'Well, let me know if anything's up. I'm sure we can work something out if you're struggling.'

'Don't worry. I'm feeling much better now.'

'Good,' said Lionel. 'Because I need you to be at one hundred per cent at the moment. I can't do everything round here. You know it's a small team with more cuts coming, and I need to be able to rely on every member.'

'Don't worry, I'm completely on it,' said James. 'I won't let you down.'

James went back to his desk, determined not to do anything he was paid to do. He made himself a cup of tea without checking if any of his colleagues wanted one, and then sat down again. On his computer there was an email from Graham Oakley.

Hi James,

Just touching base, haven't heard from you for a while. Just to say, HR have been on to me about Guy's replacement, and I'm obviously keen not to have the role unfilled for any length of time.

I guess you're still considering things, but if you could give me some indication soon (i.e. in the next week or so) whether you want the job that would be a big help. We don't have to finalise starting dates, terms etc, but once I know for sure that you're coming, I can at least tell people here, and halt any recruitment process.

All the best,

Graham

James read it through carefully. Growing up is a process of making compromises, closing down opportunities, narrowing options. He understood that – it was partly how he had ended up here – but that didn't mean he had to do it again just yet. There was still, he felt more and more certain, too much going on. He closed his email, and then closed his eyes.

One day London will run itself, for they were living in an age of great technological acceleration and political stagnation. Traffic lights will flicker on and off in response to vehicle numbers and the mobile phones trying to cross the road. Buses, trams and trains will steer themselves across town, deftly avoiding one another and stopping at unmanned stations run by highly accomplished ticket machines. Electric photo sensors will track the swiping of microchip cards and embedded transmitters will relay the news to one another through interoperable protocols. Things won't need to bleep or flash any more – information will invisibly and silently radiate across the warm sky in a billion little data packets, all backed up on a server farm just outside of Basingstoke. And everything else, everything that can't be automated or computed or ignored, will be done by the immigrants – men and women of indeterminate skin colour and legal status, and who will never dare to speak.

All those labour- and social-interaction-saving devices. All those invisible machines, all that networked intelligence. The city was getting worse, all the statistics said so – there were more robberies and murders and everyone was getting angry and anxious. But it was also getting so much *cleverer*. It was absorbing information, gigabytes and terabytes of it, and it was processing it, it was applying coefficients and evolving weightings. And the more information it processed, the cleverer it became.

One day, too, there wouldn't be any planners. Cities were full of humans and humans were too complicated for other humans to know how to deal with them. It was better left to the computers. Not just desktop PCs, but gigantic calculating machines of the kind that you only ever came across in out-of-date science fiction, and which would sit in the basement of City Hall and every day make a hundred billion calculations. They would compute air pollution, noise pollution, medium-term flood risk, waste disposal rates, levels of new company formation, housing stock supply, peak-hour congestion levels, the value of the visitor economy, the net rate of migration and the proportion of cyclists who wore helmets. They would make allowances for multiplier effects and positive feedback loops and non-linear sensitivities, they would undertake ingenious statistical analysis and relentlessly run through powerful algorithms, and then they would make optimal decisions – decisions that no one could fathom but which would invariably be correct – although in any case, it would be too difficult for any human to judge one way or another. And in Southwark Council, the only people with any jobs left to do would be the ones who could mend the computers and write press releases about how well it was all going. The only people left would be Ian Benson and Alex Coleman.

'Well what the fuck did you expect?' said Rachel. 'You're behaving like a knob. You even smoke cigarettes like a knob.'

They were outside now, and Rachel was smoking cigarettes. James was trying to smoke one too. He was practising, for when he next saw Harriet.

'I'm not behaving like a knob,' said James. 'I think that's unfair.'

'You looked like you were on sleeping pills for most of last week. And that last report on retail you sent me was dogshit, you must have written it in about four minutes. And you haven't been in the pub on Friday for weeks now – people notice these things. Remember: all we talk about is the people who aren't in the pub with us, and it's not as if anyone ever says *nice* things.'

'All right, I hear all that. But it's just a bit much to get criticism from Lionel, that's all. I mean – he's fucking *Lionel*.'

James was swearing a lot more these days as well. Swearing and smoking – it wasn't clear at this point if he was growing up or just behaving more and more like a teenager.

'Lionel isn't stupid,' said Rachel. 'He might not be able to do much planning any more, but he can still recognise a problem when he sees one. He's got a sixth sense for spotting major fuck-ups. That's why he's been able to last so long.'

'Hold on – are you saying that I'm a fuck-up?

'I'm saying you're a *potential* fuck-up. That's all. And Lionel knows it.'

James didn't much like the sound of that. After all, it wasn't as if he lacked ambition. That was the good thing about hierarchies: there was a clear path, an established step-by-step route between where he was now, and where he wanted to be. He could chart it out on a sheet of paper – a brief description of what he could reasonably expect to be doing at thirty-five, at forty, at fifty, at sixty, along with the associated salary and benefits. But all that depended upon him having a career in the first place – on not fucking up. Or, at least, not unless he had somewhere else he could go.

'What are these cuts that people have started talking about? I didn't think they had anything to do with us.'

'Well, now – there's my point. If you'd been putting the hours in with us at the pub you'd have heard about them. At the very least, you ought to take me out for our drink.'

'But I thought we'd gone through all that.'

'There's talk of another restructure. Nothing like as big, but it might impact on Environment and Planning. They need to trim the budget by half a million.'

James blew out his cigarette smoke irritably. Down the road, smoking in their own huddle, stood several overweight members of the post room, with their natural allies from the Facilities Team. He looked at them wistfully. Yes, they faced dangers and diseases – bad teeth, proletariat cancers, deep-seated nutritional problems – but they were safe from so many things: from organisational restructures, Strategy Delivery Assessments and from old university friends in high-income tax brackets.

'This Felix you've been hanging out with. I'm not sure he's good for you.'

'Felix? You haven't even met Felix.'

'I don't have to. You've been going on about him enough. He sounds sinister, the sort of person that would fuck you up for his own amusement.'

'That's rubbish. He's just a friend, that's all. It's good to be going out with different people for a change. Doing different things. I can't spend my whole life in the Red Lion. I don't want to look like Lionel in twenty years.'

'You know, you need to give Lionel a bit more credit,' said Rachel. 'He's held down that job for ten years. He's survived elections; he's survived restructures. He's put up with politicians and the most awful pricks. There's a reason for that. Don't underestimate him.'

'I don't underestimate him. I'd like him to work harder, and be a bit more dynamic and he could support us more and not look so knackered all the time, but I know his strengths better than anyone. I've been working for him for years now. He's a good friend, basically.'

'And that's another thing: you shouldn't trust him too much either. That's one of your biggest faults. It's an endearing one, but it's still a fault. You know what they used to say in the war: never trust a survivor until you know what he did to survive.'

James looked out across the street he knew so well. It was getting warmer – people were going out more, and as a result they were breaking more rules. Cars were driving in cycle lanes and cyclists were jumping traffic lights. Pedestrians were failing to control their dogs. Even Rachel flicked her cigarette butts on to the pavement, for street cleaning was the responsibility of another directorate. It all looked so very different from his masterplan poster.

'Okay, so you're saying I should neither underestimate nor trust Lionel.'

'I'm saying you should respect him, but you shouldn't think of him as a friend – it's not helpful. He's your boss. I'm giving you some very good advice here. God knows why, you don't really deserve it.'

James was tender-minded, a sentimentalist, sensitive to the realities of suffering, but also to its symbols. This, along with everything else, would need to change. He could see that, and it had nothing to do with Felix – it was what his profession demanded. To try to understand what happened in a single street in a single day would crush the toughest mind, but there was a whole city that needed to be understood, appraised and treated. If he couldn't be a computer processor, then he could at least be more like Rachel.

'Should I trust anyone we work with?' said James, throwing his cigarette to the ground.

'No, probably not.'

'But I can trust you, right?'

Rachel turned to look up at him. Her eyes were steady and loyal. They were, he realised, also surprisingly pretty – a gentle light brown, with good-humoured flecks and long eyelashes that curled upwards like her black hair.

'Oh yes. That's all right. You can trust me.'

12

15 March

Boroughs should take an evidence-based approach to managing the night-time economy.

— *The London Plan*, Section 4.37

There was no denying it, he was making tremendous progress. It was less than two months since that wretched night in that wretched restaurant, since he'd met Felix and surrendered to his counsel, and now, here he was – in a sex club in Soho. It was a testament to the advice of his mentor, but also to his own determination and strength of will. Above all, it was a testament to the power of planning.

As part of this, he was getting much better at the worrying-about-money thing. It was just as well: if you were going to fret about spending money in a place like this, then you might as well just leave now and take the night bus home. He had already bought a small round of unremarkable drinks that had cost over twenty pounds, and he knew there was every chance that Felix would order a cocktail next time. But he was starting to be more courageous about it. He was learning to rationalise personal consumption on a different, more sophisticated, non-rational basis.

It was important not to be churlish about money for, with characteristic generosity and skill, Felix had designed an entire evening for them. And it was Felix, of course, who had suggested it in the first place. He had been quite right, of course, James should have done this years ago. It was yet another rite of passage that he'd somehow failed to complete in his twenties, and was still well worth doing now. True, London was no longer one of the world's premier capitals of the sex industry, there was far too much Asian competition, but it was still a world city with open markets, high-income residents and a steady flow of immigrants in need of employment. And it still had Soho, which James had first heard alarming stories about from sixth formers while revising for his GCSEs in the library at South Leicester Grammar School, but which, in all those years of living in London, he had never investigated any further.

But here he was at last and, actually, he had done more than just go to a sex club. He had in fact *joined* one. That, as Felix and Carl had explained, was how these places generally worked. So James now, and again at some cost, had a lifetime membership to the Black Kitten on Poland Street. He even had a black plastic card with his name printed on it in gold letters. It hadn't taken very long to arrange – an almost pretty woman had efficiently typed his details into a laptop computer, taken his photograph with a digital camera and produced a card for him then and there on a desktop printer. A cloakroom attendant who looked like he was dying from tuberculosis but had wonderful manners had taken their coats, and then gently pointed them down a wide flight of red-carpeted stairs.

But downstairs, after all that, it hardly felt like a sex club at all. For one thing, and this was an obvious giveaway, there were other women there. Well-dressed professional women who had, presumably, paid to be there. In fact, he wouldn't have been completely surprised to bump into Alice. Something else he hadn't been expecting was that the room was well lit, and James was looking at the audience carefully – he was starting to pay more attention to them than to the girls on the stage. Not that they would have minded – the kinds of people who came to this place were sufficiently attractive that they actually wanted to be seen by other people. They weren't on their own or in suspicious little huddles; they weren't, and he could see this might be a problem, pornographers.

Meanwhile, the woman onstage wasn't really undressing at all – to all intents and purposes she was doing a piece of contemporary dance. The music was difficult to process, without an obvious melody or rhythm. People were clapping appreciatively, but not for anything that was remotely arousing or even enjoyable: they seemed to be applauding her for acts of technical difficulty and creative interpretation. It was very much like something funded by the Arts Council. Her costume was a particular source of dismay – a disorientating drama of velvet stockings, peacock feathers, multi-coloured hair clips, silk scarves and hooped bracelets. It was difficult to be sure what was really going on, but James was convinced that she was actually wearing more clothes by the end than when she'd started.

'This wine isn't bad at all,' said Felix.

Carl grunted. 'I didn't come here for the wine.'

'What do you think of the place?' said Felix, turning to James.

James wasn't sure what to say. It was telling how quickly his excitement and fear had evaporated. There didn't seem anything here to get worked up about. Even Rachel probably wouldn't have minded: it wasn't exciting and it wasn't frightening, and it certainly wasn't erotic. It was much like anywhere and everything else – not all that good and too expensive. It was a shame: it was actually mildly gratifying how disappointing everything was. Perhaps it was a sign that he was growing up.

Another girl came onstage. She had cropped black hair, and was dressed in a dark pinstripe suit, with an umbrella and bowler hat, which, after a minute or so, she elaborately removed. She had a button nose and was undeniably pretty, but to no discernible purpose. She might as well have been an award-winning piece of contemporary fiction. James and Carl both turned to look at Felix to see if he could explain it to them.

'What you need to realise,' said Felix, 'is that there is an art to eroticism. And, like all the arts, greater study and understanding leads to richer appreciation and enjoyment.'

James turned back to the stage and tried again. It occurred to him that the girl's act must contain some kind of satirical content, and that she was parodying the international banking system. Maybe she was going to do something horrendous and symbolic with a roll of bank notes. She started to loosen her tie. She did, James noted, have very pretty bare feet, but that didn't compensate for the black moustache that was pencilled above her lip, or her straight hips and short legs or the fact that she was wearing a suit.

It needed Carl to get them out of this mess. Like the parable of the Emperor's New Clothes, somebody had to point out to everyone else that they weren't the only person to have noticed that the woman they were all looking at wasn't actually naked.

'What the fuck is this dogshit?' he said. 'We've been here for almost an hour and I haven't even seen any tits yet. We urgently need to go somewhere else.'

'I'm in total agreement,' said James.

'I'm actually enjoying this,' said Felix. 'But very well, come on. I've got somewhere else for us to go.'

They didn't have to go very far. Felix led them out and they turned into Berwick Street, and then into a poorly lit lane, where there was a micro-cluster of strip bars, flamboyant specialist retailers and two more sombre wholesalers, both claiming to export across Europe and the Middle East. Between these was the 'XXX. com Club' in white plastic lettering on a black plastic board with a half-hearted ring of red and yellow light bulbs around the doorway. Its name was senseless, and presumably dated from a time when website addresses were considered exotic. Little attempt was being made to attract customers, and the principal function of the stout man standing outside the door seemed to be to stop people coming in rather than to entice them. But maybe that was a good thing – it was hard to be sure how the market signals worked in this industry.

Carl wavered. 'Are you sure this place is any good?'

'It's the sex industry,' said Felix. 'Nobody knows anything, and competitive pressures are weak. But last time I came here it was excellent.'

They went in, and Felix led the negotiations with an under-nourished woman behind the counter. The strange thing was, this place was even more expensive: the relationship between class, quality of service and money had broken down. There were no application forms or membership cards – instead they paid twenty-five pounds each to be allowed in for the night, and had to order at least one drink every hour.

Felix and James sat in a leather booth in the corner of a room that didn't seem to have been refurbished since the economic boom before last. The lighting was eccentric, and the mirrored walls were speckled and blackened and incapable of reflecting anything other than ghosts and psychic disturbances. Carl came back from the bar with a bottle of white wine, perplexed and bad-tempered.

'This just cost me a hundred pounds. It was all they had. And do you know – I'm not even sure if it's got any alcohol in it. I think it might be fucking grape juice or something.'

'Yes,' said Felix. 'I was afraid something like that might happen.'

Carl slumped down next to them. The smell was familiar and unpleasant, like a small house where a big dog lived. There was a pinball machine in the corner, maybe the last one in Westminster, but it had been discarded rather than curated, and James knew that it wouldn't work. There were no women in the audience here, and while that was to be welcomed, it was troubling how few men there were either. But it wasn't completely empty – at a table nearby sat a group of East Asian businessmen. Almost certainly, though you could never be sure, they were Chinese.

'Now that,' said Carl, with an emphatic jerk of the thumb in their direction, 'is a very bad sign. As a rule, we don't want to be enjoying the same things as those bastards.'

James looked at them carefully. He had to admit, they were disgusting. Overweight with awful glasses and grey suits bought at tax-free airport franchises, they looked like they worked in town planning for Shanghai City Government, although more likely they were electronics millionaires. They weren't even watching or drinking anything. Instead, conforming entirely to their ethnic stereotype, they were fidgeting with handheld devices and trying to take pictures of each other. There could be no clearer sign that they were in the wrong place.

After a long period of inactivity and gradually increasing disquiet, some upbeat music started jerkily, and a girl came onstage. It was a disheartening start. She was Eastern European, but not in a good way. It looked like she was from Serbia or Bosnia – strikingly tall, with square shoulders, a clump of muscles around her abdomen, and a tattoo of a tiger on her thigh. She seemed to be full of hurt and hostility, which was almost certainly justified, and she commanded the stage like an actor in a Shakespearean history play as she pulled off her blouse and bra. Her breasts were too large for her chest, and her teeth were too big for her mouth.

'That wasn't exactly encouraging,' said Carl. 'She was formidable, I'll give her that. But really – a woman like that needs to be serving in the navy rather than taking her clothes off onstage.'

The Chinese businessmen applauded, but the cultural divide was too great for James to tell if they were being polite, appreciative or ironic. There was a pause. The music stopped, then started, then stopped again.

'At least we saw something this time,' said James, who still wasn't sure how he should benchmark his expectations.

'I fear,' said Felix, 'that this place may be under new management since I was last here.'

'Soho is going down the tubes,' said Carl. 'This used to be a world-class cluster for the sex economy. But it's all been fucked. We're losing our competitive advantage. You can bet those Chinese fuckers will be doing business in Paris next year.'

James took a gulp of his sweet white wine. He was probably right – just like manufacturing and finance and everything else, it wouldn't be long before the Chinese became experts on pornography, and selected different suppliers. An unwelcome light came on. Nothing much seemed to happen for a while. Felix and Carl started to discuss oil prices. Some more Chinese men arrived. James got his mobile phone out, but couldn't get a reception. Carl went to the toilets and reported back that they were almost certainly the worst in central London. And then, suddenly, the lights went off again, the music came on again, and a girl padded on to the stage.

This time the disaster was unequivocal. She looked *British*, possibly even Welsh. She had big feet and the kind of sturdy legs and arms particularly ill suited for this sub-sector of the entertainment industry. There were other issues too, the freckles and moles on her shoulders, the broken capillaries on her shins, but the main problem, the insurmountable difficulty, was her age. Protected by her make-up, distorted by the stage lighting, it was impossible to be precise, but it was all too easy to be accurate: *she wasn't young.*

Felix and Carl were twitching in indignation, but James felt something else, something far more deadly: he felt sorry for her. It was so unfair that she had to do this. How could it have happened? A particularly unfortunate labour market failure, a breakdown in demand and supply had led to a sub-standard product being presented to a group of discerning consumers who had just paid a great deal of money on the expectation of something of considerably higher quality. And now here they all were, feeling uncomfortable and unhappy and cheated.

'Jesus Christ,' said Carl. 'I can't bear this.'

'Don't worry,' said Felix. 'I can see that this place is problematic. I've got somewhere else for us. I was holding it back until later, but if need be we can go there now.'

'What about the wine?' said James.

'Fuck the wine,' said Carl. 'I'll put it on expenses or something. But I'm not staying here to drink it.'

'Come on,' said Felix. 'I'm afraid Carl's right. We have to go immediately.'

'Hold on,' said James. 'We can't just get up and go while she's still onstage.'

'We're fucking going,' said Carl.

'A market only functions efficiently if it has enough information,' said Felix. 'And if we don't leave now and express our dissatisfaction, then we're withholding information from the market. It's how markets work. It's how the world gets better.'

The logic was unassailable. What was James going to do? Felix and Carl were already walking out, and James could hardly sit on his own, staying to watch her take off her bra on the grounds of social democracy. It was such a shame. The woman was still dancing, she had no choice, but by now she must have been aware of the unhappiness she was causing. The Chinese were talking loudly and watching a film on an iPad as James walked across the room, his head down.

Outside, back in the alley, an emergency conference had been called.

'Okay,' said Carl. 'That was an expensive fiasco. I'm thinking of going home.'

'No, don't worry,' said Felix. 'It's all in hand. I wanted us to do Soho for the sake of James's education, but I always thought we would end up somewhere else.'

'Really? Where are you thinking? I'm starting to lose faith with the project.'

'Well, I'm up for it,' said James. 'I'm up for anything.'

'Of course you are,' said Felix. 'We all are. And as long as we stay that way, I promise that the evening will be successful.'

'Christ, okay then. Let's do this. But the next place better be fucking good.'

Carl channelled his disgruntlement into negotiating a stunningly good price with a Pakistani minicab driver, and they clambered into a small saloon car that smelt rich and beautiful – of dark chocolate, fresh mint and strong cannabis. This time they were going much further: they were going east. James should have known – it was inevitable that this would happen at some point in the evening. The West End of London had become tamed and over-regulated. It was the fault of people like James, the planners, who had only succeeded in filling the town centre with coffee bars and sandwich shops and driving all the good stuff elsewhere. But the East was different, it was the future.

Everyone knew that: Felix, the venture capitalists, the technology start-ups, the advertising agencies and the strip-club owners. The driver took them out of Soho, through Clerkenwell and into the City fringes, and then Felix took over, for specialist knowledge was required. They travelled through obsolete high streets and long-standing regeneration priorities, past failing churches and flourishing mosques, across Dalston Junction and onwards, deep into the heart of Hackney.

And then, unexpectedly, at a forlorn street corner somewhere near London Fields, Felix instructed him to stop, and they disembarked outside a shoe shop. A few weeks ago, James would have been confused – after all, this was obviously a premises with A1 rather than D3 usage. But he knew better now. He trusted Felix, and he trusted London. He was a regulator and he spent much of his life devising rules that people ingeniously evaded or simply ignored, and as a result London blundered on. It was high-functioning anarchy. People slept in commercial office space and ran businesses from their homes, they dealt drugs in their front rooms, opened all-night bars in warehouses and they established sex clubs in the basements of shoe shops.

'Are we entirely sure about this?' said Carl. 'Because I don't know how on earth we get back from here.'

But the cab had already gone, and they were on an empty street peering into a window display: a row of black and brown leather shoes, arranged without imagination, and all of which seemed to be on special offer.

'Well, let's just hope the sex bar is cross-subsidising the shop, rather than the other way round,' said Felix.

There was no signage or low-frequency lights, and no one guarding the entrance. In fact, displaying a confidence that James considered to be reckless, there wasn't even a door. There was simply a gap at the top of a flight of dimly lit stairs, which seemed to offer little prospect of going anywhere but to a storeroom, but Felix strode down, undaunted by the darkness or danger. At the bottom of the stairs they opened a door, walked past a young man who was reading a graphic novel, and found themselves in what was actually a storeroom. Or, at least, it clearly had been until very recently, for there were still empty shelves running around the walls, a small pile of shoeboxes neatly stacked in the far corner and wooden crates that had been repurposed as seats and chairs.

'Ah good,' said Felix. 'It looks like things have already got started here. I think we're going to be okay now.'

'Thank Christ for that,' said Carl. 'Let's get some drinks, sit down and see what they've got to show us.'

And now, thirty minutes later, James could feel confident that he was enjoying himself. Onstage, things were being done properly and girls were continually getting undressed in front of him. They weren't necessarily as good-looking as in the first place, but that was okay because they were all immensely attractive, they had far less clothes on and James had had a lot more to drink. It also helped that none of them were actually on the stage for very long. They bounded on good-naturedly in high heels, danced a bit, unclipped their bras, wriggled out of their knickers, pouted provocatively while clutching their breasts and skipped off merrily. It wasn't exactly dancing, more a kind of rudimentary, highly energetic jiggling about, and it didn't look as if it required much in the way of training, but it was compelling. It was, in fact, and at long last, *pornographic*. And it took no longer than four minutes, like a perfect pop song. There wasn't enough time to inspect the quality of their skin or the whiteness of their teeth in any detail, or to wonder if they were paying any tax or receiving income support benefit while doing this.

There were eight of them, the racial variety was impressive and one of the good things was that they quickly came round again and again, although in no particular order, like an iPod Shuffle. They each had their favourites. Carl, typically, liked a big-breasted Jamaican girl and Felix, of course, preferred a little Korean with a bob of black hair and boyish hips. And James had fallen for one who looked, though he knew this was probably unlikely, like an Israeli who was doing this in order to pay for her tuition fees while studying for a Masters in Fine Art at Goldsmith's College, and who, when she wasn't onstage taking her clothes off, wore little round glasses and liked to read poems by E.E. Cummings.

All the girls were smiling beautifully. It might be stretching it to say they were enjoying themselves, but they seemed determined to make the best of the circumstances, and had a marvellous work ethic. They looked cheerful, in good health, and with no obvious signs of physical coercion or drug addiction. Crucially, they were exactly the right age. Not so young as to make him feel ashamed of himself and, even more important, not so old that he felt ashamed for them. They had been born at the end of the twentieth century, but they were twenty-first-century women, and it didn't take too much imaginative effort for James to persuade himself that they were empowered, that they had come to this country through legitimate immigration channels, and were taking their clothes off in front of him purely as a consequence of informed career and lifestyle decisions.

Despite there being no entry fee, the crowd was much better here too: well mannered, unconventionally dressed and morally desensitised without being psychopathic. The market imperfections and barriers to entry were working to their advantage for people had come here not because they could afford it, but because they knew about it. There were no businessmen on a trade mission from Asia and no construction workers or investment bankers, both of whom had a tendency to ruin things like this. Rather, everyone looked as if they worked in the digital media industries: pop music directors, website designers and people who make video games for mobile phones. These were people who took their leisure seriously, and who had carefully researched and prepared before choosing to spend their Friday night here.

Even Carl was impressed. 'Well, it's good to see that we can still put on a decent tit-and-fanny show. Maybe the country isn't completely ruined after all.'

Felix and James nodded approvingly. Yes, perhaps after all, it was still a hopeful time to be alive and to be living in London. The city was still young – the girls onstage were proof of that. The planners and regulators and developers had done their worst, but London's entrepreneurial energy, its immigration lawyers, middlemen and criminal ingenuity had triumphed and, as a result, the sex industry was here, generating employment and prosperity for the people of East London.

'They say that all art aspires to music, but surely what it really aspires to is pornography,' said Felix. 'It is not the transcendental, but the deeply elemental that truly brings us joy and wonder.'

'Is that your way of telling us that you've got a lob-on?' said Carl. 'Well, it's cost us about three hundred quid, but I'm glad we got there in the end. Let's get some more drinks.'

The pricing structure was entirely different from the other places. There were no membership fees, and they weren't obliged to order any bottles of wine. However, while the transparency was to be welcomed, James suspected that it was still costing them a fortune. It was difficult to know for sure as Carl was expertly handling the money, and every so often all they had to do was give him another ten pounds, some of which he then put in a jar on the table. As long as they did this, it seemed likely they could stay there for as long as they liked.

That was the main thing, because whatever the cost, James didn't ever want to leave. Here surely was all that one ever needed for a successful evening. The room was under-furnished, but not like in the last place which made you suspect it was about to close down, but in an East London way, as if it had just started up. The exposed brick walls had been freshly whitewashed, without any misjudged ornamentation, and nothing was broken or malfunctioning. The lavatories were well managed, with bolt locks on the cubicles, and the bar at the back of the room was pleasingly rudimentary with no electronic till, serving a limited range of spirits and bottles of lager from countries with low levels of per capita GDP. It was true that James had counted at least a dozen breaches of environmental, buildings and health and safety regulations, and that as a responsible planning officer and citizen he would have to ring a colleague in Hackney Council and get the place closed down, but that was something to think about next week. For the moment, it was all about the moment.

'One of the good things about getting older is that young women become more attractive,' said Carl reflectively. 'I'm sure that they weren't all as good-looking as this when I was in my early twenties, but now I would fuck any girl under the age of twenty-five, unless she was disabled or something.'

'That's a lovely sentiment,' said Felix. 'You're quite right: all young people are beautiful. But fortunately, hardly any of them ever realise. It stops them from being insufferable.'

As James looked, the girls onstage were becoming prettier and prettier. Their teeth were getting brighter, their lips larger and their smiles less ambiguous. More and more often, they seemed to be catching his eye, and throwing him generous smiles. They must have been doing it to the others too, of course he knew that, but there was no doubt that their eyes were resting on his the longest. Was it because he looked more handsome? Better still, was it because he looked more affluent?

It was some time before James noticed that Felix's hand was on his leg. He must have placed it there very gently, but now he was warmly squeezing his knee. Thinking about it, it wasn't really such a surprise. Something like this was bound to happen. *Because I am human, nothing human is alien to me* – isn't that what Felix had once said? And Felix was, undeniably, a fellow human. There should be nothing alien about humans, male humans, touching one another. He needed to just sit back and be cool with it. At the same time, though, it was very important that he didn't encourage him to do anything else.

'Of course,' said Felix. 'There is another place we can go where we can do more than just look at girls. Somewhere a bit more innovative.'

'You mean gay?' said Carl.

'Is it further east?' said James.

Felix nodded. 'Yes, quite a bit further. I'm afraid we'd need to go beyond Hackney.'

'Fuck that,' said Carl.

'Well, I'm up for it,' said James, safe in the knowledge that it wasn't going to happen.

'Fuck that,' said Carl. 'I've got a girlfriend at home, remember. Why the fuck would I start chasing around Essex with you benders. Let's just stay here.'

'Well, let's have another drink and think about it,' said Felix. 'We're in no particular hurry.'

'I'll get some more beers,' said James.

As he said this, he got quickly to his feet and Felix's hand fell away before coming to lie on the table. That was, James felt, a better place for it to be.

'Good one,' said Carl. 'And why don't you get a round of vodka shots while you're at it.'

'Good idea,' said James, and headed towards the bar.

Being happy, leading a rich and rewarding life: it's difficult. It requires organisation, hard work, deferred gratification and a talent for cultivating small pleasures. It takes a huge amount of *planning*. You need to nurture friendships with nice and interesting people, read popular science books, prepare wholesome meals for yourself, get to know your neighbours and go for walks in the countryside. To really make it work, you should ideally also go swimming twice a week, volunteer to do things for the benefit of the local community, become informed about the world and develop reasonable opinions that can be defended at supper parties. And yet, the problem was, at the end of all this, you will never, ever feel as mightily good as James was feeling right now. Maybe that's why the dipsomaniacs drinking tins of cider outside the public library in Crystal Palace were always smiling. They had discovered the secret of happiness on planet Earth. It was just a matter of getting the internal biochemistry right, of being drunk and feeling loved. That wasn't necessarily the same thing as *being* loved, of course, but provided you felt like this and were in a place like this, then did it really matter all that much?

13

21 March

Every opportunity to bring the story of London to people and ensure the accessibility and good maintenance of London's heritage should be exploited.

– *The London Plan*, Section 7.32

'So James tells me that you're his favourite and most brilliant colleague,' said Felix.

'Oh God, really? Is that the best he can manage?' said Rachel.

They were in the John Stuart Mill, a pub in Bloomsbury that looked much like the Red Lion in Southwark. James had chosen the venue – not on the grounds of convenience or cost, but rather on the basis of history, memories and emotional attachment. In short, he had chosen poorly.

Of course, it wasn't as simple as just being in Bloomsbury. As any town planner could have told you, they were in the Bloomsbury Conservation Area: fifty hectares of streets and squares with protected planning status. It would, James knew, have its own preservation strategy and detailed rules and instructions governing window frames, the height of lampposts and the dimensions of shop signs. The local planning officers would have to spend their time arguing about satellite dishes and loft extensions, and dealing with the Area Management Committee, which would be composed of highly educated, bad-tempered residents who spent their lives protecting the local heritage, opposing social-housing developments and increasing the value of their properties.

'James – you're receiving the highest quality advice from both the public and private sector. I hope you're finding it illuminating.'

'And what's the consensus?' said James.

'I'm not sure there is one,' said Rachel.

'Well, whatever happens, I think the main thing is that the process is a very good one,' said Felix. 'You can be confident that you're going to make the right decision. And I'm confident that you're not going to go.'

'Deputy Director,' said Rachel. 'If you don't fuck it up, you could be Director in four years. They must really like you up there. It's a unitary authority, isn't it?'

'Yep, it has been for about ten years.'

'That's very good,' said Rachel. 'Deputy Director at a unitary at the age of thirty-two. It normally takes people a lot longer than that.'

'Obviously I've only got a limited understanding of what you're talking about,' said Felix, 'but it tallies with everything I've been saying: James is a talent.'

It hadn't been James's intention, but they had been talking about the job in Nottingham. It shouldn't have been a surprise, after all, Felix and Rachel were his advisors and they were giving him advice. There were some difficulties with this, for they had different worldviews and conflicting values and priorities. The overriding problem, though, was that until this evening Rachel hadn't been aware that there *was* a job in Nottingham.

'You've clearly been discussing this together for a while,' said Rachel. 'But Felix – I'm not sure you're really aware of what a good opportunity it is.'

'That might be true, but my advice has been of a different kind,' said Felix.

'Well, yes, but rather an uninformed kind.'

'James, sorry to speak as if you're not in the room, but I think we have to accept that he has made great progress over the last two months.'

'You mean that you've taken him out clubbing and he now likes football.'

'Well in the modern world, those aren't trivial achievements.'

'You know, Nottingham wasn't that bad,' said James. 'I was pretty happy there.'

'That's my point – you were happy. No one ever does anything of significance when they're happy.'

'I'm worried that you're not taking this seriously,' said Rachel. 'This job is a big deal. You don't get offers like this very often in town planning. You could spend years in London trying to get to this level.'

'Do you know your accent is a total delight? I could listen to it all day. You sound like a 1980s Labour MP.'

James looked out of the window, slightly wishing that he *wasn't* in the room. Across the road was a crescent of Victorian red-brick houses, all with white sash windows and blue wooden doors with brass letter boxes, and none any higher than the permitted three storeys. There were mature plane trees planted at regular intervals, and broad pavements with black railings and high kerbs.

'Sorry about the pub,' said James. 'I haven't been here for ages and I'd forgotten what it was like.'

'Yes, it is a bit gloomy here. You don't often get to see walls this colour any more.'

'The pub's fine,' said Rachel. 'But I've never liked Bloomsbury. It's so dead. Give me Southwark any day. Nothing ever happens round here.'

But James knew otherwise – lots of things happened here, or at least they had. For up the road and over the square, on the edge of the conservation area, was his old student hall of residence. As with everything else, it looked exactly the same. It was here, in the last months of the twentieth century, that James's parents had driven him from Leicester, his sister feeling carsick and the boot filled with everything they could possibly imagine he would need, little of which proved to be useful. His mother had been excessively anxious, and his father had got lost twice on the North Circular.

James himself had been no more than a proto human. A skinny eighteen-year-old whose bones hadn't yet stopped growing, with naive hair, a face that was too soft and optimistic, eyes stuck behind terrible glasses. He might have fled if it hadn't been for the fact that the first person he had met, Carl, had looked even less impressive, with white plasticine arms and an outcrop of spots on his chin that would stay with him until he turned twenty-one.

'So do you want the usual?' said Felix, holding up his glass.

James nodded, and Felix went to the bar.

'So the usual is gin and tonic now?' said Rachel. 'It's what my granny drinks.'

'It's not like that any more. Some friends of Felix rebranded it.'

'That was good of them. Where would we be without advertising executives?'

There were some students here tonight, sitting on benches around a long wooden table. Tuition fees and mass graduate unemployment didn't seem to have dented their spirits, and they were being as annoying as ever. In fact, they were probably worse than before, because instead of books they now had mobile computers and media devices, and instead of looking like beat poets from San Francisco, they were dressed like rap singers from Los Angeles. James shook his head. Few things were more likely to make you feel sad and old than coming to places where you had once been happy and young.

'So I hope this isn't a set-up. If it is, then it's not going to happen.'

'Don't you like him?'

'He's charming and posh – the things that I least like in a man. And he's too small – I like men to be at least four inches taller than I am. Plus, if that wasn't enough, he's almost certainly gay.'

'I don't know why you would think that – you barely know him. He's always flirting with girls.'

'Christ, you really don't have a clue, do you.'

James finished his drink. Maybe Felix was gay, and maybe he wasn't. It was probably some kind of progress that people couldn't even tell any more. The key thing was not to get weird about it. Yes, something a bit strange had happened in the club, but so what? It was nothing he couldn't handle. Being comfortable with having gay friends was one of the things that all grown-up heterosexuals were now expected to do.

'Well, whatever, gay or not, I can't believe this is the guy who's been keeping you away from the Red Lion.'

'It's nice to do other stuff. It's been good for me. I needed to develop a bit, to live in London instead of write strategies about it.'

Rachel rolled her eyes. It was one of the things she sometimes did in planning meetings.

'Anyway, never mind me. You've cut your hair,' said James.

'No, men never get that right. I've just had it redone and tidied up a bit.'

'Well, whatever you've done. It looks very nice.'

'Thanks. It won't last. It never does. I've got Midlands hair. Just like the working class, it can't be oppressed for ever.'

James and Rachel looked at one another for two seconds, each assessing the other. She did look different this evening, and it wasn't just the hair. She had done other things – a brighter lipstick, possibly something cynical with eyeliner. She looked slimmer too, in a black blouse and bright green skirt. She didn't look like she did on a Friday night, elbows at the crowded table, the pints of Guinness, bowls of chips and warm air reddening her skin and thickening her face.

'So, the Nottingham job. When did they speak to you?'

'Not very long ago. Just a few weeks,' said James.

'So no one else knows about it?'

'No, I didn't want to tell anyone at work.'

'But you told Felix?'

'Yes, I told Felix. I thought it would be good to talk about it with someone who, you know, wasn't on the inside.'

'You couldn't trust me to keep quiet?'

'Well, I just didn't want to tell anyone at work. You know what it's like. I didn't want Lionel to get worried. You know how he takes these things, and I didn't want it all coming out in the pub one night.'

'Is that what you thought? I wouldn't have told anyone.'

'No, I know. Sorry. I should have told you.'

Should he have told her? Probably not. He had done the wrong thing for the right reasons. It was hardly the first time.

'In any case,' said Rachel, 'I don't think Lionel would be as bothered as you think. No one is indispensable.'

'No, I know that. Of course I know that. But I just didn't want it to wind him up.'

'All I'm saying is that people threatening to leave isn't a big preoccupation at the moment. Lionel's got other things to worry about.'

Felix returned with the drinks.

'Rachel, James – you're two of this city's most able planners. I know James has explained this to me, but this pub – can't we do anything about it? It needs a radical overhaul.'

He had kissed Alice in this pub, ten years ago. He had kissed her in many parts of Bloomsbury, but this one had been different. It hadn't been their first kiss, but it had been their most significant because it had been in front of so many other people. It had been public, and with Alice that was always what mattered most.

Without mobile phones to help them, everyone had gathered there on a sunny afternoon in early June, straight after their degree results had been announced. James had just discovered, to his enormous relief, that he had got an upper second and Alice, to her enduring disappointment, had got exactly the same. Carl had got a lower second, but that didn't matter because it was in maths, he hadn't done any work, and he had already been offered a job at a bank. Adam was less concerned than any of them – he had a place at law school and was already talking about work experience and graduate trainee schemes. It would take James and the others many years to understand what Adam had already realised that afternoon: that they weren't students any more.

So there they all were – all of them together, with their second-class degrees and first-class futures. People were bound to start kissing one another. Of course, Alice had already kissed Carl and probably done a bit more with Adam, not to mention with her activist friends from Yemen and Pakistan. But this was different. It was a public declaration. And while exam results and white wine may have generated her heightened emotional state, James was to understand that there was more to it than this, that it was something that Alice had given some thought to, and decided would happen, something that James would now need to go along with. And so she had kissed him standing up, slowly and in front of everyone, with mock ceremony and deadly seriousness.

There had been a round of applause and cheers. Adam had immediately ordered a bottle of champagne. And James had felt a surge of relief and thanks at having been chosen. She wasn't so very pretty, not back then, and there had been plenty of girls who might have been more suitable, who he would have preferred to go out with. But from that moment James accepted that he would have to be Alice's boyfriend, and that it was something he would do without hesitation or doubt. It was, he now saw, an important life lesson: you had to be very careful not to go out with someone you didn't love, for there was every chance that you would fall in love with them.

'That's the East Midlands,' said Rachel. 'I'm from Wolverhampton, the West Midlands. It's completely different.'

'Yes, sorry. I've never really totally grasped the whole Midlands thing.'

'You know,' said James, 'his geography might not be very good, but Felix is actually a kind of planner, like us – you know, an advertising planner.'

'Oh yes, I know. Such a creepy profession – the way they try to manipulate people into wanting things they don't need.'

'Well, someone has to. Just imagine what would happen if people weren't being manipulated by us advertisers?'

'Wouldn't they just make their own choices?'

'That's exactly the problem. If you just leave it to the people, they make terrible choices. They go around murdering philosophers, electing tyrants and drinking the wrong brand of coffee.'

'God, I think you're being serious. In fact, I'm starting to worry that you've been serious all evening. You're a total disaster.'

Rachel's new red lips were smiling. James wasn't sure what he had wanted from the evening. Had he wanted Felix and Rachel to like each other, to become friends? Well, that had never seemed very likely but at least, now that they weren't talking about his future any more, they seemed to be getting on.

'I'll get some more drinks,' said James.

James went to the bar. It hadn't changed in the slightest. What with being located in the heart of a conservation area, the pub had thrived on the lack of competition. Planning controls had meant there had been no new market entrants, and no need to innovate or improve. As a result, the pub was as well preserved as Bloomsbury itself, and dated from a time when all that English pubs ever did was serve two types of beer, terrible white wine and roasted peanuts. The service was slow and cumbersome, for the barman was not an alert young East European or a highly competent New Zealander, but a well-fed, middle-aged Englishman. He had a red beard and wore a burgundy sweatshirt with the pub name in yellow italic letters. James was sure that he'd been there when he was a student ten years ago, possibly becoming promoted to bar manager at some point.

When he got back, Rachel and Felix were arguing, but in a good way. They weren't discussing macroeconomic policy or the European Union, they were having what seemed to be a highly entertaining disagreement and Rachel was laughing – a nice gentle laugh, not like the one she used in the Red Lion.

'So I've been trying to explain town planning to Felix,' said Rachel. 'But without much success. I'm starting to wonder if he's as clever as he thinks he is.'

'Oh I know,' said James. 'He thinks our profession is worthless because we don't own things.'

'That's right. Ownership is everything. It's the basis of all political economy.'

'That's not how it's done. It's much more about regulation and use than ownership.'

'Well, regulate this pub then. Turn it into a Moroccan restaurant or a vodka bar or something.'

'Planners shouldn't really be intervening in the market in that way,' said Rachel. 'We can't go around telling people how pubs and shops should be run.'

'Oh, that's just an ideology, a spell cast by the ruling class to mask historical contingencies. The state can do as much as the people want it to.'

It was easy to forget, but Felix was actually a Marxist. It was one of the first things he'd told James. It was actually essential to his worldview – a deep understanding and unwavering position on the structural underpinnings of economic relations that enabled him to say and do all sorts of extremely right-wing things.

'Well, it's a Thursday night. I think we should make the most of it,' said Felix.

'What were you thinking?'

'Let's go to my club. Erica will be there and after her last outing I'm sure she'll want to explain herself.'

'That sounds exciting,' said Rachel. 'Do you know I've never actually been to a private club.'

'Oh my God, Rachel – you'll absolutely hate it!' said James. 'I can't wait to see the faces you pull.'

'Can you dance there? James – you've never taken me dancing before.'

'Actually, this might be tricky,' said Felix. 'On busy evenings, I'm only able to take one guest along.'

'Oh,' said James. 'Couldn't we all go? I'm sure you can get us both in.'

'Well, we could try. But I wouldn't want to risk it. I've slightly blotted my copybook with the very pretty doorwoman, and I suspect she isn't in the mood to grant me any favours.'

'We don't have to go there,' said James. 'We could always just have another drink here.'

Felix didn't say anything, but as if by way of reply turned his head to look across the room. The barman was doing a newspaper crossword and drinking a pint of bitter. There was a burst of noise and clapping of hands, for the students had got excited about something that was happening on one of their computers.

'No, don't worry,' said Rachel. 'I'd hate to make you stay here on my account.'

'I don't think we can stay here much longer,' said Felix. 'It's becoming intolerable.'

James would have to make an ethical decision. He could see that. And like most ethical decisions, it was actually quite easy. He had accepted someone else's decision in this very pub all those years ago, but he didn't have to do it now.

'Felix, you go to the club. I'll go with Rachel to the station.'

'Really? Are you sure that's what you want to do?'

'You don't have to,' said Rachel.

'I'd like to,' said James. 'We can walk together.'

They all stood up to go. James picked up Rachel's coat and handed it to her.

'I guarantee that the club will be highly entertaining tonight,' said Felix.

'Well, let me know what's going on there and I can always come and join you.'

'Very well. I'll call you.'

Outside, Felix vanished immediately into a taxi. James and Rachel crossed the road and headed northwards. The original cast-iron streetlights glowed softly as they walked past the bookshops and tearooms that had closed for the day, past the tennis courts and private parks, and out of the conservation area, into the noise and dirt of London.

The two planners walked side by side, through the southern borders of Islington. Much of it was ruined and there was little that could be done, but still they tried to understand. The text was huge and unreadable, but they poured over it. They studied bus timetables, revolving advertising boards, late-night traffic flows, estate agents' windows and franchised coffee shops. Like code breakers, they looked not for meaning but for structures: repetitions and synchronicities, patterns and frequencies. They noted the oversupply of B1 office space and under-provision of C3 residential, and they speculated about regeneration strategies, the size of retail units and affordable housing targets.

They came on to Euston Road, the city's first bypass, the east-to-west carriageway built to run through the villages and fields on the edge of London, stretching from Marylebone to Essex. Like all bypasses, it had been controversial and ultimately unsuccessful, destroying farmlands and doomed by everything that came afterwards.

'Shall we have another drink?' said James.

'Yes, there's a pub just here.'

Rachel led them along the road, taking his hand as she did so, until they came to a pub just across the road from King's Cross Station.

'This place is awful,' said James.

'You've been hanging out with Felix too much. It's fine. I sometimes come here if I'm waiting for a train.'

But the pub wasn't fine at all – you didn't need to have studied much economic geography to know that. It was a railway pub, with transient and uninformed customers who didn't return often enough to be valued. During the week it was used by salesmen and at weekends by football fans from the north of England. Its only competitive advantage was its proximity to three major railway stations and, other than television screens, the owner had never made a significant investment in anything likely to improve the consumer experience. The lighting was primitive, the female toilets unadvisable and the chairs made from aluminium. The barman had a red nose and looked a bit like Lionel and in the corner were two alcoholic Scotsmen who had got off the train from Edinburgh ten years before but never managed to get any further. Above their heads was a large sign reminding patrons of the unlawfulness of drug use and violent behaviour.

'So you didn't really believe that about the doorwoman? That was so obviously just a ruse to stop me from coming.'

'Why would he do that? I thought you were getting on well.'

'Because he wanted you to himself. Because he's gay and doesn't like women.'

'Well, I guess everyone is a bit gay. There are degrees, aren't there, like everything else. He's never said anything.'

'Fuck knows. He probably doesn't even know himself. I'm increasingly coming to the conclusion that all men under the age of forty aren't worth the bother. You're all so useless and self-absorbed.'

They sat looking at each other across the small, unsteady table-top. Rachel was looking prettier than James had ever seen her, but she was no Harriet – her legs weren't rubbing against his, and her hands remained around her drink. So if anything was going to happen then it would need James to take the lead. But the problem, of course, was that he was a planner. He could give advice, take a view and have opinions, but he couldn't make decisions.

'You're not going to Nottingham, are you?' said Rachel.

'No, I don't think so.'

'But it is a really great opportunity. You should feel pleased that they want you.'

'I know, I am. It's just not the right time.'

'Well, I'm glad,' said Rachel.

'Are you really?'

'Yes, of course I am. The office wouldn't be the same without you.'

James drank some of his gin and tonic. It didn't seem to work the way it had before. Instead of warming and strengthening him, he could feel it softening and curdling, making him feel older and weaker. Perhaps it was a drink for grandmothers after all. Or perhaps it only worked if you drank it in wine bars and private clubs.

James's phone beeped. There was a message from Felix: 'I think you should come now.'

Felix was different from James and Rachel, and always willing to take command. In certain industries, it had always been understood that a bad decision was preferable to no decision at all – particularly advertising, where there was little verifiable distinction between the

227

two. Felix made calls – whether it was on the value of a brand of toothpaste or the quality of the girls at a strip show. And because he made his calls with authority, in an upper-class voice or curt text message, people tended to follow.

'Are you being summoned?' said Rachel.

'Well, not summoned, but yes – I think I might head down there. That is, if you haven't got any other plans.'

But of course she didn't. The problem, of course, was that Rachel was a town planner too.

'Well, I guess you ought to get going then.'

'I don't have to go. I don't have to do anything.'

'No, you should go. I should go. It's late.'

Rachel was standing up and buttoning her coat. She was doing it very quickly, but it was hard for James to tell if she was upset with him or not. Maybe she just wanted to go home.

'Aren't you going to finish your drink?'

'No, I'm fine. This wine is horrible anyway. I think I'll just head off now.'

'You would have definitely hated the club,' said James.

'Yes, I'm sure.'

They walked out together, the barman nodding sadly at the only remotely attractive and economically viable couple in his pub, and now they were back out on the Euston Road. They turned to face one another and to say goodbye.

'Well, I'll be off then. The station's just there,' said Rachel.

'I really like your hair,' said James.

'Yes, you told me that earlier.'

'Oh yes. Well, see you in the office tomorrow?'

'I've got some days off. I won't be in again until Wednesday.'

'Oh? You didn't say. Are you doing anything exciting?'

'No. No plans. Maybe I'll do some spring-cleaning. I've still got unused holiday that I have to take before the end of the month.'

'Oh, okay. Well, have a great weekend then.'

They moved closer to say goodbye, and as they did so, James kissed her. It was a hesitant and incoherent kiss – technically poor and open to misinterpretation. He was too tall, and he needed Rachel to raise her face up to his, but either she was unwilling or was no more skilled than he was, for her lips did no more than brush ineffectively against his. Alcohol wasn't going to help either – they had drunk just enough to get into this situation, but not enough to do anything about it. It was no good – somebody had to take the lead, just like Alice had done all those years ago. But there was no one chairing, they had no agenda or PowerPoint to guide them. James turned one way, Rachel turned the other and in two seconds they were apart again, facing one another as if nothing had happened.

The traffic on Euston Road had picked up, and a double-decker bus drove past at speed. Rachel shivered in the breeze and took a step back from the road, and also from James.

'Goodnight then,' said James.

'Yes, goodnight.'

Rachel turned towards King's Cross station. James went the other way, back into town, walking headlong into a Thursday night. In the countryside, as James knew, you were up against the weather, which amplified your mental state and physically obstructed and buffeted you. But it was so much worse in the city, where the whole economy was against you. Every interaction and regulation made things difficult to progress, and unlike Felix he had no natural talent for attracting taxis. He stopped at street corners, he waited by road junctions, he held out his arm against the oncoming traffic and wondered why nothing happened. The gin and tonics were starting to work at last, but only to make him bold enough to feel bad-tempered.

It was a full fifteen minutes before he was in the back of a taxi going south and checking his phone again. He had two text messages. The first was from Felix: 'Am making my peace with the doorwoman here. Suggest you stand down.'

Well, it was fucking inconsiderate, but maybe it was for the best. James had to go to work tomorrow, and not in an advertising agency. Did he really want to stay up late, drink more gin and listen to Felix make prophecies about Western civilisation? Besides, if he was really doing something with the doorwoman, then so much the better – it would certainly make things easier all round if Felix was sleeping with women rather than touching his knee.

The other message was from Rachel: 'Sorry to be dopey, but was that meant to be a KISS kiss??'

Before he could think of a reply she had sent another one: 'Whatever it was meant to be, it was nice. See you next week xx'

14

26 March

In estimating provision from private residential or mixed-use developments, boroughs should take into account economic viability and the most effective use of private and public investment.

– *The London Plan*, Section 3.71

The office of Galbraith & Erskine was in Canary Wharf – the land of the developers, built by the private sector for the private sector. All that government had ever done was decontaminate the land, build an underground line, hand over the property rights and then get out of the way. It was the biggest thing to have happened in London in thirty years and James had written an essay about it for his A levels. But again, somehow, he had never actually made it here before.

It was now quite important that something happened here, for the night before he had sent Graham Oakley an email telling him that he didn't want the job in Nottingham. It was a friendly, direct, well-written email, and had taken only three minutes to write, read once over and send. He was learning to be more decisive, that most attractive of male qualities. He was changing, he was becoming a more successful human being and a less effective government administrator, but he needed to do it faster – his kiss with Rachel was proof of that. For what it was worth, he was probably becoming less nice as well, but in truth that should probably have happened a long time ago. The private sector, working with developers, meetings in Canary Wharf – these were all logical next steps.

He had arrived early, and found a coffee bar at the top of the square. But unlike everyone else there, he wasn't studying his phone, he was sitting on a stool by the window and making a survey. Around him were some of the tallest buildings in Europe and none of them were more than twenty-five years old. With no small-minded local authority to get in their way, cheered on by investors and the Docklands Corporation, the architects had done whatever they wanted. They had taken the blueprints from Hong Kong and built upwards – it was all they knew how to do, it was the only way anyone could tell if a building was good or not. And now, or so he'd been told, they were all going off to the Middle East to do the same thing there, to build gigantic towers that couldn't be corrupted or damaged by the people who lived there. By the end of the century, every city in the world would look like this. Well, maybe he should just accept it – become one of the people who got well paid for making it happen, rather than badly paid for failing to stop it.

Nobody dawdled in Canary Wharf, everyone had a purpose and moved quickly across the squares, anxious not to be in the open air and unproductive. There were no post offices for people to huddle outside, no library steps where tramps could drink cans of cider. There was no graffiti or litter either – the public space was respected and well cared for, probably because it wasn't actually owned by the public. It wasn't really used by the public either, except to walk between the towers and then in July to eat lunch from boxes of sushi. A hundred yards away, ignored, was the river Thames.

All of the people that James could see made a significant contribution to the wealth of the nation while making the world a worse place to live in. They worked in business services, and spent their lives helping international corporations to pay less tax, acquire commercial rivals, exploit monopoly positions, evade environmental regulations and skirt legal responsibilities. They were central to the functioning of the modern economy. Twenty thousand other people travelled in every day to make them coffee, serve them lunch and guard the buildings. It was, everyone had agreed, a tremendous success, the sort of place that Laura would approve of. To his right, in a tower on the corner of the square, was the law firm where Adam worked.

James too was here on business. Although not, strictly speaking, Southwark Council business. He had got better at this, and hadn't bothered calling in sick. He had just put 'external meeting' in his calendar and left the office without telling anyone. He hadn't told Felix either. Felix would only have warned him against it, and then given an illuminating but unhelpful lecture on modern business practices. It was the problem with having a friendship on a pro bono basis – you only got the advice and guidance that he wanted to give you. And, anyway – what did it have to do with him?

Felix Selwood. There was no doubt he'd come into James's life at the right time, that he had helped him, been generous, and that he knew some valuable things: strip bars, drug dealers, aesthetics, metaphysics and what was going to happen to capitalism. But were they really going to be friends? In theory, there were good reasons why James ought to feel grateful to Felix, but of course he felt no such thing. He knew that just because there was such a word as gratitude, it didn't mean that it existed. Not really, and certainly not between adult men. If you gave someone what they desperately needed, then all you ever got back was relief and resentment. Anyone who worked in the public sector knew that.

No, if anything, it was Felix who ought to thank James. For two months James had been, just like Erica had said, one of his projects. He had allowed Felix to boss him, to instruct him, practise his speeches, elaborate on his worldview. There were few greater pleasures. Whatever other motives he might have, and there could be all sorts, that would be plenty. It was time that James got to do some things for Felix – to buy him expensive drinks, introduce him to useful business contacts and make informative pronouncements on the property market. It would serve him fucking well right.

He hadn't told Rachel either. He hadn't spoken to her since that night in Bloomsbury, but he knew she wouldn't want him to be here – for sound reasons, but also probably some selfish ones as well. If he was ever going to try and kiss her again, then it would be so much easier if he worked somewhere else and earned more than her, but that didn't necessarily mean she'd be celebrating his success. After all, he never did for any of his friends. But you had to look out for yourself in this world, no one else was going to do it for you. That was the true message of Canary Wharf.

James rose abruptly. He was still early, but he needed to get going, for Canary Wharf was no place for brooders. It was a place where people got things done, where decisions were made and deals were struck. He left the coffee bar and marched diagonally across the square. There was no doubt, he fitted in well – dark suited with briefcase and square glasses, his head up and focused on the task ahead. The spring air was thin and mild, and he was caffeinated, confident, purposeful. It was, for once, a good cause: he was doing something for himself instead of the council, instead of for Lionel.

The doors of the tower opened silently before him. Inside, it was like being in a small airport. There were security guards and electronic gates, a marbled bank of receptionists with headsets. There was a coffee shop identical to the one he'd just been in, and a large copper-plated cube suspended on a steel rod, an abstract artwork, which looked exactly like the type of thing that town planners put in the middle of shopping centres, except this one hadn't been vandalised. He gave his name, showed some identification and was efficiently processed and directed towards a lift.

This lift wasn't anything like the one at Southwark Council. It was the size of a bedroom, no one needed to brush against anyone else, it didn't judder and it had a screen on a wall with business news. It didn't occur to James for the slightest moment that it might get stuck between levels for two hours, and it took no more than twenty seconds to take him all the way up to the thirtieth floor, three-quarters of the way to the top. His confidence still perfectly intact, James stepped out directly into the reception of Galbraith & Erskine and strode on.

'Yes, hello, can I help you?'

Only now did James falter. The receptionist who looked up at him from behind the crescent desk was unnervingly magnificent, almost impossible for James to describe without romanticising or dehumanising. She was a gypsy princess, with black hair, ferocious white teeth and red lips that took up almost all her face. Her dark eyes were serious, but her smile so large and friendly it was incoherent, as if James was an old friend.

'Hello, I'm James Crawley. I'm here for a meeting with Robert Wenham at three. Sorry, I'm a bit early.'

'Okay, just wait here and I call him.'

She had a Spanish accent and imperfect grammar – displaced from the mountains of Andalusia by the European financial crisis, she was now stranded in London's service economy. She was exactly the woman he wanted to be holding hands with when he next saw Alice.

'Don't worry. Please sit down and I'll tell Robert you're here. Would you like tea or coffee?'

'No, thanks very much. I'm fine – I don't need anything.'

'Robert will be out in a minute. Just let me know if you need anything.'

Unable to think of anything else he could talk to her about, James went to sit down on a soft leather chair. On the low table in front of him were neatly arranged copies of the *Financial Times*, the *Economist* and *Property Week*. On the walls above was a series of large and beautiful photographs of Galbraith & Erskine projects from across the country. There were apartments in Glasgow on the banks of the river Clyde, Victorian warehouses in Manchester converted into creative studios, a business incubator in Oxford, a block of pastel-coloured flats in Stratford overlooking the Olympic Park and neo-Georgian town houses on the edge of Basingstoke.

There was none of the naive hope of James's Sunbury Square masterplan poster. They may not have had a significant affordable housing component, they may not have been supported by local community groups, but they had all happened: these were photographs, and they hadn't been created on a computer. It wasn't Metroland either – none of them had been built for the aspiring middle classes with limited means and imaginations, desperate to look like each other. Galbraith & Erskine's buildings were as confident, diverse and ambitious as the people they had been made for.

'James – it's good to see you,' said Robert. 'Thanks so much for coming over. Let's go into my room. It's just here.'

Robert's office was just as James had thought it would be: attractive, busy but uncluttered, designed to motivate and encourage effective decision-making. It wasn't as pretentious as an architect's, and it wasn't anything like as depressing as being in a local authority. It was, James thought, a room he could be comfortable with, and had lots of space – enough for James to recalibrate Robert's seniority within the company. For surely, in that respect at least, it worked just like the public sector.

'This is Paul. He shares the office with me. It's just the two of us at the moment.'

There was a third desk in the corner – a conspicuously empty one, with a cover over the computer screen. Perhaps, thought James, they had it in mind for him. It seemed a perfectly reasonable supposition.

'Can I get you anything to drink?' said Paul.

'Just water, if that's okay,' said James, determined to answer every question as appropriately as possible.

Paul nodded. He was younger than James and looked well designed for long-term subservience and steady career progression. His light brown hair was cropped short, his face slightly freckled, and his eyes blue with only a dash of cruelty. He wore a pinstripe suit, which James didn't care for, but was bound to be expensive. James very badly wanted to know how much he earned.

'Some water sounds good. It can get very dry here.'

Above Robert's desk was a large map of London, just like Lionel's. But it was more than decorative – it was dotted in coloured pins, yellow Post-it notes and arrows drawn in felt-tip pen. There was a cluster of red pins around the southern borders of Southwark. It was gratifying, in a way: even if the residents weren't bothered, over in Canary Wharf the things he did were being followed closely.

'Ah yes, the battle map,' said Robert. 'As you can see, we've got interests all over London – particularly in your patch.'

'Yes, I can see that,' said James. 'It looks like the whole of South London seems to be interesting you at the moment.'

'That's correct. We're still interested in the east of course, everyone is, but we see inner South London as being the major driver of residential growth over the next ten years.'

'Southwark, Lambeth, Lewisham, Greenwich,' said Paul. 'The opportunities are there, but it's a question of how willing the boroughs are to make things happen.'

Looking towards the window, James could see that the tower was on the western edge of Canary Wharf. Directly beneath them, away from the business headquarters and landscaped squares, things were more complicated, with a wide range of obstinate market failures. It was the Isle of Dogs, in the jurisdiction of Tower Hamlets, and contained all the things that you couldn't find in the Docklands any more: post-war housing estates, medieval street plans, ramshackle graveyards, organised crime, disgusting pub lunches, psycho-geographers, religious maniacs and communist politicians.

'Yes, the view is great isn't it?' said Robert. 'They keep trying to reorganise the seating here, but I refuse to move. I like being reminded of all the work to be done.'

Robert was just as friendly as he had been at the football match, but there were details that James hadn't noticed before. He was, for instance, at least two inches taller, while the eyes were narrower and his voice louder. Maybe it was because he had home advantage. They made some small talk. James had been expecting this, and was well prepared. Besides which, he was also getting better at being less prepared. They talked about Chelsea and their prospects in the FA Cup. They talked about how successful Canary Wharf had been, possible new developments on the north side and all the things that were going wrong in the Olympic Park.

The receptionist returned with a tray of both carbonated and still bottles of water, and tumbler glasses containing lemon and ice cubes. She gave them all the loveliest of smiles, making sure that James received the very largest. He had failed to protect Erica from Rick, but maybe if James worked here, he could rescue her from the developers.

'Thanks, Margarita, that's great,' said Paul. 'Don't worry – we'll serve ourselves.'

'So, you've seen our map,' said Robert. 'It's no secret we're trying to do things in Southwark. And I was struck when we met by some of the things you were saying. They weren't the sort of thing you often hear from a town planner in London.'

'Well, as I said, I'm interested in making things happen, and getting things done. It would be great to hear more about what your thinking is.'

Robert gave a short speech about his ambitions and plans. It was, thought James, a pretty good one. There was no doubt that he understood South London. Not in the same way that James did, he wasn't a planner. He didn't talk about economic clusters, regeneration priorities, housing densities or unemployment rates. Instead, he talked about property values and construction costs. He wasn't guided by well-meaning targets and strategic frameworks, but by market forces and prices – and it meant that everything he said was clear and to the point. As well as being better paid, it was, James realised, so much easier being a developer.

'Yes, I can see what you're saying,' said James. 'I think there's a real cross-over with what I've been trying to do.'

There was a knock at the door and Simon Galbraith entered.

'Simon!' said Robert. 'I didn't know you were going to join us.'

'Sorry – I didn't mean to interrupt. I just wanted to say hello to James.'

James rose to his feet and they shook hands. He was wearing glasses, delicate ones with rimless frames that didn't in any way diminish the power of his blue eyes.

'Really good to see you. How do you like the office?'

'Oh, yes, it's great. I love the view.'

'Yes, I thought you'd appreciate it. Sometime I'll have to show you the view from my room on the other side. I often think it's a shame that town planners don't get to work in places like this. You always seem to be tucked away in those squat municipal buildings where you can't see anything.'

'We've been talking about what's happening in Southwark,' said Robert.

'Ah yes, of course – Sunbury Square.'

'We were just about to get on to that.'

'Well, yes – that's right,' said James. 'There's no reason why we shouldn't be able to work together. After all, fundamentally, we work in the same sector. We may have different priorities, but we all want to see the same things happen.'

This was pretty much what he'd said to them at the football, but now it seemed that more was expected of him. There was a pause. Simon nodded his head, but didn't smile. Robert took a piece of paper from his desk and handed it to him.

'So do you think you could help us with these?'

James looked at the sheet. There were eight questions, most of which he could answer there and then. If they had bothered to download and read his masterplan then they could have found the information themselves. But the last two were more difficult. In fact, they weren't really questions, they were requests to do something.

'We're only looking for a bit of friendly advice,' said Robert. 'There's no pressure or anything.'

But of course there was pressure, there was great pressure. These people were the real thing – they were *businessmen*. They weren't bureaucrats and do-gooders, and they weren't like Felix's advertising friends either – they didn't spend their time dreaming up zany websites and brand strategies. Every single thing they did incurred a cost and needed to make a return, and that included this meeting.

'Yes,' said James. 'I'd be happy to help. I can give you the answers to these tomorrow morning. But you know that the height restrictions are fixed, and I can't alter specifications on the affordable housing or key-worker allocations. That would need to be a policy decision.'

'That's helpful,' said Robert. 'Of course, we don't want you to do anything that you're not comfortable with. It's just about trying to speed things up.'

'So on the social-housing issue, would that need to go back to council members?' said Simon.

'No, it shouldn't do. To a certain extent, the composition of individual mixed-use developments can be done at the discretion of executive officers, but not at my level. Although I can make recommendations.'

'So you're saying we'd need to have a conversation with Lionel Rogers?' said Simon. 'Or should we go higher than that? If need be, I can put in a call to someone.'

'No, I wouldn't do that,' said James. 'Your best bet would be to talk to one of the housing associations who have already submitted an expression of interest. I can give you the contacts. What we're expecting are consortium bids from commercial and not-for-profit partners.'

But Simon didn't seem particularly interested in that piece of advice.

'Yes, of course, the housing associations. We know them all well.'

'We prefer not to have to work with them if we can help it,' said Robert. 'Most of them seem to be more bothered about hitting targets than accruing genuine value.'

'We're much more interested in inward investment,' said Paul. 'In bringing jobs and prosperity into your borough, rather than just managing decline and shifting low-income groups from one patch to another.'

Simon and Robert both nodded their heads, and James could see that Paul would rise and rise in Galbraith & Erskine, that he was surely headed for senior management. Did he have a planning qualification? Almost certainly not. More likely, he had studied economics or finance, maybe even philosophy – something that taught you how to be cold-hearted in a way that came across as sensible and wise.

'You're not saying that Sunbury Square has to be delivered by a housing association are you?' said Robert.

'No – even if we wanted that, we couldn't do it. Our tender process doesn't allow us to exclude or specify any partners. It's just what we're probably expecting.'

'The Bermondsey developments. None of those had a housing association attached, did they?'

'No, they didn't.'

'So there's no reason why this one should have to.'

'No, no reason. It's just what we're expecting will come back to us. As I said, some housing associations have already been in touch.'

'You mean they've submitted bids?'

'No – not yet. No one has. But there have been informal meetings.'

'Meetings ahead of a competitive tender?' said Paul.

'Well, meetings like this one, I suppose.'

There was a pause. The atmosphere had become brittle. It wasn't like being in a meeting with Rachel and Neil Tuffnel. There was no munching of chocolate biscuits while people tried to come up with friendly things to say to one another.

'So, just to be clear,' said Robert, 'provided we could demonstrate the various outputs that you're looking for, there's no requirement for us to be in a consortium with a housing association or anyone else.'

'That's right.'

'And although the council has overall targets, the outputs for Sunbury Square can still be negotiated with senior officers.'

'Yes. To a certain extent, yes.'

'Right,' said Simon. 'I've got to head off. I'm meant to be in another meeting. But this has been very useful.'

Simon rose, and nodded to Paul.

'James – we must see you again soon. Either here or at the football, of course.'

He left the room, and Paul followed him out. James had the impression that they were now going to talk about what he'd just told them.

'It's not like Simon to take such an interest in a project at this stage,' said Robert. 'I think he really likes this one. He likes you too.'

Robert and James talked some more. They talked about a proposed development off the Old Kent Road and an application to turn a school in Peckham Rye into flats, and made some speculations about the retail property market. After a while they began to talk about the football again and Robert checked his email. It dawned on James that there was no longer a good reason for him still to be there. In his briefcase he had a copy of his CV and two of his best research reports, but they wouldn't be needed. The interview was over.

Margarita said goodbye tenderly as James left the office and travelled back down in the lift. There was no doubt, just like at the football, he had been looked after beautifully. They had been generous hosts, they had shared confidences and listened respectfully to him. But something hadn't happened. Had he done anything wrong? No, he didn't think so. He had been helpful, he had spoken openly and generally behaved, as far as he could tell, like a businessman. In fact, if anything, he might have been a bit too helpful. No doubt, he had passed the test, but the problem was – he wasn't sure now if there had actually been one. He had expected things to be a bit more resolved than this. Ambiguity and miscommunication, meetings that finished inconclusively – this was the kind of thing that went on at Southwark Council. It wasn't the sort of thing he thought that property developers did.

James passed back through the entrance, which was just as busy as before, and out into Canary Wharf again. The sky was darkening, but people were still crossing the squares, moving briskly between the towers. Lights were coming on, the coffee shops were emptying, but the bars were filling up, for even Canary Wharf had a night-time economy. It wasn't hard to visualise himself here – no longer in the Red Lion with Rachel, but in a modern, well-lit bar with blond-wood seating, drinking a bottle of chilled white wine,

exchanging market intelligence with Paul, Robert, Margarita –
maybe giving Adam a call and getting him to join them, and then
ordering a large Mediterranean mezze platter on expenses.

It wasn't hard to visualise, but was it going to happen? In any
case, did he really want to work for Galbraith & Erskine? He wasn't
so sure that he did now. Drinking wine with Margarita was one
thing, but he wasn't convinced that hanging out with the likes of
Paul would be a recipe for long-term happiness. The crucial thing
was how much they got paid. It needed to be a lot: there didn't
seem much point in still earning significantly less than Adam and
Carl, but no longer being able to look down at what they did for a
living.

There had been, he could now see, a lack of clarity in his objectives. What he had really wanted most of all was for Simon Galbraith
to like him. But that didn't seem like an especially sensible ambition. What did he want his affection and admiration for if it wasn't
to get a job? As he walked down into the underground station
through the fast-moving and efficient private sector crowds, it
occurred to him that maybe he should have spoken to Felix after all.

15

28 March

In a city as dynamic as London it is impossible to anticipate all the ways in which change will happen.

– The London Plan, Section 8.8

'Okay,' said Felix. 'What we've got to do now is put them all together.'

Art, recreational drugs, anonymous sexual encounters, high-end shopping, financial irresponsibility, alcohol free at the point of purchase. It was what cities were for, it's what they were – an agglomeration of reckless promises. And it was what London did better than any other city. It was still the capital of possibilities and unsustainable desires, the place where you could commit an unlimited number of mistakes and moral atrocities.

That was, if you thought about it, what planning was all about: to let liberty flourish, to design a place in which people from all around the world could come and make themselves unhappy in as many ways as possible. And nothing, absolutely nothing he could think of, better exemplified this than where he was now. For James was at the opening of a visual art show in East London. He was at a private view – an event attended exclusively by trendsetters, opinion formers, thought leaders and, unusually, a town planner from Southwark Council.

For once, the venue was everything that James had hoped for. For nearly a hundred years it had been a printworks. Steel beams still passed above their heads from which brackets and belts would once have hung, connected to cast-iron printing presses and their crates of paper, binding machines, refuse bins and tanks of ink and glue. But those had all gone – rendered uncompetitive by East Asia and replaced by white walls and economically productive empty space. It was, thought James, exactly the kind of B2 light-industrial site that was ideal for an art gallery – the planning permission would have been an easy decision.

James had gone straight there. He no longer needed to meet up beforehand for a heart-warming gin and coaching session. Unlike with the book launch, the nightclub or football match, James was going alone. Well, not quite alone – he had taken Harriet with him. It wasn't exactly a date, he was through with those, and anyway he'd decided that the concept was flawed. Rather, it was an evening out to which he had happened to bring along an attractive young woman. It was, as Felix might have said, an intelligent piece of repositioning.

Of course, he had thought about asking Rachel to come. But they had only seen each other once that week, in a waste-management meeting, and besides, she would have hated it here. But what did that say about her?

'This place looks ace,' said Harriet. 'It's totally my sort of thing.'

Outside, James knew, East London was unravelling. The factories had closed, the bankers had fucked up, the buildings were falling down and the buses had stopped working. Everyone was going mentally ill. But that was okay – because he was on the inside. He might not be that far away, but he was insulated from all the ones who had to queue, all those people in shopping centres who still drank beer in carpeted pubs and in public consultations said that crime was their biggest concern. He was with the artists, the creative entrepreneurs and the middlemen who made everything work. The only criminals here were drug dealers, and they had all been invited. It was London's cockpit, the East. It wasn't Soho where the story had now come to an end, and it wasn't Camden – it wasn't indiscriminate and tasteless. It wasn't even like Clerkenwell, which had got too clever for its own good. It wasn't necessarily very strategic, but nonetheless it was the direction that London was moving in – the visual artists and the town planners, the ones that were any good, all knew it.

'Felix! It's so good to see you. It's been absolutely ages.'

'Harriet – I didn't know you were coming.'

Felix looked at James with a craftily raised eyebrow, as if he had done something that he would regret. That was, of course, perfectly possible. The main thing was that he was making decisions, even if they were ill advised, and that Harriet was looking very pretty. Possibly more dishonest, but definitely pretty – the weeks in Morocco had lightened her long hair, put deep round freckles on her forearms and darkened her face, so she could hide her inconsistencies better than ever.

'Well, you needn't look so grumpy about it. James invited me. It serves you right for not calling me any more.'

'Well, never mind all that,' said Felix. 'Let's get a drink. Ah, here we are.'

A woman walked past with a tray of beautiful drinks – tall slim glasses containing a range of pastel-coloured liquids, sprigs of dark-green mint and slices of unexpected fruit.

'All the drinks are vodka-based cocktails,' explained Felix. 'It's being sponsored by a drinks brand that we're relaunching. They need to be associated with prize-winning contemporary artists instead of Glaswegian alcoholics.'

James nodded. 'That's very good planning,' he said.

He sipped his cocktail. Apart from the vodka, he had no idea what was in it, but it was a nice pink colour, and sweet and strong. He could probably drink about ten of them. Harriet had seen someone across the room and disappeared. James wasn't surprised. She was highly social, capable of interacting in a number of original ways, and anyway – didn't she have at least a bit of a degree in art history?

'Well, you look very good,' said Felix. 'Harriet is looking good too. I like her brown. I just hope she doesn't do anything that damages your brand capital.'

'Not at all, she'll thrive here.'

It was a Thursday night, the greatest night of the week. Friday nights were for out-of-towners and weekends in London were an intractable problem, but Thursday nights were for everyone that mattered. And how would he deal with tomorrow morning after all these cocktails? Well, if the worse came to the worse, he would simply call in sick again. And what could Lionel do about it? It wasn't as if he was going to bump into Ian Benson and Alex Coleman *here*.

Felix came over and introduced him to someone, who in turn introduced him to an artist called Derek. Again, it was nothing to worry about. He was short, had a northern accent and thankfully didn't want to talk about art. In fact, as Felix had told him, only bankers did that. All that artists ever talked about was money. Derek was sufficiently naive about how government worked to think that James might be able to help him in some way and was interested in all the different kinds of money which required filling in application forms: Arts Council grants, residency awards, bursaries, British Council travel funds. It was exactly the type of money that James was comfortable with, and he was soon giving advice. Making it up as he went along, just like they did in the private sector, he made the ingenious suggestion that artists could qualify for local authority key-worker status, and that he could get subsidised accommodation in new developments. Derek, who was currently living with his sister in Croydon, was deeply impressed.

Having built up his confidence with this quick win, it was time to move on to the next room. This one had even more going for it. It was a large bright room, full of horrible paintings and beautiful women. But, encouragingly, it was striking how unattractive the men were. A lot of them looked like they had studied Computer Science at university. They had thick-framed glasses, dry skin and unstrategic hair. They looked physically weak, shallow-chested, short-legged and incapable of protecting the people they cared for. It wasn't that James was just missing the point. He probably was, but that wasn't the point. The point was, at a fundamental level, he was the best-looking man in the room. He was, in fact, good-looking. It was a new and important insight, and worth pausing to think about. People had, from time to time, told him so, but for some reason he had never believed it until now.

'Hello, what's your name? We've met before haven't we?'

A woman had come suddenly into his line of vision, and was now standing directly in front of a painting of a bunsen burner, which he had, in any case, been struggling to make sense of.

'Yes, I think we have. I'm called James. Your name is Felicity, you work as a newspaper columnist and we met at a book launch a couple of months ago.'

'Oh, very well done! Yes, I remember. You were with Felix. Is he here tonight?'

'So you cover art as well as books?'

'Of course! I'll be found wherever the beautiful people are.'

There was, James could tell, plenty of irony in what she had just said, but still probably not enough. For Felicity herself was anything but beautiful. It was yet another sign of the progress he had made that he had no doubts about that. He was getting more confident making ethical and aesthetic judgements – they were, he was starting to realise, very often the same thing. Things he hadn't noticed about Felicity when they had met before were clear now – her slanted face, the small gloating eyes. And her deep voice, which he had once been so impressed with, was clearly just the consequence of too many high-tar cigarettes.

'Well, maybe you can write something about me,' said James. 'I'm sure your readers would enjoy hearing about the glamour of local government.'

'Hmm, I'd have to work in an angle somehow. Maybe if you did something scandalous. Readers aren't really interested in public-sector types unless they do something wrong.'

There was a tap on his shoulder and James looked round to see Harriet beaming at him. She had brought someone with her: a sinister old man, as tall as James, and therefore eerily tall, with milk-white skin and slow-moving features. He wore dark glasses and a black leather hat with a wide brim.

'This is Jacob. He says that he's the most important person here,' said Harriet. 'And the way to tell that is because no one knows who he really is. You can't even google him!'

'Good to meet you,' said James, reaching out his hand. 'Are you an artist?'

Jacob smiled. A comic book, twisted smile, and extended a long hand with curved fingernails. He was almost certainly the oldest person there – his skin was pulled back tightly and his skull was starting to show through his face. It was possible that he had been in the Nazi Party.

'Of course he isn't an artist,' said Harriet. 'I told you – Jacob's really *important*. He doesn't make art – he buys it. He's a collector.'

'Jacob, Harriet – this is Felicity,' said James.

'Hello,' said Felicity, who didn't seem to have any idea who Jacob was either. 'And where are you from?'

'Switzerland,' said Jacob. Or he might have said 'Stockholm' or 'Stasiland' or 'Swindon', for his accent was thick, and his voice was thin.

'Are you thinking of buying something here?' said James.

'Oh James, don't worry about all that boring stuff. Come with me – Jacob has given us a present.'

Taking his arm, Harriet pulled James away and towards the nearest bathroom. In her hand was an ominous little leather pouch. James couldn't help but feel pleased at leaving Felicity stranded with Jacob – it was exactly the kind of thing that people used to do to him.

'Jesus,' said James. 'Who is that freak?'

'Oh, don't be such a meanie. He may look like Lord Voldemort, but he has the heart of Dumbledore. He's been looking after me while you've been flirting with that awful woman.'

They went into the disabled toilets, which were generously sized, marvellously clean and suitable for a wide range of purposes. There was a cumbersome but reassuringly secure bolt on the door, and a helpful little ledge to rest their drinks on. A couple could spend a comfortable evening here.

'I'm so pleased you brought me here,' said Harriet. 'I'm having such a good time.'

'I know, I thought you'd like it. But what's up with Felix?'

'Oh, don't worry about him,' said Harriet. 'He's probably just jealous of how handsome we look together.'

James nodded. Harriet might be on to something – he was, still, and despite all the evidence, convinced that she was wiser than she looked. She certainly had plenty of life skills – you could tell by the way she was skilfully preparing Jacob's cocaine in the corner. Leaning against the door, he thoughtfully drank some more of his cocktail. This one was an unsettling orange, the same colour as the logo for Lambeth Council. It was carbonated, and fizzed like an unwholesome vitamin drink.

'Here,' said Harriet, standing up to face him. 'Now why don't you kiss me?'

Harriet's wide, curving mouth was coated in cocaine. Like a naughty girl who had been licking cake mixture, a great deal of white powder had been captured unevenly but comprehensively around her wet lips. It was, James knew, going to be much more than a drugs experiment — it would be an important life experience, and he had to make the most of it. It was not a moment to be tentative or considerate. Firmly holding her face in his hands, he gave her exactly what he hadn't given Rachel: a selfish and wholly successful kiss, his lips pressed against hers for a full minute. The kiss was like the very best modern art — complicated and discordant, a jarring combination of lurid and provocative tastes and striking for its brutal symbolism and subversive use of physical aggression.

He pushed down, and felt Harriet push forcefully back up. She was strong and he needed to make full use of his long arms and big hands to hold her in place, and to push further into her mouth. She writhed and gasped and then, just as he was starting to worry that he was hurting her, she pulled her head back with a jerk and smiled. Her lips were pink again, her face flushed. It was often a mistake to interpret someone through their eyes, but it was difficult when they were as close and powerful as this. Harriet's were bigger and greener than ever, and glowed with excitement and promise. James couldn't help but also notice that at least thirty pounds' worth of cocaine powder was now all over the toilet floor.

'There now, wasn't that fun?' said Harriet. 'Now, why don't you go back out and look after Jacob? A girl in a cubicle does need a certain amount of privacy.'

James unbolted the door. He suspected that she was now going to take more cocaine. But what could he do? Even when she was telling the truth, she behaved as if she was lying. Besides, he'd had more than enough and was ready to go back out there. He could pick up with Harriet later – for the moment there was an adventure to be had in the gallery. He felt energised, liberated, *deregulated*.

'Oh, and you better give Jacob this back,' said Harriet, handing him the pouch. 'I don't think there's much left, but I'm sure he won't be cross.'

As James walked across the gallery, he realised that he'd found his art form. It was visual art, with a strong emphasis on the contemporary. It was obvious. Literature was, thankfully, being killed off by the Internet. Science merely gathered further evidence of the universe's indifference and mankind's degradation. Cinema was just sensory stimulation, and could now only aspire to pornography. Theatre, music, dance – these were crude and primitive art forms, of interest primarily to anthropologists. But visual art had transcended all this – disembodied truths that had avoided the traps laid by realism, capitalism and technology. It didn't even need to worry about ideology – it *was* an ideology.

Yet when he got back to the first room it didn't seem quite the same as before. The lights were brighter than he remembered and it was surprising how crowded it had become. Maybe the event hadn't been as exclusive as he'd thought. More men had arrived, tall ones in black trousers, not all of whom looked as if they were artists. Also, with his new, enhanced powers of cognition, the paintings were so much easier to understand. The problem, though, was that now they didn't seem anything like as good.

'Ah – I've been looking for you,' said Felix. 'It's time I introduced you to some arts public relations people. You'll find they're very much like those charming women you met at the book launch, but paid even worse. James – are you all right?'

'Yes, hold on. Give me a moment. I'm just feeling a little bit light-headed.'

Felix looked at James with his sceptical eyes, concern and doubt shimmering across his face. 'What on earth have you done to yourself?'

'Harriet gave me some of this,' said James, holding up the black pouch, 'and now I feel a bit odd.'

'Let me have a look at that.'

Felix dabbed a finger on some specks of white powder and made his diagnosis immediately.

'Uh oh,' said Felix. 'This isn't normal cocaine. It isn't drug dealer's cocaine. This is *art dealer's* cocaine. How much did you take?'

'I don't think I had all that much.'

'A line? Two lines? Any more than that and you're going to be in serious trouble.'

'I don't know. It was difficult to tell.'

'And where's Harriet? Did she have some? I've seen her on this kind of stuff before. It's not pretty.'

James felt giddy. The sensation wasn't especially difficult to understand – it was simply a superabundance of biochemical activity. Across his body, chain reactions were breaking out as every complex molecule simultaneously did something reckless and stupid. His nerves were twitching, his blood vessels shrinking, his synapses spiking and neurons firing. He was burning up great quantities of energy. Metabolically, it was hard to imagine that anyone could be more alive than he was just now and yet his great fear was that it would result in sudden death.

'Yes, Harriet had quite a lot I think. I don't know where she is.'

'Okay, you wait here. I better go and find her. Try not to get into any trouble.'

But waiting in one place wasn't going to be possible. His legs were trembling and his eyes straining. His teeth were gripped tightly together and he was clenching his cocktail glass so firmly that it was in danger of breaking. He could feel muscles tensing and contracting, his long bones shuddering. Looking at works of art wouldn't do. He badly needed to interact with another human being, to get into a fight with a man perhaps, or sexually assault a woman. Maybe he should go back and find Felicity. And then, suddenly, he saw someone he knew.

'Alice?' said James. 'I didn't know you were coming tonight.'

Alice looked startled – not actively displeased, but certainly more bothered than she had any right to be. James could see her clever, complicated face try to absorb what it meant. Well, she'd better get used to it – bumping into James at things like this was something that would happen more often from now on.

'Well, this is a surprise. How very nice to see you. Are you here with Adam and Carl?' she said.

'No,' said James. 'I'm here with some other people.'

Alice nodded, as if that was exactly what she expected him to say. There was no doubt she looked great, different but even better than the last time. Her hair had changed again – the fringe had gone and it was darker, so that her black, disbelieving eyes were more conspicuous. She looked alert and ever-so-slightly hostile, as if she was on the cusp of losing her temper or, more likely, saying something witty and remarkable.

'What have you been up to then? Do tell – it's been ages. It's been such a manic year.'

'Yes, me too. Work has gone crazy – we're basically rebuilding half of London.'

'Really? That sounds very grand.'

Before Alice could say any more, James embarked on a short, dazzling summary of the Sunbury Square Masterplan. It was what Felix would have called an *elevator pitch*. He was vague about its location and precise about its ambitions. He gave a measured overestimate of its budget, size and significance, and lightly passed over operational issues. No one could have heard him without coming away with the impression that James was in complete control of his brief.

'Gosh, that sounds very impressive. I should get someone at the paper to do something about it.'

'I actually have a press officer working for me – a young man called Alex. But yes, of course, I'd be very happy to talk to someone about it.'

James took a long and deep drink. He was sure he was saying brilliant things, but it was possible that he was saying them too quickly. A waitress walked past, and he swapped his cocktail for another – a blue one this time, which looked as if it might be more soothing.

'Are you okay?' said Alice. 'You look a bit rattled.'

'No, I'm fine,' said James. 'Just a lot going on at the moment, you know how it is.'

One of the very few people who had actually been looking at the art walked over to join them.

'Now, James,' said Alice. 'I'd like you to meet the significant other in my life. This is Sam. I've got to go and talk to someone for work, but I think you'll get on well together – both of you are dedicated public servants.'

James looked at him with wild interest. He wasn't just shorter than James, that was to be expected, he *was* short, with a neat, compact body. And while he would acknowledge that Sam looked healthy, he could see there was no great strength there – it was more a case of not eating red meat and playing badminton once a week. He was wearing a charcoal-grey suit that was no more expensive than James's, and he had a round face and round glasses.

'Oh, right, and what do you do?' said James. 'Are you in Whitehall?'

'No, at the moment I'm working at Camden Council, in social services.'

'Oh, so you don't work in the media?'

'God – no fear,' said Sam. 'The media? No, that's Alice's thing. I wouldn't go near it.'

James, the listener, wasn't really listening. He was finding it difficult to concentrate. He raised the blue cocktail to his mouth and fished out an ice cube. He was overheating, and he needed something to help cool down. Alice was right – he felt fucking rattled.

'So, you're not a lawyer, or a doctor?'

'No, but I do work with a lot of them.'

'Are you a psychotherapist?'

'No, though I often work with them as well. Like I said, I work in social services.'

'So you're a social worker?'

'Well, not technically. I'm actually training to be one. I'm studying part-time, but yes – that's the plan. At the moment, I'm more involved on the management and policy side of things, but I'd like to be more frontline.'

James looked at him in wonder. A perfectly objective judgement of Sam, accounting for all possible traces of rivalry and envy, was that he wasn't good-looking. He was probably clever and good at his job, driven by strong moral purpose and a humane worldview. But he wasn't good-looking.

'Alice said that you worked in town planning?' said Sam. 'That's really interesting. I've just started working with some planners myself on a new integrated health scheme. It's fascinating to see the approach they bring.'

It occurred to James that he was behaving oddly, but so long as he was aware of this, it couldn't be that serious. It was only if he didn't know when he was being strange and aggressive that he ought to worry – in which case, of course, he wouldn't anyway. Carl had been right that evening when they had gone clubbing – cocaine made you clever, which meant that this stuff must make you *really* clever.

'So, are you Jewish then?' said James. 'Is that what's going on?'

'Uh, no,' said Sam. 'No, I'm not. I'm not quite sure what you're getting at.'

Sam was looking at him in a way that James didn't especially like, but there didn't seem much he could do about it. He didn't seem cross – he had patient eyes and a social worker's concern for another's well-being. Sam didn't even need to be Jewish – he was just the most grown-up person there, and James knew that the one thing that all women want in a man, the single most essential and attractive quality, is for him to be a grown-up.

'Well, good to meet you – was interesting to talk. I ought to go and see where Alice is.'

James wasn't sure if he had vanquished an enemy or suffered some kind of obscure but damaging defeat. It was something to be thought through later. In the meantime, he felt a great need to move on quickly – not to retreat or run away, but to be somewhere else.

He went into the third and final room. It was much smaller and quieter. This was a good thing because he needed to be on his own for a bit. He was, he was reasonably certain now, feeling unwell. Surely this couldn't be cocaine? Either that or Marcus's stuff hadn't really been cocaine at all. Or perhaps it was just a question of how much money you spent on it. In which case, it served him right – he should have learnt by now that anything given to him for nothing was bound to be extremely expensive. The truth was, he didn't really know anything about recreational drugs. Nor did he know anything about the contemporary art sector, literary fiction or professional football. He didn't really know enough about anything – except for Southwark Council's social-housing policies. He thought he had for a while, but now he knew otherwise. That was the problem with cocaine – it made you clever, clever enough to realise that you weren't very clever at all.

There were no paintings here. Instead there was a sculpture, or maybe it was what was known as an installation – a little irregular grouping of rods and circles arranged in the centre of the room. They were so slight and delicate, that he wondered for a moment if they were plants. They reminded him of the projector images he had seen in the nightclub – geometric lines and abstract shapes, which quivered together in little clumps. He walked up closer. They were devoid of colour or texture or meaning, and because of that could be trusted.

The sculpture was rotating. But unlike everything else in the world that was made of metal and moved, it wasn't going to hurt anyone. Instead, it did nothing more than gently sway back and forth in wide, irregular arcs. If anything, it seemed to want to befriend him. He couldn't detect any electric motors, although these days such things were invisible and made no noise. More likely, he guessed it was simply made of aluminium or some alloy so light that it took no more than an air conditioner and passing bodies to be animated.

From time to time, James peered into the room behind him, but each time it was hopeless. He had lost his sense of perspective, and the scene was two-dimensional, congested and essentially unnavigable. He could still understand the pictures on the walls, but everything else, everything human, was a mystery. Why had everyone come here? Was anyone apart from Jacob actually going to buy anything? How did all these people earn any money? Maybe it wasn't just the cocktails: maybe the whole thing, maybe all of London, was being paid for by Felix, as part of some gigantic, real-life advertisement.

It didn't help that his hearing had been damaged. Not that he heard less now – in fact, the opposite seemed to have happened.

He could now hear *everything* – the chink of cocktail glasses across the room, whispered curses in the corners, the twang of insincerity in Felicity's voice, the clicking of Alice's shoes, and echoes from where the old printing presses used to be. He badly needed to sober up, or else have another drink – to do something about all the drugs and confusion that were leaking through his body.

It was difficult to tell how long he had been standing there. He hadn't been checking his watch, and his body was incapable of monitoring the time. He was sure that the arms of the sculpture had undertaken a full rotation at least a dozen or so times, but there was no way of knowing how fast they were moving. All he knew was that it was much better to be here than anywhere else.

But now, from the room behind him, he was aware of other noises – noises that anyone might hear. Noises that had probably been going on for a while, and which he could no longer ignore. They were wild and frightening, and it was clear that something terrible was happening. He didn't want to go back. It was calm in here, and he sensed that once he looked round, once he went back into the room, things would never be calm again.

There were footsteps and he turned round to see Felix. He had been expecting that.

'James, I think your guest may need some assistance.'

He walked back into the room. No one was waiting for him, but there they all were. There was Alice who, after all these years, was still able to cause him great harm, and her boyfriend, whom James wouldn't be able to compete with for another twenty years. There was Felicity, who was laughing unpleasantly. There was Jacob, the art collector, who was in a corner poisoning a young woman. There was Derek, the artist, who had seemed so cheerful an hour ago, but now looked as if he was weeping.

Most disturbing of all, though, in the centre of all this, there was Harriet. In some ways, he had to concede, she was looking better than he'd ever seen her. She looked like an Amazonian warrior – more ferocious, alive and dangerous than anyone else in the room. Her hair was long and her mouth more powerful than ever. But the problem, the insurmountable difficulty, was that she had just destroyed at least two works of art, and was attempting, with great violence, to dismantle another one. It was essentially a terrorist situation.

Given all this, it was surprising how well behaved everyone else was being. They were watching in respectful silence, while a woman who seemed to have a position of authority stood in the centre of the room. James wasn't sure if she was the gallery owner, or just taller and more handsome than anyone else. But in any case everyone, except for Harriet, seemed to be doing what she told them.

Two policemen arrived. It was, he had forgotten, East London – there were police everywhere, to deal with all the people who didn't go to art galleries. One was a stout Anglo-Saxon, with short fair hair and big ears who looked a bit like his flatmate Matt, and the other was a slender young South Asian, with long eyelashes. Taking their command from the tall woman, they methodically began to apprehend Harriet – one of them wrenched the canvas from her and the other one took her firmly by the wrists.

'Help me,' said Harriet. 'James – help me. They're hurting me. Help me. Fuck. Please help me.'

James didn't have any choice. If she had been screaming, he may have been able to ignore it, but she was asking for help, and so he would have to help her. He would have to intervene – it was what planners did, an unfortunate compulsion of duty. He spent most of his life observing, but essentially he was an interventionist – it was his job to get involved. Plus, he was on very strong drugs, which were impairing his judgement.

James was never able to fully describe what happened after that – not with anything as primitive as words, which in any case had never been his strength. A five-million-pound work of contemporary art, an avant-garde jazz opera or a beautiful game of pinball might represent it with more precision and clarity. Striding into the centre of the room, he could at least take advantage of his height. Policemen weren't tall any more, and he was able to tower above them, to configure himself into an imposing and belligerent position. But, and he had forgotten this, although he was very tall, *he wasn't all that strong.* Nor did he have any technique or training for this kind of thing – after all, he had gone to a fucking grammar school.

The policemen released Harriet and rushed towards him, while James clenched his fists and threw his arms forward without any great skill. It was, therefore, bad luck that the first thing to happen was that James punched one of the policemen directly in the throat. It was, everyone could see, an act of terrible violence and there was a gasp of appreciation from the room. Surprised and hurt, he had not so much fallen but squatted down, in obvious distress and pain. James wondered if he should now try and help, or else maybe start to kick him.

It was a shame that the officer that James had felled was the young Asian rather than the large white man. Not just symbolically – it might also have given him a chance to escape. For the one still standing was stronger and much better at fighting. He attacked James with great ferocity and competence. There were no idiotic punches, instead he seized James by the shoulders and pushed him hard into the wall. James in turn grabbed his chest and pushed back as hard as he could, and as he did so, another canvas fell loudly to the floor.

And then, suddenly, just as they'd got started, they both stopped as if by mutual agreement. The fallen officer slowly raised himself and started to unstrap something from his belt. The other one took a step or two back. James, who hadn't really known what he was doing from start to finish, put his hands up in the air.

'I think you had better come with us,' said the policeman.

James nodded. That did seem the sensible thing to do. It had to be more sensible than fighting. The rest of the room was no longer quiet. There was a very loud and disagreeable humming, as everyone started talking at once. As far as James could tell, the consensus seemed to be that he had disgraced himself, but not in a good way – not in a contemporary art way. There was no need for him to be held – he very badly wanted to get out of there. His head down, he walked out between the police officers and into their car.

What with his geography degree, his certificate in town planning and his detailed knowledge of building standards, James was in a better position than most to analyse the spatial arrangements of his police cell. He wondered if it was any larger than the statutory minimum. It certainly felt small, but there again he was so very tall.

It was, James thought, probably an encouraging sign that they hadn't taken much interest in him when he had arrived at the police station. An officer with very good manners had taken his details and asked James to empty his pockets. Another one had taken his phone, his shoes and his trouser belt, and escorted him to the cell. A minute later, he returned and kindly gave him a plastic cup of water and a grey cotton blanket. After that, they seemed to largely forget about him.

But for someone who was still trying to cope with the after-effects of cocaine, a night in a police cell was hardly ideal. He needed to embark on a long, meditative walk, but he could cross the floor of the cell in just three steps and there wasn't much else he could do, except sit on a narrow bench. It would have been easier to put up with if they'd locked him up with Harriet, but she had fled. He wouldn't have thought it possible, but she had managed to evade arrest. It occurred to James that that was a serious offence, although probably not as serious as punching a police officer.

It was dark and cold – it seemed a very long time ago that he had been overheating in an art gallery. The Metropolitan Police Service probably procured ten thousand grey cotton blankets each year, with unit cost being the only consideration. It was insubstantial, not large or thick enough, and offered very little warmth or comfort. Another problem was that it was also incredibly noisy. He had hoped that the prisoners in the other cells would be asleep or morbidly depressed, but in fact they were making dreadful sounds, like primates in a Victorian zoo. He was almost certainly the best-behaved prisoner in the whole building. Meanwhile, out on the streets of East London he could hear sirens and horns, shouts of rage, drunken chants and threats of violence, maybe even a helicopter. For a moment he wondered if a riot or an attack on the station was taking place, but no – it was just the sound of the greatest night of the week, the sound of a highly successful urban economy.

As he huddled on the concrete bench in the corner of his concrete cell and listened to the sounds of the city being destroyed, James suddenly realised that he did have a worldview. It wasn't quite a revelation, for he'd probably always had it. It probably wasn't a philosophy either, and it might not be worked through enough for Felix, but it did have the advantage of being easy to articulate: *people were fucking hopeless*. It wasn't just that they were terrible and cruel bastards, although they often were that as well, and the problem wasn't death-knowledge or insatiable longings – the main problem was that they just weren't any good. They were incompetent at living, they couldn't be trusted to reason effectively, and almost everything they wanted made them unhappy.

It wasn't obvious why this was the case – it could just be a cosmic misfortune or the deep strategy of a wanker God or, more plausibly, that humans had evolved to live in an entirely different set of circumstances from the ones they now found themselves in. Fuck knows. The important point was that it was true: they were no good at making decisions that would maximise the well-being of themselves or those around them. And so they shouldn't be allowed to.

Immediately afterwards, he fell asleep. Perhaps it was all the vodka cocktails or maybe, as he'd hoped all those months ago, with revelation so came peace. He slept deeply, without dreaming, but not for that long, as deciding when to wake up wasn't his prerogative. It must have been no more than six hours later when another police officer opened the cell door.

'Okay, you're going to have to get out now. We need the cell for someone more important.'

James padded down the corridor in his socks, following the officer back to the front desk. His possessions were already waiting for him, in a neat little pile.

'Is that it then? Is it all right for me to go?'

'Yep, you can go for now. I'm sure we'll call you back in here before long for a proper chat.'

He was, thought James, exactly what you'd want a London policeman to look like. He was big and black, with a wide smile and flat shiny nose.

'So you'll be charging me?' said James, not entirely sure what that even meant.

'We'll give you a call. It depends if anyone wants to press charges and what the witnesses say. You may just get a caution. Although young Ravi might have something to say as well.'

'Ravi?'

'Ravinder. The officer you lamped. If he wants to take it up, then you'll be in trouble. We don't take that kind of thing lightly.'

No, James could see that. It wasn't like working in town planning, there was solidarity here. The class system wasn't going to do him any favours either. If he was an Etonian who had gone on the rampage at Oxford it might be a different matter. Plus, as ever, he was far too *old* – this had been a young man's crime and might have been treated as one if he had in fact actually been a young man.

'Don't worry too much. We've got enough going on. Come back as soon as we call you, say sorry, bring flowers and a box of chocolates. It's not up to me, but I'm pretty sure you'll just get a caution and that will be the end of it.

James put his shoes on and left the police station. He was, he had to admit, completely satisfied with the level of service he had received. The cell might have been small but it was clean, and the officers had been well mannered and highly trained. He felt the early morning sun and the air and his spirits, exhausted as they were, gave a little surge. He couldn't quite understand why he didn't feel much worse than he did. He was on Stoke Newington High Street, and he knew that somewhere not all that far away must be his favourite sex club, but the only geographic landmark he could recognise was the sun, plump and warm as it rose above the City of London. He started to walk towards it, southwards, towards Southwark. He was, despite all that had happened, not without hope.

He turned his phone on. There was nothing from Felix but there was a text message from Harriet, sent just before midnight: 'That was a bit mad! What happened to you? Hope things okay xx'. He sent a message back: 'I've just got out of police station. Are you ok? Where did you go?'

If nothing else, she ought to be impressed with that. He had, after all, spent a night in a police cell and he had done it for her. That was quite a gesture – heroic even, by modern standards. But when the phone rang in his hand ten seconds later, it wasn't Harriet. It was Rachel.

'Jesus Christ. You're in so much fucking shit it's almost unbelievable.'

16

29 March

The decisions we make about our city now will shape the quality of life of those who come after us and their view of how successful we have been in our stewardship of the city.

— *The London Plan*, Section 1.56

'I could go into a lot of detail, and if you want me to I will, and we'll get someone from HR here. But there are essentially two ways to do this. You can resign now, and I'll look out for you as best I can, or we can fight each other for the next six weeks. In which case, make no mistake, I will completely fuck you.'

It was nine o'clock, and James was in Lionel's office, much like any other morning. Rachel was there as well – for, in accordance with Southwark Council disciplinary procedures policy, he had been allowed to take one other colleague with him. But so far, the only person to have really said anything was Lionel.

'Bear in mind, I'll have the entire organisation behind me. I've already had the chief exec on the phone. He wants your head.'

Lionel was incapable of ferocity – as with so much else, his talents in this regard had been spent a long time ago. The best he could do now, the most fearsome thing he could do, was to speak in a certain gruff style as if he was a man who was always sure of himself. But that didn't mean he wasn't cross.

'Surely you can't just fire me for this?'

'Christ no,' said Rachel. 'This is the public sector. You have to practically commit homicide before that happens.'

'Nobody's talking about you getting fired. Let's try not to use that word. But understand that you still have to go.'

'But it's not as if I did this in the course of work. I was at an art gallery, it wasn't a public consultation or anything.'

James turned to Rachel. The drugs had left his body, he was reasonably confident about that, but the problem was, they had taken all the good things with them: nutrients and vitamins, brain chemicals, white blood cells, possibly his soul. As a result, one of his greatest powers, the ability to listen and concentrate in meetings, had deserted him. That was a shame, because it was probably the most important one he had ever been in.

'James has got a point. But I know what you're going to say. Somewhere in section five of his contract it will state: "Any officer who conducts himself in a manner which in the reasonable opinion of Southwark Council's executive management brings himself or the organisation into disrepute or threatens the good standing of . . . blah blah blah."'

'That's exactly right. Look, we can go legal if you force me, and we can have it out. But, like I said, it will end up hurting James more than it does us.'

It wasn't wholly clear if Rachel was representing his best interests or not in these negotiations, or in fact if they really were negotiations – after all, the major decision didn't seem to be up for debate. Instead, Lionel and Rachel began to discuss his leaving terms. He could always have called the trade union, but rather unwisely, not long after Felix had told him they were a twentieth-century relic, he had stopped paying his subscription.

'So if he resigns now, he could still get his three months' notice?'

'I'd have to talk to HR to get it confirmed, but it shouldn't be a problem.'

'And you wouldn't want him to actually work that period out?'

'No. Nobody wants him to still be in the office by the end of the day.'

'Maybe he could work from home?'

'I don't really think that would work. I think it's best if he just goes. As long as his files are all in good order, then we don't have to worry about a handover or anything.'

'And what about a reference? You'll still give him one, right? He's going to need that whatever happens.'

There was a pause, which James didn't like in the least bit. He wanted very much for this to end. If he could just get out and sit down on his own for a while, he might be able to heal and to think. In fact, what he could really do with right now was to have his prison cell back.

'James,' said Lionel. 'Can I have a word with you on your own – without Rachel?'

James nodded. There seemed little point or scope for refusing. Rachel began to say something, thought better of it and quietly left the room.

'Lionel, I'm really sorry about what's happened.'

He tried to hold Lionel's gaze. As ever, James was stooping his shoulders, but now it was being done out of submission rather than kindness. Lionel looked as if he was thinking hard, but it was James's impression that he was simply waiting for an interval to pass, so that when he did speak the force would be all the greater.

'The problem is,' said Lionel, at last. 'I don't even want to save you.'

'Lionel, I'm really sorry.'

'Are you aware of how much trouble you've caused me?'

'I know, I know. I'm so very sorry.'

'I'm not even talking about your antics last night.'

'What do you mean?'

'You've been speaking with developers, haven't you?'

'No. Well – yes, you know we all deal with them. It's part of the job sometimes.'

'You've been speaking to Simon Galbraith.'

His body had been empty, but now James could feel it softly filling up again with something. He wasn't sure what. It felt like cold morphine, the opposite of adrenalin, something that made him congested and slow-moving.

'Yes, I met him at a football match not long ago.'

'You just met him once?'

'Well, once or twice. I met him another time as well.'

Thinking on your feet, making stuff up, lying – it was something that people in the private sector were so much better at. James's body had gone cold, but his head was hot – prickly, as if exposed to a great heat – and he didn't know what to do with his eyes. Lionel, on the other hand, had rarely looked calmer.

'How do you know I met Simon? Have you been speaking to him?'

'Oh, I know Simon Galbraith. I've known him for years. I know him so well that he gave me a friendly call two days ago to tell me what a nice, ambitious young man you are, how helpful you've been, but that he was a bit concerned with how open you were about various matters – so much so, that he was wondering if he ought to mention it to a senior council member whom he happens to know.'

'But why did he do that? I don't understand,' said James, although it was all too clear what had happened. He'd been fucked over – by the richest and most charming man he had ever met.

'Because he's a *developer*. He's a bastard. And he wants very much to do things in this borough, which means that he wants to stay friendly with me. Unless you could have been more valuable to him than my goodwill, then you were fucked.'

'I didn't really tell him anything he didn't know already. Honestly I didn't.'

Lionel decided not to say anything for a while. He looked around the room airily – another gimmick, just like his melodramatic pauses. Was it possible that he was enjoying this? Lionel, so ineffective in all those meetings, was good at something after all. He was good at sacking people.

'You know, he's always asking me to go to the football with him. Either that or it's Wimbledon or the theatre or something. That's how these people work. Once you owe them something, you're in trouble. Once you enjoyed his hospitality and wanted to please him he had you. And, do you know what's really bloody annoying? Because of you, now I *do* owe him something.'

'So is that really why I'm going? I've worked here for nearly four years, and I'm going to have to leave for saying some things to a developer who I barely know?'

'No, not really. You were probably fucked anyway. Your nonsense last night saw to that. You've lost your job. What I'm telling you now is that you've screwed your career as well. You won't get a reference from me. You could have been a good planner. But I think you're going to have to do something else now.'

It had never been difficult to pity Lionel – he was, after all, pitiful. And if he could pity him then James had thought that, when the time came, he could destroy him, he could replace him. Not for what he'd done, but for what he was – for what he was like, for his non-aerodynamic personality, corduroy hair, brown shoes and 1970s accent. He was called Lionel, and he wasn't even Jewish. But it wasn't going to work out that way after all. It was Lionel who was going to destroy him.

'You better clear your desk,' said Lionel. 'We can sort everything else out later, but I think you better just go now. You'll get your three months. Someone from HR will be in touch with you.'

That was it. His last ever meeting at Southwark Council was over and, for once, it hadn't overrun. James got up to go. Lionel had already turned away, and was pretending to do something on his computer.

Rachel was waiting in the corridor. He looked at her with trepidation and a sudden gust of hope. Would she save him somehow? Was that still possible? No, of course not – and it wasn't just that Rachel couldn't help him, she *wouldn't*. He could see that. And maybe she was right not to. She was looking at him curiously but not tenderly, her arms folded and with an authoritarian plumpness around her mouth.

'You didn't hear any of that did you?' said James.

'Believe me, I was desperately trying. What did he say?'

James shook his head. 'I don't want to talk about it.'

'No, I can imagine. But I'm guessing you fucked up even more than I thought you did.'

It was such a shame, what had happened. It wasn't a tragedy, it probably wasn't even an injustice – it was simply a shame. Every life gets the disaster it deserves and his was a small one, for he had lived his life without any great scale. But, and this was the point, his capacity to withstand it was also small. The character and defences to protect him from what had happened were even less than his misfortune.

'People know about it. That's the real problem. Never mind Lionel – senior management must have already read about it. You know the Comms Team monitor stuff like this all the time.'

'The gallery was full of journalists, bloggers, Internet twats. What have they said?'

'Here, listen to this one. It's probably the most problematic, because it actually mentions your job title. Well – Lionel's job title. You can imagine what he made of that.'

Rachel read aloud from her mobile phone. *'There was unexpected drama last night at the opening of a new exhibition at the Shaw Gallery in Whitechapel. James Crawley, Director of Planning at Southwark Council, was detained by police after attempting to vandalise several of the works on show with an unidentified young woman. It is not clear what the motives for the attack were. Many of the attendees were under the impression that they were witnessing a piece of performance art, and it was only when the police—'*

'Fuck, okay, stop reading. I don't want to hear any more. For one thing, I can't bear all the exaggerations and factual inaccuracies. Where did they get the idea that I'm the director here? None of that will actually go in the newspapers, will it?'

Rachel shrugged. 'Search me. Personally, I wouldn't have thought it was much of a story, but I guess that's what the Internet is for. I don't think your parents are going to read it in the *Daily Mail* if that's what you're worried about.'

'I bet what you've just read was written by a poisonous witch called Felicity. I hardly know her, but she would have loved the chance to do me over – she's that sort.'

'No,' said Rachel, peering into her phone. 'That was written by someone called Alice Baum.'

James nodded silently. He probably should have guessed that. It would have had nothing to do with him being peculiar and hostile with her boyfriend. It wasn't vengeance or high drama, that had never been her thing – and anyway, he wasn't important enough to her for that. It was just a good little story.

'Well, I guess you better get your things. Much better to do it quickly, before everyone turns up. I'll walk out with you.'

She was right – the office was almost empty, and that had to be a good thing. For the last time, he looked up at the bright overhead lighting that you couldn't moderate, the square windows you weren't allowed to open, the grey computers and black telephones. He looked at the kitchenette, with its sink full of unwashed mugs. It had been a depressing place to work but it had at least been restful, it had been safe. There were, he suspected, many worse jobs than being a planner in a local authority.

Ian Benson was sitting at James's desk, typing things into his computer.

'Just deactivating your hard drive and switching your accounts off. It's council policy. No hard feelings. Have you got any personal files you want me to back up for you?'

'No, don't worry. I never used it for anything other than work. And I never saved anything on the desktop either – all my files are on the server.'

'That's very commendable,' said Ian. 'Not like the others. It's a shame you're leaving.'

James started to clear his desk with a black bin liner. It didn't take long – he had also been one of the very few to adhere to the office clean-desk policy. Nor did he have many possessions. There were no framed photos of loved ones or pictures of baby elephants. Almost everything on the desk was the property of Southwark Council – apart from the electric stapler, which he had bought for himself, and his own little planners' toolkit – dividers, compass, triangle and coloured pencils, which his parents had given him as a present when he got his first job, but he'd never actually used. As he could have told them, it was all done on computers.

'I googled you just now,' said Ian. 'Got an absolute shit storm. You're famous, basically.'

James nodded. You didn't have to be much of a planner to know that it was not meant to have turned out like this. So much for the vision, so much for the strategy. Although, despite everything, he still didn't know for sure if he had overplanned it or not.

'Maybe see you out clubbing again one night?' said Ian.

'Yeah, maybe,' said James. 'Thanks for everything.'

Rachel and James got into the jerky, treacherous lift that still hadn't been serviced. They travelled down and through reception, moving against the thick flow of Southwark Council finance managers, policy officers, regulators, inspectors and administrators arriving for work. The men in charcoal suits, the women in long dark skirts, all looking in a way that James had never quite noticed before: purposeful, necessary and salaried.

And now they were outside, standing on the steps for the last time. Rachel lit a cigarette, but James had quit smoking. He looked out on to the busy street, where everything was still conforming closely to his worldview: drivers stuck in queues beeped their horns pointlessly, cyclists went through red lights and pedestrians dropped litter. The rush-hour traffic hadn't peaked yet: as they both knew from Neil Tuffnel's studies, this wouldn't happen for at least another twenty minutes.

'You'll be fine,' said Rachel. 'There's a whole world out there. God – in six months' time you'll be saying it's the best thing that's ever happened to you. That's what everyone who loses their job always says.'

But James wasn't so sure. After all, he was James Crawley and he was a town planner. What else was he going to do? Sit on a beach in Vietnam selling hair bands? Secure venture capital investment for a high-growth nano-technology start-up? The truth was – he wasn't going to be fine. He was actually pretty badly fucked.

'At least we got you three months' notice. That will keep you going for a bit. You know, Lionel didn't have to do that.'

'And what about after that? Do you think I can get back?'

'Well, obviously not here.'

'No, but somewhere else. I can still be a planner, can't I?'

Rachel blew out cigarette smoke and paused to think. But, unlike with Lionel, he didn't think she was doing it for effect.

'Look, it's the public sector. You can be incompetent and lazy. But you can't fuck up in the way you did. What did Lionel say to you?'

'I don't really want to talk about it. But he's not giving me a reference.'

'Well, whatever, your problem is that you are no longer regarded as a safe pair of hands. And in public administration, that is always a basic requirement. No one wants a planner, however brilliant, who smashes up artworks and gets into fights with the police. The whole point of being a planner is that the public have no idea who you are.'

Rachel was right. Even in places like Nottingham, especially in places like Nottingham, that kind of thing mattered. Could he go and work for a developer? But that seemed unlikely too – it was influence rather than planning skills that they were interested in. Developers didn't give a fuck about skills. He wouldn't be going to many more football matches now. Nor was it likely that he'd get invited to many art exhibitions either. Although he could, he supposed, still go to the odd book launch.

'You know what – this isn't necessarily going to make you feel any better, but it looks like I'm going to get a promotion out of this. Lionel had a word with me before you came in.

Nothing's settled, but he wants to enlarge my role, and give me some of your responsibilities. It helps him out, what with the budget cuts.'

James nodded. Yes, he could see that. It made a lot of sense. No need to replace him with someone new. No recruitment costs or redundancy payouts – from the perspective of the public good, it had worked out rather well.

'Christ – the others are going to be in a state about you going like this. It's not the kind of thing they're good at dealing with. Neil is going to most probably pass out.'

'I know, I know. I'm sorry. Christ, what a fuck-up.'

'Well, don't worry about that now,' said Rachel. 'I'll give them all your love. We can arrange leaving drinks or something when things have quietened down.'

James checked his phone. There was a text message from Harriet: 'OMG! Crazy night!! I'm OK. Felix took me back to his place. Hope you don't mind xx'

Did he mind? He probably would a great deal at some point, but not yet – there were too many other things to mind about. At least biologically, things were starting to stabilise. He was starting to feel normal again, neither saturated with bad chemicals or emptied of all the good ones. The problem with that, of course, was that he was now beginning to feel terrible – almost as terrible as he ought to be feeling. There was still no word from Felix. Or maybe, that was the message? He was, after all, a master of communication. He had first contacted him with a two-word email, maybe Harriet was the medium he'd chosen for saying goodbye.

'Look, you'll get over this. I guarantee it. You'll be able to walk back into the Red Lion for a drink and laugh about this in a couple of months. And you'll be earning so much money with your new job that you'll be buying the drinks.'

'I don't think that's ever going to happen. I don't want to talk about it, but I don't think Lionel and me are going to meet again anytime soon.'

'Lionel will be okay. He's upset more than cross. I'll talk to him about your reference when he's calmed down. You know, believe it or not, I think he had it in his head that you were after his job. That's the kind of thing that sends him over the edge.'

'And what about you?' said James.

'Me?'

'Will I see you again soon?'

They looked into each other's eyes for a moment and James offered up a smile. But it was much too late now. There had been too many mistakes and bad decisions, too many things that had either been done badly, or else not at all. Rachel looked away, back towards the street.

'Yes, of course,' said Rachel. 'There's no reason why we can't be friends.'

'That would be nice.'

'I'll call and we can go for a coffee or something. I'll still need someone to rant to about this place.'

Rachel flicked her cigarette stub on to the pavement, and turned to go back inside. She gave him a hearty, non-metropolitan shake of the shoulders. It was almost an embrace, full of warmth and strength, but it was no more loving than the one he had got from Angus at the football match.

'Well, you know how it is. I've got a housing meeting to go to. That new guy from the community team is going to be there. Honestly, you're the lucky one.'

'Oh God, yes – him. Useless. Hope it goes okay.'

'It'll be okay. *You'll* be okay. I'll give you a call in a couple of weeks.'

'Yes. Goodbye.'

'Goodbye.'

The world is urbanising. James had been taught that at school when still quite young, and he'd never forgotten it. Cities were terrible, everyone knew that – they spread diseases and made people ill, they brought people too close together, so that they did harmful things to one another and to themselves. But still they came. All round the world, people were coming. They were coming to Sao Paolo, they were coming to Lagos and to Shanghai, and they were still coming to London. Most of the world was emptying, but the parts that mattered were filling up. The human race was agglomerating for the next, maybe the final, stage of the drama. And against all this, against the masses with all their problems and unreasonable demands, their malice and squalid hopes, there stood nothing other than the planners – the regulators and the lawmakers. The best intentioned, but not the bravest, with the wisdom to know that something had to be done, but not the means or the strength to do very much about it. There weren't very many of them, there was no way nearly enough, and now there would be one fewer.

James walked down the road with his plastic bag of possessions, which was awkward to hold in his hand, but too light to hoist over his shoulder. He was heading north, towards the river, but he had little idea what he would do when he got there. He looked up. It was an unusually bright spring morning and the sky, at least, looked exactly like it did in his masterplan poster.

A NOTE ON THE AUTHOR

Tom Campbell read history at Edinburgh University. *Fold*, his first novel, was published by Bloomsbury in 2011 to critical acclaim. He lives in London with his wife and three sons.